Then that silhouette began to change.

There came a shriek of tearing metal. Something growled.

Heart pounding against his rib cage as though it were trying to break free, Artie forced himself up and back. He scrambled on his hands and knees, agony spiking through his head, making it almost impossible for him to stand.

Then it was above him.

Artie's breathing came too fast, and he had the coppery taste of his own blood in the back of his mouth. It had been a man, standing over him. He knew that. But now it was something else. Its eyes blazed orange in the dark, its wet snout gleamed. Its fur was sleek, with muscles rippling beneath it.

It growled. But that growl sounded like a laugh.

The wet snout dipped down, he felt its hot breath on his throat; then teeth ripped his flesh with a sickening tearing sound.

It was the last sound Artie heard.

Prowlers Series
by Christopher Golden

Prowlers
Laws of Nature (*coming soon*)

Available from Pocket Books

For orders other than by individual consumers, Pocket Books
grants a discount on the purchase of **10 or more** copies of
single titles for special markets or premium use. For further
details, please write to the Vice President of Special Markets,
Pocket Books, 1230 Avenue of the Americas, 9th Floor,
New York, NY 10020-1586.

For information on how individual consumers can place
orders, please write to Mail Order Department, Simon &
Schuster Inc., 100 Front Street, Riverside, NJ 08075.

PROWLERS

Christopher Golden

POCKET PULSE
New York London Toronto Sydney Singapore

The sale of this book without its cover is unauthorized. If you purchased this book without a cover, you should be aware that it was reported to the publisher as "unsold and destroyed." Neither the author nor the publisher has received payment for the sale of this "stripped book."

This book is a work of fiction. Names, characters, places and incidents are products of the author's imagination or are used fictitiously. Any resemblance to actual events or locales or persons, living or dead, is entirely coincidental.

An *Original* Publication of POCKET BOOKS

 POCKET PULSE published by
Pocket Books, a division of Simon & Schuster, Inc.
1230 Avenue of the Americas, New York, NY 10020

Copyright © 2001 by Christopher Golden

All rights reserved, including the right to reproduce this book or portions thereof in any form whatsoever. For information address Pocket Books, 1230 Avenue of the Americas, New York, NY 10020

ISBN: 0-7434-0364-9

First Pocket Pulse printing April 2001

10 9 8 7 6 5 4 3 2 1

POCKET PULSE and colophon are trademarks of Simon & Schuster, Inc.

Cover art by Anna Dorfman

Printed in the U.S.A.

For
Tom Sniegoski

ACKNOWLEDGMENTS

Thanks are due most especially to my editor, Lisa Clancy, for her enthusiasm (particularly references to crack) as well as to my agent, Lori Perkins. As always, my love and gratitude to my wife, Connie, and my wonderful boys, Nicholas and Daniel.

AUTHOR'S NOTE

Those readers familiar with Boston may note that I have taken certain liberties for the sake of my story.

I won't tell if you won't.

PROLOGUE

The taste of a child's blood.

The subway train shrieked as it entered the Government Center station, brakes squealing in pain. The boy shouldered his backpack and stepped off the train and onto the platform amid a tumble of humans, going about the business of their lives. It was after 7:00 P.M. and most were going home. Not this boy. From the heft of his bag and the set of his gaze he was on his way somewhere other than home. Books in there, probably. Maybe a night class.

The man waited until the milling about had ceased. Just before the doors closed, he stood, clutching his slim, stylish briefcase in one hand, and then stepped off the train. He allowed his eyes to glaze over with the numbness of the commuter, but his heart began to beat faster and there was a sureness in his step. A hunger.

This was not his stop.

The boy moved on. Eric Carver followed.

Several different train lines passed through Government Center, a labyrinth of tunnels leading from one line to the other. Numerous staircases led up to various surface exits. When the boy headed into a narrow passageway that would eventually take him up, Eric Carver followed. Several people passed, going in the opposite direction. Then they were alone.

The only noise in the tunnel, other than the distant wailing of trains, was the echo of Eric's footfalls, the sound of the leather soles of his seven-hundred-dollar imported Italian shoes striking the filthy tiled floor. Alone like that, the boy sensed him.

The young, even among humans, had an uncanny sense of self-preservation.

The boy glanced nervously over his shoulder several times as he made his way along the passage toward a stairwell that would take him up. Up to the darkness. To the night. Up to the moon.

Eric could taste the boy's blood on his tongue, feel his teeth tearing the young flesh. He picked up his pace, working to keep the vague, blank expression on his face. He even swung his briefcase a little. And he whistled. A happy tune. It was from a Disney cartoon, he knew. "Hi-ho, hi-ho, it's off to work we go."

It was a long stairwell. Perhaps as many as one hundred steps. As soon as the boy started up, Eric knew it was time. He began to run, though the sound of his shoes on the tiles was quieter somehow. Still, the boy heard him coming and looked back. Eric glanced at his watch and swore, a performance meant to indicate that he was late for something important.

The boy saw. His eyes would tell his brain and his brain would tell his body that there was nothing to worry about. But his heart would begin to hammer in his chest, and in the depths of his mind he would *know*. The young ones always knew. That was why they were such a challenge.

Like a fellow actor in the same bit of absurd theater, the boy glanced at his watch. He did not swear, but made a little *tsk*ing noise with his tongue, and then began to hurry up the stairs.

Eric smiled. He liked the boy. The scent of fear rolled off him in waves.

At the forty-seventh step, Eric gauged that he needed only seven more to overtake the boy, perhaps eleven if the boy panicked and began to sprint.

As he mounted the fifty-second step, Eric tensed, preparing to lunge at the boy.

Then he heard laughter. With an upward glance he saw a trio of young women of various shapes and sizes descending the stairs toward them. One of them muttered a vaguely sexual remark and the others tittered again. Eric growled deep in his chest, but continued hustling up the stairs. On the fifty-fifth step, he passed the boy. On the fifty-sixth, he turned to glance at him and flashed him a bright, toothy grin. A knowing smile.

Lucky boy, he thought. Even though he did not speak the words aloud, he knew the message was clear. The fear in the boy's eyes was not the reward he had hoped for that night, but it would tide Eric over until another opportunity arose.

In his heart he had known that he would lose the boy. That was best. The child, no more than eighteen, had been too tempting to ignore, but taking him there would have been too great a risk.

On the other hand, it would hardly have been the first time Eric had nearly compromised his safety for irresistible prey.

He reached the top of the stairs and walked out into the night, still swinging his briefcase, still whistling happily. The half-moon was bright in the clear, cold March sky, and it pulled at him, tugging painfully at his flesh, as though prying and digging into him to reveal the truth of Eric Carver, the secret within the man.

It was late by the time Eric returned to his apartment. He had boarded the T again and ridden it to Copley Square, then wandered about for a while, prowling, sniffing at the city. Eventually he had found his way to Morton's. It always amused him how many people had trouble finding the place. An office tower sat above it, all glass and steel, and simply by looking at it one would never imagine someone might have put a restaurant in the basement—well, if it weren't for the sign, of course.

But the smell. The succulent odor of cooking flesh was irresistible. Eric ate at Morton's at least once a week. Whenever he descended into the basement restaurant, the mâitre d' would always find a table for him, never mind that he had no reservation. Mr. Carver, a regular customer, was well known to the staff at Morton's as an excellent tipper, a wine connoisseur, and a lover of steak eaten raw enough to break federal health guidelines.

Nobody minded breaking a few rules for Eric Carver.

Tonight he ordered the super porterhouse, very rare, along with a baked potato and a salad. The wine he drank came from his own personal reserve, a service the restaurant offered only to its most valued customers. Eric Carver was relatively young, or at least he appeared to be. In only a handful of years he had become one of the highest paid attorneys at Gallows and Winter, where he was already a junior partner.

He was a mover and a shaker.

He was more than that as well, and perhaps people sensed it. Some did. It always fascinated Eric that of those who sensed something unusual about him, some shied away while others moved closer, as if sticking their heads in the maw of the lion.

After dinner Eric went home alone, as he did most often. There were women. A great many women, in fact. Some of them had even been to Morton's with him, and he had taken a significant few back to his apartment. But none of them ever went there a second time. Alone with Eric, they invariably found him a bit too . . . wild. Polished as he might be in court or at a deposition, within the confines of his own lair he was, to say the least, a little rough.

On the far side of Copley Square not far from the Boston Public Library there stood an ornate Catholic church that had been closed and sold off in 1957. The nave and transept had been transformed into office space, to no one's great surprise. But the seven-story bell tower, with its medieval interiors, its stained-glass windows and its 213 steps from top to bottom, had been sold to a private developer and transformed into a luxury apartment. For someone of an athletic nature, of course. And Eric Carver was nothing if not athletic.

He walked across the park at Copley Square, shying away from the paved paths where couples strolled hand in hand. A crew of teenagers cruised past, one on a skateboard and the others marching with a bounce that was half-dance and half-challenge. Eric chuckled at the spectacle of the young ones, at the airs they put on, thinking themselves so dangerous.

At the other end of the square he crossed the street and reached into his pocket for the keys to the church tower. An old man walking his dog along the sidewalk was nearly yanked off his feet as his yippy poodle began to bark in alarm and haul on its leash.

Eric pulled out his keys and jingled them in his hand. He smiled at the man, baring his teeth. The dog stopped, crouched into a defensive posture and bared his teeth also.

"You oughta have that pup looked at," he told the geezer. "Got a nervous condition or something."

The old man frowned and ducked his head as he moved off, the dog very enthusiastically pulling him onward. Eric heard him mutter to the poodle, barely above a whisper. Still, he heard it. The words were unkind, but Eric ignored them. He had enjoyed himself tonight. One frail old man and his dog weren't going to change that.

Weird smell to the dog, though. He'd noticed that. It was unusual for a house pet to have such a raw odor, such a feral scent. Even as Eric turned the key in the lock at his front door, he tried to shake the smell from his nostrils and could not. He pushed the door open with his knee, left hand clutching his briefcase, right hand holding the keys, and he glanced one more time along the sidewalk toward the old man and the dog with the wild scent.

It wasn't the dog.

A hand that was barely human whipped out from inside his apartment, grabbed Eric by his thick brown hair and painfully hauled him inside. Powerful hands slammed him face first against the door, closing it. It was too quick for him to get a look at his captor. Huge, powerful hands. He felt the beast behind him, heard it sniffing him, felt the moist heat of its breath on his neck.

Then the hands let him go and he turned to see the beast. Shadows fell across his face, but his green-and-yellow eyes glistened just the same. Wet, like an animal's. The face was hard and stubbled and a trio of identical white scars marred the left side, from temple to jaw. The beast snorted.

Eric pulled himself up to his full height but was still seven inches too short to meet him eye to eye.

It was dark in the stone-and-wood foyer at the base of the tower, but Eric could see perfectly well in the dark. Far better than a human. The beast was not alone. Others were all around him, there in the shadows. One of them, a beautiful black woman with blazing orange eyes and hair dyed blood-red, crouched on the steps. Eric counted seven of them. He sniffed the air and realized there were more upstairs, in his lair.

A low growl began deep in Eric's chest, but it was cut off instantly as the beast grabbed him again. Thick fingers splayed against his chest and slammed him back against the door. The beast lowered his head to stare at him, green-yellow eyes blazing.

"You know who I am?" the huge creature snarled in a voice like snakes gliding across sandpaper.

Eric could not help himself. He looked down at his shoes, too frightened to meet the cruel gaze.

"Tanzer," he whispered. "You're Tanzer."

"You heard what happened in Detroit?" Tanzer rumbled.

Shuddering, afraid he might wet himself, Eric nodded. In the dark around him the others shifted, moving closer, circling him. Closing in. The black woman with orange eyes tossed her fiery hair back and grinned, showing her teeth, like a shark's.

Tanzer pressed harder on Eric's chest until he could not breathe. The beast's talons dug in; Eric could feel them through his suit.

"It's going to happen here," Tanzer told him. "What you've been living is a lie. A charade. It's over now."

Eric wanted to balk, wanted to shout *"No,"* tell the beast that he had made this life, carved out his hunting ground. All he could manage was a tiny shake of his head. "This is . . . my lair," he said, ashamed at how weak he sounded. "You're not supposed to—"

"Do I need to piss in a corner to mark it?" Tanzer roared. With one swift movement he reached down and unzipped his pants. "Because it *is* mine, Carver. I bring you the wind and the wild. It can bring you life as you've never known it, or it can hunt and kill and eat you. Call of the wild, boy. What's it to be?"

They were all around him, panting in the dark. Tongues flicked out to lick lips in anticipation. One of them was even drooling. Eric could smell their blood, and the animal scent of them was almost overpowering. The wildness.

Slowly he raised his eyes to Tanzer's. Then he leaned forward, just an inch or two, and threw his head back, exposing his neck. Tanzer opened his massive jaws, hot breath coming fast, and closed his sharp teeth on the smooth flesh of Eric's throat.

"You are mine," Tanzer told him. "And we are yours."

He moved away, and one by one, the members of the pack, even the weakest of them, took his throat in their jaws.

Carver was the lowest in the order of the pack now. But in time he might rise above some of them.

The charade was over. The moon was high.

The beasts were loose.

C H A P T E R 1

Glass shattered.

The clientele of Bridget's Irish Rose Pub hushed for a heartbeat to glance in the general direction of the sound. A waitress had dropped a beer mug. Instantly the chatter of the crowd resumed, people tossing back pints of Guinness on draft or digging into steaming, succulent servings of shepherd's pie. Bridget's pub served a hell of a shepherd's pie.

Nineteen-year-old Jack Dwyer hustled the short distance from the huge cooler to the long oak bar, two cases of Budweiser long-necks in his arms. The customers who came to Bridget's tended to want draft, and they tended to want it Irish, or the next best thing. If not Irish, then Sam Adams. But there were still plenty of people to whom Bud was the king of beers. The long-necks were heavy, and Jack had built up considerable biceps and shoulder muscles over the years carry-

11

ing kegs and cases out of the cooler. He'd never lifted weights in his life, didn't need to.

Still, "strong" was a relative term, and the cases were heavy, and the veins stood out in his arms and neck as he carried the beer toward the bar. Plenty of regulars frequented Bridget's for dinner, but others came in just to drink. Despite the crowd milling about—Saturday nights the pub was packed from mid-April on—he spotted half a dozen he recognized, some he even knew by name.

Jack only saw him in profile, but the goon standing at the end of the bar, blocking his way, didn't look at all familiar. He was maybe six feet tall, which beat Jack by an inch or two, needed a shave, and had slack features that indicated he'd had three or four too many.

"Bartender," the guy said a little too loud.

Over the Saturday night ruckus, nobody heard him except the twentyish couple who sat on the nearest stools waiting for a table. Bill Cantwell was down at the other end of the bar, pulling a pair of pints for a couple of Celtics fans with their eyes glued to the TV bracketed to the wall behind the bar.

"Hey!" the goon snapped. His hands were on the edge of the bar, his body almost completely behind it now. "Bartender!"

Jack was leaning back, holding the beer cases against his body, putting the weight on his neck and shoulders. The guy was in his way.

"Excuse me," he said, loud enough, but with as little inflection as possible.

The guy rounded on him, wobbly on his feet. He glared blearily down at Jack with his lip curled up, his eyes narrowed. "'Hell's your problem?"

With a sigh, Jack held in the angry retort that was on the tip of his tongue. "Just trying to get the beer through. If you'll give the bartender a second, I'm sure he'll be right with you."

The drunk snorted dismissively, turned around still blocking the way, and called out for the bartender again.

"Hey," Jack said, and he bumped the guy with the cases of beer he was carrying.

Furious, the man attempted to shove him away. Jack slid easily out of the way and the fool stumbled past him. His path was now clear.

"Thanks," Jack said, smiling pleasantly.

"You little—" the guy began, as he reached for Jack.

With a grunt, Jack knocked away the guy's hands with the cases of beer, then put them down on the floor behind the bar with a clank of glass against glass. As he was standing up, the guy reached for him again. Not to take a poke at him, but to pick him up like a rag doll.

Jack slapped his hand away, pointed at him, snarling: "Customers are not allowed behind the bar, *sir*. The bartender will be with you in a moment. And when he is, *sir*, he will tell you that you have had too damn much to drink and that you should go home before you get your ass thrown out of here or hauled across town by Boston's Finest. *Sir*."

The guy glowered, nodding a bit woozily. There was

spittle on his chin and he clenched his fists and started toward Jack again. Jack tensed, ready for it.

"Is there a problem here?" a deep voice boomed.

Jack paused, let out a breath. The drunk blinked in surprise and looked past him. Bill Cantwell had finally come closer and now stood with his big arms crossed and his bushy eyebrows pinned together in a scowl. His beard and hair were more salt than pepper these days, but he was still as formidable a presence as he had been when he played center for the New England Patriots fifteen years earlier.

"You gonna let this punk talk to me like that?" the drunk sputtered. He tried to stand up straight, make himself a little more imposing in Big Bill's presence. He failed miserably.

"What do you think I should do about it?" Bill asked, amused.

The drunk liked that. Nodded to himself. "You oughta fire 'im, treatin' a customer like that. Dock his pay at least."

Bill shook his head slowly. "I don't think I can do that, my friend."

"Why the hell not?" the drunk said with a sneer.

"For one, Jack's right. Only staff behind the bar, and I can't serve anyone who's obviously so drunk he probably only stumbled in here 'cause the last place stopped serving him. That'd be you. The other reason I can't do that is 'cause Jack here is one of the people who makes the rules and signs the checks. See, he owns fifty percent of this place."

The drunk was dumbfounded, staring at Bill in disbelief, then glancing at Jack, then back at Bill. Jack smiled.

"If I was you, I'd move on out of here without raising a fuss," Bill went on. "See, Jack wasn't kidding about throwing you out. He's a kid, sure enough, and polite as can be, just like his mother taught him, but he'll break you in half if you get in his face. I've seen it happen."

Still smirking, the drunk glanced doubtfully at Jack, who kept smiling. But it was a cold smile, and he was bouncing just a bit on the balls of his feet.

Once, twice, the intoxicated fool opened his mouth to say something. At length, he turned away. "Chrissakes," he muttered under his breath, "all's I wanted was a beer."

Together, they watched him set off for the door. Rather than walk along the bar—the easiest way out— he weaved in and out among the tables, bumping a chair here and there. Patrons glared at him angrily and two older women watched him aghast as he pushed out the door.

Jack raised his eyebrows and shook his head. "I don't get it," he said. "It's like they see the word *pub* and think it's somewhere they can drink till they puke. I mean, c'mon, have a look around. This is a nice place."

With a sigh, he looked up at Bill. "Thanks."

Bill nodded, chuckling to himself. "Anytime, tough guy. Now get that beer out of my way and into the ice before I fall over and break an arm."

"Or the floor," Jack muttered, then squeaked a protest as Bill whapped him lightly on the head. "All right, all right. Can't take a joke."

Both of them were grinning.

Bill went back to pulling pints, and Jack started stuffing Bud long-necks into the iceboxes under the bar. He was down there on the scarred wooden floor when Courtney found him.

"Are you hiding down there or working?"

The last of the Buds had been stashed away, so Jack stood up and faced his sister across the bar.

"What's up?" he asked her.

Court was twenty-eight, but looked older, despite the spattering of freckles across the bridge of her nose. There were lines around her blue eyes and at the corners of her mouth, and she had cut her sandy blond hair to shoulder length a few years back just to save time in the mornings. On their own, Jack knew those things would not necessarily have made Courtney Dwyer look older than her age. But once you added the cane . . .

Court rapped on the bar with the lion's head on her black cane, which had once belonged to their maternal grandfather, Conan Sears. "Earth to Jack. You're gonna be late."

His hands were damp from the ice and he wiped them on his pants even as his sister's words sank in. "What? Oh, wait, what time is it?"

With a sigh, Courtney held out her watch so he could see the hands. Twenty past seven.

"Damn!" he snapped. "Artie'll be here in ten minutes."

"You'd better change, then. You don't want to be less than beautiful for dear old Artie," Courtney teased.

Jack's head spun. He glanced around the bar, then out onto the floor of the restaurant. It was busy. Waiters and waitresses hustled, faces intent, and up at the front at least a dozen people stood waiting for tables and glaring at Wendy, the hostess on duty.

"I . . ." His voice trailed off. He glanced at Courtney. "Are you sure you don't need me? It's pretty busy."

A look of mock horror spread across her face. "My God, Jack, I don't know," she said in a fluttery voice, a hint of their late mother's brogue hiding in there. "What do you think, Bill? Can we spare the lad for the night?"

The burly bartender topped off a pint of Bass from the tap, slid it over to a customer, then moved down the bar toward them, looking patiently bemused. "What are you two going on about?"

"Our boy's got a hot date," Courtney told Bill.

Jack sagged against the bar. Nobody could make him feel twelve years old again the way his sister could.

"Oh, really?" Bill said, puffing up his chest and crossing his arms. "And do we get to meet this girl, or are you hiding her from us? Not good enough for her, are we? Or is she not good enough for us?"

"Kill me," Jack mumbled, and let his forehead slam down on the bar. He bumped it against the wood several times.

"Her name's Kate," Courtney said. "She's one of Artie and Molly's friends. Has her eye on our Jack, this Kate does."

"Can I go now?" Jack pleaded, forehead still on the bar. He could feel the grain against his skin and a damp spot where someone had set a glass not too long ago.

"I don't know if we can do without you," Courtney replied.

Jack laughed, stood up, and walked out from behind the bar. "I get it, Court. But if the place falls down on you, don't blame me."

"Be a gentleman tonight, Jack," Bill called after him.

With a shake of his head and a grin he could not hide, Jack held up his left hand and shot Bill the finger, blocking the gesture from the view of the patrons with his right. "You played professional football, buddy. I've heard about those locker rooms. Don't tell me about being a gentleman."

"Hey!" Courtney snapped, chiding him for real this time. "Watch that."

Jack's only reply was an expression of perfect who-me? innocence.

Bridget's Irish Rose Pub was two blocks from Quincy Market in downtown Boston. Most of the buildings around it were residential, though more businesses had sprung up in storefronts in recent years. Once upon a time the tourists and locals who swarmed Quincy Market had seemed to exist in a kind of box, and the neighborhoods on either side had been invisible beyond the walls of that box.

Over time, however, that had changed. The streets around Bridget's were cleaner, the buildings brighter, and more often than not, couples discovered the place by strolling hand in hand along the sidewalk. In reality, only a small percentage of the Quincy Market crowd wandered down that way, but it was enough to turn a once struggling neighborhood pub into a thriving business.

The transition had taken time. Others might have thought of Courtney Dwyer and her little brother as persistent, but the truth was, they'd had no choice. Bridget's was all they had in life and they'd had to make what they could of it, despite the odds and the mortgages and the times bankruptcy had loomed.

As Jack changed clothes in his bedroom on the top floor of the building he and his sister owned, he looked at the framed picture of his mother on the bureau and silently thanked her. It was a ritual for him, something he did whenever the photo caught his eye.

Nine years she had been dead, but he still lived by Bridget Dwyer's example every day. One look around his room was testament to that. The bed was made, clothes put away, and there was very little clutter except for the stacks of western novels ready to spill out of the overstuffed bookshelf. His mother had taught him that if he could keep his house in order, he could keep his life in order. That was her way of looking at the world.

Sometimes it worked, sometimes it didn't, but it comforted him.

Jack's greatest regret was that she had not lived to see what her little pub had become.

"Wish me luck, Ma," he said, his voice low.

With a light touch to his pockets to confirm the presence of his wallet and keys, Jack left the room. On the stairs he looked at his watch—7:45. He was running late, but not so late that Kate would be offended. He barely knew the girl, but he didn't want her to get the wrong impression. They had met three or four times, when he had been out with Artie Carroll and Artie's girlfriend, Molly Hatcher. Kate was cute but quiet. Apparently not so quiet that it kept her from telling Molly she'd like to see more of Jack, though.

Not a bad thing, he thought.

It was worth a shot, anyway. Through high school, Jack had never dated much because of his responsibilities to the pub and to his sister. But he'd been out almost a year now, and since school was no longer part of the equation, he figured it was time to get himself some kind of social life.

Jack was nervous. He hated it, but there was nothing he could do about it. As he opened the door that led down into the restaurant, he surveyed himself one last time. A shower and a fresh shave; his short, bristly hair barely needed a brush. He wore decent-looking black boots that Courtney had bought him for Christmas, a pair of Levi's, and a white T-shirt under an olive-green V-neck sweater. No jacket. He wondered if it would get cold, but shrugged off the thought. Better to be cold than to carry a coat around if it was too warm.

One deep breath, then he stepped out on to the landing at the top of the steps, locked the door behind him, and went down into the maelstrom of the restaurant. Bud Trainor was taking dinner orders at a table for six. Missy Keane and Kiera Dunphy were going in opposite directions burdened with trays of appetizers, twisting to slide back to back like ballet dancers or synchronized swimmers. Food service as an Olympic event.

No Courtney.

Jack glanced around, turned to look back toward the kitchen. The swinging doors were beneath the stairs he had just descended, and he spotted his sister just in front of them, talking to Tim Dunphy, Kiera's brother, who was the best cook they had. He looked agitated and rubbed the stubble on his shaved head as he spoke. The tattoos up and down his skinny arm seemed to dance with the motion.

Courtney shook her head, leaned on her cane a bit more than usual, and flexed her bad leg unconsciously.

With a tiny curse under his breath, Jack hurried toward them. "What's wrong now?" he asked.

"Friggin' Marty," Tim grunted. "Cut his hand 'cause he was drinkin' before work again." He turned back to Courtney. "You gotta fire the guy. Seriously, c'mon. Bad enough some of these guys get in pissing matches 'cause one's from Dorchester and one's from Southie, but I can't use guys I can't depend on."

Courtney's expression was grim. She had never

understood how people could hate each other just because they lived in a different neighborhood in the same city. Yet Tim had somehow managed to keep the peace in his kitchen. The least she could do was handle a problem like this. "I'll take care of it."

"Where's Marty now?" Jack asked.

"Went to the friggin' hospital," Tim said, rolling his eyes. "Now I'm short one guy."

Jack looked at Courtney. "I could—"

"I'll take care of it, I said!" his sister snapped.

Her eyes were harsh, but Jack knew she was not really angry with him, only frustrated. The words she had not spoken were just as clear as the ones she had: *I've been doing this since I was nineteen and you were still in grade school, Jackie. I'm not an invalid.*

He took a breath, still concerned, but saw that she would brook no argument.

"Artie's at the bar. He's been waiting for you twenty minutes," she said quickly. "You should go before he breaks into song or convinces Bill to give him a beer just to shut him up."

Jack laughed, then Courtney and Tim joined him, and the tension had passed. They would work something out. They always had. He turned and moved swiftly through the restaurant, dodging customers, servers, and busboys, becoming part of the ballet himself. Artie was sitting at the far end of the bar, near the enormous frosted windows that faced the street. He was eating popcorn from a bowl and jabbering at Bill Cantwell, who was staring at Artie in a combination of amazement and dismay. More than likely, Artie was waxing poetic on one of his many favorite subjects, from gun control to the legalization of prostitution to conspiracies in the U.S. government.

Artie was something else. It wasn't really that those issues meant a lot to him, he just liked to have things to talk about, to get a debate going. That had always been his nature, but even more so since the previous fall, when he had begun his freshman year at Emerson College, studying broadcasting. As Jack approached, he heard Artie's rambling and knew the topic was gun control. He smiled. Artie had been born and raised in downtown Boston, just like Jack. Boston Catholic High School boys. But to look at him less than a year after graduation, one would think he'd been raised in southern California. His blond hair was long now, and shaggy enough that he perpetually needed a haircut. He didn't dress like a surfer. It was April in New England, after all. But the ripped, hooded Boston College sweatshirt he wore with jeans and battered high-tops fit his new persona perfectly.

Artie had always been eccentric, though, so despite the fact that his new look had surprised other friends and even Artie's parents, Jack barely noticed. Artie was just Artie. And his girlfriend, Molly, didn't seem bothered by his quirks either.

"Hey," Jack said.

Without glancing around, Artie threw a kernel of popcorn over his shoulder and it hit Jack in the face. Then he turned quickly, feigning remorse.

"Oh, sorry, bro. Didn't see you standing there." Artie grinned.

"Sorry I'm so late. Things just got—"

"Nuts, I know. It happens, man. Just to you more often than others. It's your life, you gotta live it. We oughta get moving, though." When Artie spoke, his sentences all seemed to run together, as if his mouth had gotten ahead of his brain.

Jack looked around. "Where are the girls? Are we meeting them somewhere or—"

"Nah, they're double-parked across the street. Didn't think you'd be so backed up. Not that there's any parking around here anyway, right?"

"They've been outside all this time and you didn't think maybe you should tell them I was running late?" Jack asked, thinking Kate was probably ready to go home.

Artie frowned, looked at Jack as though he had been insulted. "Jack, come on. They're smart girls. They'll figure it out. We should go, though. Molly's patience isn't infinite, y'know?"

"She's in love with you," Jack replied archly. "She must be pretty patient, right?"

Artie punched him, slid off the stool, and turned back to Bill Cantwell, who had moved down the bar to hand a pair of sweating Budweiser long-necks to a couple of older guys waiting for a table.

"We'll have to finish our talk another time," Artie called.

"Yeah. Looking forward to it," Bill told him, with a

wave and a look that he usually reserved for rambling drunks and madmen.

Together, Artie and Jack walked past the frosted glass toward the front door. Jack felt surprisingly good, despite the weight of the responsibility he was shrugging off for the night. Or maybe because of it. He strolled toward the door with a calm he did not usually feel, as Artie bounced along beside him, rattling with energy as always, muttering "Hey" and "How ya doin'?" to Bridget's staffers he passed, just in case he'd met them before and forgotten.

As he pushed out the door, Jack glanced at Wendy, the hostess. Short-cropped red hair, green eyes, perfect smile, twenty-five. She was on the phone, but when she saw him she held up a finger to get his attention. "Just a moment, sir," she said into the phone. Then she covered the receiver. "Jack, we've got a party of twelve want to get in at eight-thirty. What do you think? You want to carve that kind of space out for that big a reservation?"

Jack opened his mouth to respond, to solve the problem, then shook his head and smiled. "Know what, Wendy? I'm not working tonight. You really should check with Courtney."

With that, he pushed through the door behind Artie and out onto the streets of Boston.

A free man.

Vanilla.

Her eyes darted about, scanning the people around

her as she moved along the sidewalk, on the hunt. On the prowl. Ready to spring but forcing herself to stay calm, to play it cool, to lurk among the prey, unseen. Her entire body thrummed with the unreleased energy of her carnal desire, her bloodlust.

Vanilla.

Where had that scent come from? So enticingly sweet, but only the barest whiff. With a frown, Jasmine paused and lifted her nose just a bit, sniffed the air.

There.

An almost new Toyota was parked illegally a few yards back, hazard lights blinking. The engine was not running, and the front windows were open. Through the windshield, Jasmine could see two girls. Young and tender flesh, perhaps eighteen. No more than twenty. The passenger had wild red hair, past her shoulders, and her laughter as the two girls talked was innocent and warm. The other, the driver, was colder. She was like ice, with short blond hair cut in stylish waves to frame her diamond-cut features. Her voice was full of presumed knowledge and expectation.

She was Vanilla. Her natural human pheromonal scent was masked by some sort of perfume, but it was not offensive to Jasmine's nose the way so many such concoctions were.

Vanilla. She looked cold but smelled sweet. And beneath the ice, the hot, raw vulnerability at the center of all humans.

Jasmine felt a tiny shudder go through her and the hairs on the back of her neck bristled with anticipation.

Her flesh wanted to be released, the beast within yearning to be free, but she focused enough to control the urge. Tanzer had taught her well. Her tongue snaked out and slid along her upper lip. She quivered as she took a deep breath and then let it out. After another moment she crossed the dozen feet between herself and the Toyota and crouched by the passenger window.

The girls' conversation faltered and they each shot her a questioning glance.

"Hi!" Jasmine said, light and friendly.

"Hi," the passenger responded hesitantly.

Jasmine inhaled deeply of them, of Vanilla in particular, a smile on her face.

"Do we know you?" Vanilla asked.

"Sorry," Jasmine replied, sublimating her ancient accent as best she could. "I'm just a bit lost. Can you tell me how to find Quincy Market?"

The passenger smiled and pushed her hair behind her ears. "Yeah. You could spit on it from here. You're headed in the right direction. Just . . . right down there where you can see all the people—that's it."

Jasmine thanked them. The girls looked at her oddly, but she did not mind. She had felt an undeniable temptation to move closer, to inhale that aroma. With a tiny, playful wave, she walked on. A moment later she glanced back to see that the girls were once again engaged in conversation and paying no attention to her at all. She ducked into a narrow alley between two aging buildings and headed for the fire escape. The metal ladder was not down, but she easily made the twelve-foot leap to grasp the first landing.

With a quick glance about to see that she was not being watched, Jasmine scrambled soundlessly up the fire escape to the fourth-floor landing, from which she leaped to the roof. Her muscles rolled beneath her flesh as if they had a life of their own, and as she moved she knew that her features and the texture of her skin had changed.

The beast was surging up inside her. She shook it off and moved to the edge of the roof. From there she watched Vanilla and the other girl in the Toyota for another thirteen minutes until two young men walked out of the pub across the street and slid into the backseat of the car. Their scents were interesting as well.

The engine roared to life and the car began to roll off.

Jasmine pursued it. She moved swiftly across the roof, darting with extraordinary speed through the nighttime shadows like a wraith. With a grunt she leaped a sixteen-foot gap between buildings without breaking stride, then continued on.

On the breeze, she scented others in her pack. She tilted her head back and uttered their ancient cry, throat vibrating with it. The others responded, moving toward her through the neighborhood. Below, the car took a right turn. Jasmine sprinted to the far end of the roof and leaped out into open space, arms widespread as she fell to a roof two stories lower. She hit, went down to her knees and rolled, then was up in an instant and running.

By the time her keen eyes detected others of the pack converging, two on the ground and one on the rooftop across the street, she had already identified each of them by scent.

The gray Toyota with Vanilla behind the wheel stopped at a traffic signal, then sped up with the flow of traffic when the light turned green. Jasmine's lips curled back from spiked teeth as she gave voice to the ululations of the pack once more. The breeze whipped her hair, and her legs pumped beneath her, carrying her at inhuman speed across the rooftops of the city of Boston.

The hunt was on.

CHAPTER 2

"So here's this guy, computer software sales-man, makes about three hundred thousand a year, if not more, lives in a half-million-dollar house in the burbs with his perfect perky wife and his perfect perky kids and he shows up at the church for the wedding of his best friend with beach chairs and a cooler full of Corona, and he sits in the parking lot drinking beer for an hour before the ceremony starts. Then he has to read the prayers of the faithful, right up there on the altar, and he's slurring his words."

Artie and Molly chuckled good-naturedly, consider-ing they had heard the story before. They had urged Kate to tell it for Jack's benefit, and he was glad they did. He laughed and shook his head in disbelief.

"You've gotta be kidding me," he said. "So this is your sister's husband's best friend? Did she ban the guy from the house?"

"You'd think, right?" Kate replied, rolling her head. "But, no. No ban. She just tortures the guy by telling the story every chance she gets, and she uses it to keep him in line as much as possible."

Jack watched her as she spoke, the way her hair—cut into a style that was almost jagged, all sharp, dangerous angles—revealed a soft luster whenever she tilted her head forward. She did that often, and it conveyed a sense of intimacy as if she were speaking only to him. He watched the way her icy blue eyes glinted in the dim lights, and the way her lips moved to form words completely untainted by the Boston accent the rest of them had. Kate's family had moved from Ohio to Boston when she was in the seventh grade.

They had met a few times before, and Jack had thought she was attractive and nice enough, but he had been unprepared for such a startling girl. In the environment of the Dixie Kitchen—a spectacular Cajun restaurant tucked down a side street in the South End with a decor only slightly above "dive"—a girl like Kate seemed almost out of place. "Almost" because she had the kind of charisma that could make any place her own.

"What a jerk, huh?" Artie put in.

The spell was broken. Jack smiled at Kate, a bit bewildered by her, and she flashed him a sly grin as her eyes held on his a moment longer than necessary.

Jack blinked, turned to Artie and Molly with a shocked expression. "What?" he said, aghast. "You mean when you guys tie the knot I can't hang out and tailgate at the church before the wedding bells ring?"

Artie fumbled for a response, his head sort of bobbing. The easiest way to throw him off-balance, or to interrupt him when he was blasting off on another rocket of a tangent, was to bring up marriage.

Molly did not hesitate. She whacked Jack in the arm, eyes narrowed in mock fury. "You can feel free to tailgate all you want that day," she said, "'cause you'll be out there for the ceremony, too. You won't be invited inside."

Jack shot her a wounded look. "I'll crash the service, then, Moll. How could I live without seeing you radiant in white on the day you took your vows to Shaggy over here."

"Hey!" Artie protested. Then he grinned. "I resemble that remark."

Molly sighed. On her, impatience was a beautiful thing. She was so damned smart, and yet so completely at home with that intelligence and comfortable in her skin, that the simple fact that she had always put up with the two guys made Jack love her as much as he did Artie. Sometimes more. He admired Molly, too. Her parents were divorced and she and her mother got by on next to no money. They lived in Dorchester, at the edge of a neighborhood that was all boarded-up windows and stolen cars. Just at the edge. Molly had known early on that all her smarts wouldn't get her everything she needed, so she had worked extra hard to find scholarship money.

In the fall, she'd be heading off to Yale.

Kate was going to Holy Cross.

Jack glanced around the table at his friends, and this sweet, fascinating girl they had introduced him to, and much as he knew they would argue the point, he felt excluded.

From somewhere in the back of his head, a distant memory was dredged up. *"One of these things is not like the others . . ."* The song flashed through his head, its lilting melody a powerful recollection. Then it was gone.

But the feeling remained.

Artie had been his best friend since the third grade, and he'd known Molly from the first day of junior high. They had dreams to follow, and the means to do it. Jack had the pub. Most of the time, that was okay with him; he loved the place and his sister and the memory of his mother, and he and Courtney had turned Bridget's into something to be proud of.

He knew that didn't matter to Artie and Molly. He would always be Jack to them, for they had known him at a time when he had been defined by age, not occupation. But he wondered about Kate and any other girls he might meet. How important would it be to them that he had not gone to college?

The others laughed suddenly and Jack blinked, smiling dumbfoundedly. He glanced from Artie's face to Kate's, figured one of them had said something funny, and kept smiling, though he felt awkward that he had not heard the source of their amusement.

"Hey, Jack, you want any more popcorn shrimp?"

Artie asked, bouncing a bit in his chair with his ever-present nervous energy.

Jack slid the plate across the table toward him. "Help yourself, bud." They had eaten way too much already. Alligator tail, gumbo, corn bread, jambalaya . . . and that was just him. The popcorn shrimp had been for everyone, but Kate and Molly had eaten most of it. Everyone seemed to be done, except Artie, who wolfed down the last dozen or so shrimp as the conversation turned to a movie the girls had recently seen. Artie, who had been admirably restrained when it came to political riffs during dinner, went off on a tangent about the film being racist, though he had not bothered to see it to bolster his argument.

Molly challenged him on just those grounds, and the two began to debate. It was the way a lot of evenings with the two of them ended. Jack tuned them out and gave his full attention to Kate.

She was also ignoring Molly and Artie. Her little grin was back, and Jack liked the fact that it was uneven, turned up a little farther on one side than the other. Though her features were very sharp, she had the smallest, softest dimple in her left cheek. It was a marvel, as far as he was concerned.

"I'm really glad I came out tonight," he said to her, his voice low, keeping the talk just between the two of them.

"So am I. I'm not usually the type to . . . you know, how I asked Molly to ask Artie to ask you? That seemed really immature. But after the couple of times we met, I thought I'd like to meet you again, and I didn't know how else to go about it."

Jack smiled, shook his head. Kate Nordling was unlike any high school girl he had ever met.

"You're something," he told her.

She blinked, glanced at the grease-spotted tablecloth. "In a good way or a bad way?"

"Definitely a good way."

Those ice-blue eyes turned up toward him again, met his straight on, all sincerity. "Thank you."

Jack just watched her for a few seconds. Then he gave a small shrug. "I guess it's no secret that I work a lot. Most of the time, in fact. But . . . maybe we could do this again soon."

"I could be coerced," Kate assured him.

"Good to know."

While the guys paid the bill, the girls went outside to get some fresh air. As the waiter went off with their cash to make change, Artie moved in for the kill.

"So? What'd you think? 'Cause you know Molly's going to ask me a million questions and if I don't have answers she'll crucify me." He began to ramble. "All right, Kate's a little conservative, but she's nice, right? And pretty much a babe."

Jack leaned forward to stare into his eyes. "Artie!"

Artie blinked at him, mystified.

"If you want me to answer, you actually have to—"

"Leave a space between questions," Artie finished for him. "I know, I know. Sorry, bro. So go on. You were saying?"

"*You* were saying," Jack corrected. "But, yeah, she's very cool. How do you mean conservative?"

"Conservative, bro. Politically. How many definitions are there?"

"I'd guess more than that one. And why do I care if she's politically conservative?"

"Maybe you don't," Artie allowed, though reluctantly. "I just figured you should be aware, right? I mean, whenever I bring up the legalizing prostitution thing, she goes out of her mind. She's just a little too Catholic, Jack."

"I went to twelve years of Catholic school. I can handle it."

Artie grinned like a fool. "So you like her?"

"What was your first clue?"

The waiter came back with the change; Jack left most of it for a tip before they got up and started for the door.

"Cool," Artie said mostly to himself. "Very cool. That'll make Molly very happy."

"We all want a happy Molly," Jack replied.

"Amen."

They pushed out the front door on to the sidewalk in front of the Dixie Kitchen. The girls were maybe twenty feet off to the left, and their conversation died as soon as the guys stepped outside. Jack knew that Molly had been quizzing Kate the same way Artie had quizzed him, but that was okay. Kate glanced at him and smiled, and Jack smiled back. Artie and Molly had been the go-betweens tonight, but Jack and Kate wouldn't be needing them anymore.

Kate lifted her right hand, which had hung by her side out of Jack's view, and took a long drag off the cigarette she held there. Her smile was still in place as she blew out a lungful of smoke.

Damn.

Jack deflated. The last thing he had expected of Kate was that she smoked. He tried to keep the revulsion off his face and wasn't sure if he had succeeded. Never mind that his thoughts of kissing her—and he had had quite a few at dinner—were now tainted because he knew her mouth would taste like an ashtray. That wasn't the worst part. What bothered him the most was that this girl he had thought was so amazing and different and bright would be foolish enough to smoke, knowing that the cigarette companies purposely made a deadly product addictive.

Artie had gun control, prostitution, Republican conspiracies, the spectacle of the evening news, and a dozen other topics that drove him berserk. Jack had smoking.

"All set?" Molly asked.

Jack nodded. "Yeah. Let's get going. I promised Courtney I'd be around for closing."

He didn't feel good about the lie but he knew if he spent too much more time with them his disappointment would show. Kate hung back beside him. As they walked to the car, she reached out and twined her fingers in his. Jack let her, smiled at her.

She took another drag on her cigarette.

As Kate slid behind the wheel, she tossed the butt of

her cigarette on the sidewalk. Artie and Molly climbed into the car, and Jack was about to get in the back with Artie when he felt his skin prickle. The back of his neck felt warm. He frowned and hesitated, then glanced around. Cars passed by on the road. A lot of others were parked, their interiors black, on either side of the street. A handful of people were out, most of them going to one restaurant or another, though he spotted an older man walking a brutish-looking dog a block or so away.

"Jack?" Kate ventured. "You all right?"

He surveyed the storefronts and the darkness between buildings. He took only a second, and then he shook off the feeling that had unnerved him and dropped into the backseat.

"Fine, sorry. My brain froze for a second."

They all chuckled as he put on his seat belt, but Jack didn't join in their laughter. For a moment, he had been positive that someone was watching him. The feeling was familiar, the one he would get while he was sweeping up late at night in the pub with no one around, or when he was little and woke up frightened in the middle of the night.

As Kate put the car in gear and pulled out into traffic, Jack peered into the darkness between two buildings across from the Dixie Kitchen, and blinked in surprise.

Something had moved, back there in the shadows. He was sure of it. The shudder that went through him as he thought of that figure in the dark made him feel like a moron.

It was only a dog, he told himself, *or maybe a homeless person.*

But it hadn't *moved* like a person.

He told himself to forget it, and he did. For a while.

The streets were nearly deserted and most of the storefronts were dark when they pulled up in front of Bridget's. The pub was still open, of course—last call wasn't until a quarter to one—but the kitchen was closed, so there were fewer patrons inside now. The wind had picked up, and the temperature had dropped ten or fifteen degrees. The car heater hummed.

Molly was worried.

Jack smiled and said all the right things, but there was something odd about him. Had been ever since they left the restaurant. It was driving her crazy that she couldn't put a finger on it. Artie was not just her guy, he was her best friend. Jack was like a brother to him and had always been a good friend to her and a confidant as well. He understood things about her that even Artie never had, mainly because Artie's parents were members of that freakish minority in America—happily married people.

Molly wanted Jack to be happy, and to have a social life. She knew that he rarely got out unless she and Artie dragged him to a movie or dinner, and when Kate had expressed interest in him, Molly had been thrilled. If they had hit it off, Jack would have had a chance to act only nineteen for once, and they would be a foursome when they went out, so she wouldn't feel like the token girl.

Things had seemed to be going along really well, and then *poof!* Jack got all squirrelly.

"Hey, thanks for getting me out, you guys," Jack said, as the car idled at the corner.

"Bro, you are going to have a social life if we have to drag you kicking and screaming," Artie told him. He held out a hand, and Jack shook it once, then let go.

Jack climbed out of the car. Before he shut the door he glanced back in at Artie. "Be good."

"Only in public, man," Artie promised.

Jack laughed. He went around to the driver's side door and leaned down to look into the open window at Kate. "Thanks for a nice night," he told her. "It was cool getting to know you better."

Molly winced. She could hear it in Jack's voice; something had happened to sour his date with Kate. She only wished she knew what it was. Not that she could do anything about it. For her part, though, Kate did not seem to notice.

"I had fun too. We'll probably see each other again soon," she said.

"No doubt," Jack agreed with a small laugh. "Not with these two around." He glanced over at Molly and smiled. " 'Night, Moll. Take care of our boy."

"Always," she said, smiling at him. Jack was a charming s.o.b., without ever trying. Almost without realizing it, she slipped one arm between the front seats to hold Artie's hand.

Jack bent to give Kate a kiss, but it was just a polite gesture, the sort of thing you did at the end of a date. Molly knew it, and the expression on Kate's face when Jack turned to walk away told her that Kate knew it too. That did not mean there was no chance they would see each other again—after all, Jack had seemed fine all through dinner—but it sure didn't look good.

Ah, well, nothing can be done about it now, she thought. They would have to let the relationship take its own course. Or not, as the case might be.

"You next, Molly," Kate said as they pulled away from the curb.

Molly took one last look at Jack through the rear window as he jogged to the front door of Bridget's. Artie shot her an inquiring glance. She only smiled and squeezed his hand, still turned halfway around in her seat.

"So what'd you think of Jack?" Artie asked from the back.

"Hmm?" Kate mumbled. She glanced at Molly, then looked at Jack in the rearview mirror. "Oh, sorry. Lost in thought. He's a great guy. Very my type, I think. But . . ."

"But?" Artie asked, obviously fishing.

Molly smiled. Her guy had never been one for subtlety.

"Well, what'd he say about me?" Kate asked. She smiled sheepishly. "Okay, I know how high school that sounds, but freakin' sue me! I'm still in high school for two more months, I'm allowed!"

Molly's eyes went wide and she stared at Kate, then started to giggle. "Whoa. Relax."

"He thinks you're, and I quote, 'very cool.' He likes you. That's a good thing, right?"

Kate smiled. "Right."

They drove for a little while, Molly fiddling with the radio while Artie stretched out in back, resting his eyes. He might have been sleeping; Molly couldn't be sure. Artie could take a five-minute nap just about anywhere.

"So what's Jack's story?" Kate asked, her voice low, as though she thought Artie might be sleeping and wanted to keep the conversation between herself and Molly.

"How do you mean?" Molly asked, also keeping her voice low. "You know his story. We all went to school together, but he didn't go to college so he could help manage his pub."

"I know, I know. But how did he get to that point? I mean, what happened to his parents?"

Molly pursed her lips. She did not like getting into other people's personal business, and these were questions that Kate herself should have asked Jack. On the other hand, this way Jack would not have to tell his story again.

"Nutshell?" Molly asked.

Kate nodded.

"His mom and dad opened Bridget's in the late seventies, bought the building, everything. In the eighties, his Dad got them into a bad financial hole, then took off with some waitress. I don't really know the whole story, but the guy skipped town and hasn't been heard from since. Jack's mom—that was Bridget—she made a go of it on her own. To hell with the old man, right? Bridget turned it all around; the place began picking up business. She dug them out of the hole, or at least started to."

Molly paused, glanced out her window at the streetlights flashing by and at the flat, claustrophobic overcast sky.

"What happened to her?" Kate prodded.

"Jack was ten and in the fifth grade at the time. He and Artie were already close, and Artie remembers it really well, I think. There was some kind of school play or a pageant or something. Mrs. Dwyer got coverage at the pub so she and Courtney, Jack's older sister, could go. On the way home they were going through an intersection when a drunk driver jumped the red light and plowed right into the driver's side of their car."

"Oh, my God!" Kate whispered, glancing over at Molly in horror, then back at the darkened road ahead.

"Jack's mom was killed. Courtney's leg was badly mangled. She still has to use a cane. And Jack walked away with a little cut over his eye. You can still see the scar there, if you look for it. I think he's always felt kind of guilty about that, actually."

"About what?" Kate asked.

"That he wasn't hurt worse."

On the drive through Boston's labyrinthine streets out to Dorchester, Artie did nod off a bit. From time to time the car would bounce through a pothole or one of the girls would laugh loud enough to jostle him awake. Then, contentedly, he would again burrow against the locked door, his body skewed beneath his seat belt in a way that could not have been covered by the safety testers. As he drifted back off he would hear a snippet or two of conversation. Prom. Graduation. Old Orchard Beach for the Fourth of July. Six Flags sometime in June. Summer jobs.

Plans. Molly and Kate had a lot of plans for the summer, for their lives. All of Molly's involved Artie, and he didn't mind at all. Whatever she wanted to do was all right with him. It was not simply that he was too wrapped up in his own world to make decisions about such things, though that was part of it. For the most part, though, his flexibility could be attributed to one thing: he felt lucky as hell to have Molly as his girlfriend and if his wearing a white dinner jacket to the prom made her happy, that was enough reason for him to comply.

Half-asleep, the other thing he noticed from these snatches of conversation was that they had stopped talking about Jack. That was good. Whether or not things worked out with Jack and Kate wasn't really Artie's concern. He just wanted everyone to be happy, be cool with one another, so there would be no awkwardness if they all got together at a party or just went to the movies together.

With those thoughts floating around his head, his eyelids fluttered and he slept again. The next time he opened his eyes it was to the *ding-ding-ding* that the car used to remind the driver that one of the doors was open while the engine was still on.

Molly was getting out.

"Hey, lazybones. You want to ride up front, or is Kate supposed to chauffeur you home?"

Artie looked up to see Molly leaning over the seat in front of him. Her door was open—*ding-ding-ding*—and she had a silly grin on her face.

"No, no, I'm good. Just resting a little bit. You guys were talking, I just figured I'd rest my eyes." He unbuckled his seat belt, popped open the rear door and practically tumbled out of the car.

The car was parked under a streetlamp, and Molly's red hair shone in the light. With a soft smile, she stepped into his arms and kissed him deeply. "Call me in the morning?"

Artie was fully awake now. He gazed into Molly's eyes and laid his forehead against hers. "Sure you don't want me to stay?" he asked. "It's not like you have school in the morning?"

"I have church in the morning," she chided him. "I'd take you with me, but the place would probably fall down if you walked through the front door. Never mind that I somehow doubt my mother would be pleased to find you at the breakfast table."

"Ah, high school girls." Artie sighed.

Molly whacked him on the arm and he chuckled. "Go home," she said.

"Some time tonight!" Kate called from the car.

With a last kiss, Molly turned and headed up to the door of her building. Artie watched until she was safely inside—it was a pretty rough neighborhood—then slipped into the front seat next to Kate.

"You set?" she asked.

"All except the radio," Artie told her. As Kate maneuvered a three-point turn in the middle of the street, he fiddled with the stations. "That's the one thing I'll never understand about you two. Okay, one of several million things. I mean, hello? There's more on the radio in this town than Kiss 108, y'know? Not that there's anything wrong with pop, but spin down the dial, check out something different once in a while, or God forbid click over and listen to NPR. There's still magic in radio if we give it a chance."

Kate snickered.

"What?"

"Sometimes I wonder what planet you're from," she told him.

"What's that mean?" Artie asked, a bit hurt.

With a shake of her head, eyes still on the road, Kate reached over and patted him on the leg. "Just that you're lovably unique, Artie. It's a good thing, trust me."

"All right, then," Artie replied, nodding with satisfaction. "So what do you think—NPR?"

"If you put on National Public Radio the car might explode in protest. Why don't we play it safe and stick to some kind of music, all right?"

"Coward."

They both laughed at that, but their good humor was short-lived. The most convenient way in and out of Molly's neighborhood was through a section of Dorchester that looked almost as though the apocalypse had come and gone and nobody had bothered to tell the rest of the world. Artie had been asleep on the drive out, but now that they were headed back into Boston, he glanced around anxiously.

"How could anybody live here?"

"Easy, if they don't have any other choice," Kate told him. "Or if they need to be as close to a crack house as possible."

"Aren't you Little Mary Sunshine," Artie muttered. He watched the boarded-up or shattered windows and the darkened doorways, and saw a few homeless people around. Down one dark alley they passed he saw a bunch of younger kids standing around a metal trash can with a fire burning inside.

Then they were through; the homes they were now passing were dilapidated, the property uncared for, but this was a far cry from the almost surreal danger of the neighborhood they'd just passed.

"Lovely place," Kate said. "Thank God Molly's going away to college in the fall."

"No kidding," Artie agreed. He glanced over at her. "Listen, Kate, thanks for driving tonight. If you don't want to go all the way back to Emerson, you can just drop me at a T station."

"Nah, no problem. Just don't forget my tip."

Artie smiled.

Without warning, the windshield shattered. The rock that had struck it was the size of a softball, and it hit Artie's shoulder even as he instinctively turned away.

Kate screamed, threw her arms up, too late to protect her face. The car pulled to the left, drifted, bumped up over the curb, and plowed into a telephone pole. Artie heard Kate scream again, and then the scream was cut short and the horn was blaring and it wouldn't stop, and he realized that he had slammed his head on the dashboard and blood was streaming down his face.

His vision was out of focus and his eyelids fluttered as he tried to get his bearings. He felt dizzy even though he was sitting. With effort, he managed to focus enough to figure out which direction the steering wheel was in. Kate was slumped forward, her weight straining at the seat belt. The horn was still blaring, but she wasn't leaning on it. Something had happened under the hood when they crashed, and now the horn was stuck.

Artie shakily wiped at the blood that stung the corners of his eyes and tried to look out through the shattered windshield. Just dark out there. No streetlights. Just the glass and the telephone pole. The horn blaring.

It stopped. Sudden as the rock through their windshield, the horn was cut off midscream. Artie wiped at the blood again, frowned painfully, and glanced out. Something moved in the dark outside the car.

"Help?" he croaked.

Kate's nose was smashed and bleeding, and she was unconscious. They needed an ambulance.

He asked for help again.

Frustrated, still moving in slow motion as though he were under water, Artie fumbled with his seat belt and managed to free himself. He reached for the door handle, pulled it, and tried to get out.

Without the strength or equilibrium to stand, he tumbled to the sidewalk. The side of his head thunked on the paved walk, but he barely felt it. His eyelids drooped, and he must have lost consciousness for a moment.

When he opened his eyes again he felt the pain. His skull felt as if it were made of shards of jagged glass and he was almost afraid to move. Artie Carroll whimpered there on the ground. He winced as he reached up to wipe the blood from his eyes again. He thought of Kate, but dared not lift his head to look for her.

He croaked her name weakly.

No sirens. He wanted to cry at that. How long since they'd crashed? A minute? Three? No sirens.

Something moved at the corner of his vision. He turned his head just a bit, and the pain jabbed into his skull. But he could see a figure approaching now, in the dark. There was a streetlight far off, and it cast just enough light to throw the figure into a dim, almost phosphorescent silhouette.

Then that silhouette began to change.

There came a shriek of tearing metal nearby, and he heard Kate start to scream. She was conscious now, awake and screaming. Something growled and he heard the sound of snapping bone.

Heart pounding against his rib cage as though it were trying to break free, Artie forced himself up and back. He scrambled on his hands and knees, agony spiking through his head, making it almost impossible for him to stand. Then he did try to stand, but he slipped in his own blood and struck the sidewalk again.

Then it was above him.

Artie's breathing came too fast, and he had the coppery taste of his own blood in the back of his mouth. It had been a man, standing over him. He knew that. But now it was something else. Its eyes blazed orange in the dark, its wet snout gleamed. Its fur was sleek, with muscles rippling beneath it.

It growled. But the growl sounded like a laugh.

Kate had stopped screaming. Now it was Artie's turn.

The wet snout dipped down, and he felt its hot breath on his throat; then teeth ripped his flesh with a sickening tearing sound.

It was the last sound Artie heard.

CHAPTER 3

Every Sunday morning Jack woke up early and walked the four blocks to Store 24 to get a chocolate Nestlé Quik and the *Boston Globe*. Most of the time he didn't read the paper, but the Sunday *Globe* was a sort of tradition in his family, different sections and coupons and the comics spread across the breakfast table. Some people had church. The Dwyers had the *Sunday Globe*.

Another part of the tradition was an impossibly large stack of pancakes made with Bisquick and served with Log Cabin maple syrup. Not that low-fat stuff, either.

That particular Sunday morning Jack had the pancakes ready at seven-thirty, pats of butter already melting on top, but Courtney had not yet emerged from her bedroom. He had been glancing through the book review section for any new biographies that might be of interest, but as the butter melted, he frowned and glanced down the hall.

With one last sip of his pulpy orange juice, Jack went and knocked on her door. "Court?"

"Come in," she called with obvious frustration.

Jack pushed open the door and found his sister at the small desk in the corner of her bedroom writing checks, a small stack of bills by her hand.

"Pancakes are going to get cold."

She looked up in surprise, then glanced at her watch. "Damn, we've gotta get going." Courtney signed one last check, slipped it into an envelope, then sealed it. "Smells good," she said as she grabbed her cane. Then she followed him back to the kitchen.

During breakfast she grilled him about his date with Kate the night before, which he had expected, but their talk soon turned to more pressing matters. Pub matters. Jack agreed to prepare the work schedule for the following week, post it downstairs, and then go over the bar orders. Courtney took care of ordering for the restaurant end of their business, but Jack had taken over the actual pub portion of Bridget's Irish Rose Pub when he was a sophomore in high school.

"How's it look outside?" she asked as she rinsed dried syrup from their dishes.

Jack put the syrup bottle and the juice away. "What, you sat in there paying your Macy's and Visa bills and didn't bother to look out the window?"

"Pretty much, yeah."

"Nice day," he told her, chuckling. "A real nice day,

actually, for April. Gonna be in the sixties, I think, and blue skies. I've got the windows open in my room. Quincy Market'll be packed."

"Then so will the pub," Courtney said, frowning.

"Hello? That's a good thing, isn't it? Kinda what we want? Most Irish pub owners would kill to be swamped at lunch on a Sunday."

Courtney laughed. "Yeah, yeah. I know. Just wondering if I should call Wendy and see if she can come in. I don't want to be caught shorthanded."

"We'll handle it," Jack reassured her. "If things get completely nuts, well, we'll roll with it. That's the best part. Our own circus act."

Courtney rolled her eyes. "Yeah. With no net."

"A net takes all the fun out of it."

"Go take a shower," she said. "We've got work to do."

The TV was on in Jack's bedroom as he got dressed. His hair was still wet from the shower but he pulled a shirt over it anyway. Yet another from his drawer full of short-sleeved, collared polo shirts with three buttons at the throat and "Bridget's Irish Rose Pub" sewn into the breast. This one was the most recent model—burgundy with navy blue stitching. Customers could buy them at the bar for thirty-two dollars. Employees got them at cost.

He pulled a fresh pair of jeans out of the closet just as *Sunday Today* gave way to five minutes of local news. It was 8:25 A.M. The first story caught his ear, and as he pulled on his jeans, he turned to the television with the sense of unease that always accompanied news reports of tragedy.

"Two people are dead in Dorchester this morning in what appears to be a savage double murder. Authorities say they believe the victims might have been attacked by a gang. Apparently a large rock was thrown through the windshield of the car, causing the driver to swerve into a telephone pole. The victims were then allegedly dragged from the car, beaten, and mutilated."

Jack winced, horrified. "Oh, my God."

On his nightstand, the phone began to ring. Idly, eyes still riveted to the television screen, he zipped up his pants. He let the phone ring again, ran his hands through his still-damp hair.

"Local authorities believe last night's murders may be related to at least three other killings in the area in the last six weeks, most recently that of Corinne Berdinka, a nurse slain April fourth in the parking lot of New England Medical Center. Thus far, there seem to be no other links between the victims."

The phone rang a third time. This time it caught his attention. Jack blinked, then reached out to answer it. He lifted the handset off its cradle.

"Despite the mutilation of last night's victims," said the newsman, "they have been identified as Katherine Nordling, eighteen, of Boston, and nineteen-year-old Emerson College student Arthur Carroll."

Jack froze. He closed his eyes as he turned, phone gripped so tightly his hand hurt. He felt cold all over, his skin seeming to prickle with it, as if there were icicles on him. His chest hurt and he didn't know why; then he realized it was because he couldn't breathe.

Couldn't breathe at all.

He started to shake his head from side to side in a wordless denial. He had heard it wrong. Or it was a dream. Because that just could not be. Then he opened his eyes and saw the pictures on the television screen of his best friend and a girl he had laughed with the night before.

"No. Oh, Jesus no." It was a whisper.

All the strength drained out of his legs and Jack collapsed onto his bed. On the television screen the newscasters had moved on to something else, but the pictures were burned into his head.

He found that he could breathe now. At least enough so that he was able to cry. His chest heaved with nearly silent sobs.

Then he remembered the phone in his hand. He held it up and looked at it as though it were some sort of alien artifact. And then he heard her voice. Molly's voice.

"Jack?"

Pain there, quivering and awful and alone. He lifted the phone to his ear. "Molly?"

"Oh, my God, Jack," she managed, her voice a rasp, as though he could hear the tears rolling down her face.

"Molly. God, Molly, I'm so . . ." He took a hitching breath. "What are we going to do without him?"

*   *   *

Questions. So many questions and not a single one of them seemed to have an answer.

Artie's dead. The words kept resonating in his head but they had an alien quality to them, as though they were written across his mind in some arcane ancient language that not even professors studied anymore.

Numb. Jack was just numb. He had gone into the kitchen to tell Courtney and they had cried together and she had held him so tight it was almost funny—she being so much smaller than he. She had tried to cradle him as she would an infant. Eventually she disentangled herself, reached for her cane, and hobbled across the kitchen to the wall phone. The first call was to Wendy, who agreed to act as assistant manager for the day without even asking why. The second was to Bill Cantwell, to ask him to get one of the part-time bartenders to come in and help out.

Bill asked. Jack could tell the very moment that Bill asked, for in that moment his sister, leaning against the wall with the phone clamped to her ear, had glanced over at him and begun to cry again. Only for a second, then she stood up straight and told Bill exactly what had happened.

Courtney was strong and always had been. It pained Jack to see her so strong, because he knew it did not come naturally to her. She had simply never had any other choice.

Bill got someone to help cover the bar and insisted upon coming in right away, to help them get ready to open.

Bill and Courtney were there now, while Jack sat alone on his bed, staring alternately at the palms of his hands and then at the windows with the sparkling sun and sky beyond. Nothing he saw made any sense to him. Nor did the words that kept echoing in his head.

Artie's dead.

He decided to try to say them aloud, to taste the words to see if that helped him to understand. "Artie's dead," he told his empty, open hands. Then he glanced out the window and said it again, telling the sky. His world had been irrevocably altered, and yet his own flesh and blood had not been affected in the least, the world outside had not changed. He heard a car horn blaring, a dog barking, and somewhere not too far off, a baby crying.

And *that* made sense.

It made sense that a baby should cry.

His lost and wandering gaze fell upon the framed photograph of his mother on his bureau. Jack felt compelled to go to it, as though his limbs were not his to control. He rose from the bed and walked over to the bureau and lifted the frame.

Bridget Dwyer, smiling and freckled and tarnished by hard work and a broken heart, but still filled with the faith that her life would be all right. She had the Irish Rose Pub and she had her children, and damn it, she would make sure everything was all right.

And then Jerry Coleman, a fifty-seven-year-old stockbroker with an alcohol problem, had drunkenly tried to change the radio station in his BMW, swerved across the road, and made a liar out of her. Everything was not going to be all right.

But Courtney and Jack had been their mother's children. His big sister stayed strong, though her leg was ruined and her heart was shattered. Courtney had faith, and Jack knew even at the age of ten that if there was one thing his mother, God rest her soul, would have wanted from him it was that he should have faith as well. Faith that life would be all right. He and Courtney would find a way to survive, even to thrive. They would make a life.

And they did.

Now this.

"Artie's dead," he whispered, saying it aloud again. This time he was saying it to his mother. He gripped the frame in his hands and stared at her face, searching the still eyes of a dead woman's photograph for some clue. For faith.

"Why, Mom? First you, and now . . . Artie never hurt anyone. And Kate, too. It's just not . . ."

Jack closed his eyes tight, squeezing out a single tear that slipped down his left cheek. He leaned on the bureau and pressed his forehead against the framed picture, skin on cold glass.

Aside from Courtney, Artie had been the one constant in his life since his mother died. Now for him to die so horribly, to be . . . He could barely even think the word *murdered*, but that was the truth of it.

I'll kill them, he thought to himself. *Put me in a room with them, and I'll kill them.*

That was just his pain talking, his grief and fury. For he knew how helpless he was. Even if the police got lucky and were able to figure out who had been committing these savage crimes, Jack would never get within fifty feet of them, and even then it would be in court. His best friend had been murdered and mutilated and there wasn't a damn thing he could do.

He had never felt so useless, so lost. But at least he had Courtney; at least he wasn't alone. One of the first things that occurred to him when the first wave of shock began to subside and before the sorrow began to poison him, to weaken him, to numb him, was that now Molly was truly alone. She had friends in school, and she had an aunt in Philadelphia, but her mother was a coldhearted drunk with calluses on her soul. How a woman like her had ever given birth to a being as kind and decent as Molly had forever been a mystery to everyone.

Molly's only solace had been Artie. In contrast to the terrible knowledge about human behavior she had acquired in her life, Artie was a stunning example of innocence.

But Artie was dead.

Jack nodded to himself, wiped the back of his hand across his eyes. Artie was dead, and just as Courtney had to be strong for him, he realized he had to be strong for Molly. He was all she had.

"Ah, hell, Artie," he muttered to himself.

With a heavy, hitching sigh, he put the photo of his mother back on the bureau and went to the window.

Sunday, not even noon, but there were plenty of people out there going on about their business as usual. Untouched. Untainted by murder.

The lucky ones.

There was a knock, then Courtney's voice. "Jack?"

"Yeah?"

She pushed the door open, stood there in the hall leaning against the doorframe. Courtney wore a green cotton dress with a little brass tag engraved with her name and title: manager. She looked nice, but her wide eyes still held all the pain of the day—her own and a measure of Jack's as well. She was hurting *for* him.

"There's a policeman downstairs," she said. "A detective. He wants to ask you some questions about last night. Do you want me to tell him to come back later?" she asked tentatively.

"No. Send him up. I can't help, but I don't want him distracted by waiting for me to talk to him either."

Courtney nodded and turned back toward the stairs. She left his door open.

Jack continued to sit on his bed, hands in his lap, staring at nothing. He realized, after a moment, that he still had on the clothes he'd put on for work that morning. He resolved to change his shirt the moment the cop was gone.

At a soft rap on the door, he rose to find a plain-clothes police officer staring at him, badge in hand. The cop wore jeans and a rust-colored canvas jacket, with a bulge under one arm. Dark hair and eyes, and younger than Jack would have expected, the guy was definitely still on the uphill climb to forty.

"Jack Dwyer?" he asked.

"Yeah. Have a seat."

The cop glanced around, spotted the black wooden captain's chair in the corner, and went to sit. He spent a few seconds scanning the room as he did so, and Jack wondered what it must be like, being a cop, looking at everything not for what was on the surface but for what might be under it.

Hell of a way to live, he thought. *Second-guessing everything.*

"I'm Detective Jason Castillo, Boston Homicide," the man said, brow knitted with the gravity of his words. "Your sister told me you're aware of what happened to Arthur Carroll and Katherine Nordling last night."

"Artie," Jack muttered. "And she was Kate."

"Right," Castillo said, and nodded slowly. "I'm sorry to have to speak to you about this now, but we want to work as quickly as possible. I hope you understand."

"I do." Jack uttered a tiny laugh and looked up. "Mr. Castillo . . . Detective . . . what the hell do I call you?"

The cop loosened up a bit. "How about Jace?"

"All right, then. Jace, I figure you've got a much bigger investigation than just Artie and Kate going on right now. I saw the news this morning. I'll do anything I can to help you. But why don't I cut to the chase for you? I didn't know Kate very well. We'd met in passing a couple of times but last night was our first date. She was a friend of Artie and Molly's."

"Molly Hatcher?" Castillo asked.

"Molly, right," Jack confirmed. "So I don't know about Kate, but I do know about Artie. I know more than anybody—probably even his parents. He smoked a little pot, belonged to some radical liberal groups at Emerson, and thought that guns and teenage pop stars should be banned in America. Either of those opinions could have pissed people off, as could a couple dozen others that Artie wasn't afraid to talk about."

Jack did not understand the emotions filling him, or the weird rippling energy that ran up and down his spine. Then he knew what it was. It was anger. And Detective Jason Castillo was in the way. Jack stood up from the bed, stalked across the room, then turned to face Castillo.

"What I'm getting at here is that Artie didn't have any enemies. Not really. Oh, there was a kid who stole his lunch every day for a week in junior high. Artie told on him. I know for sure that guy's been arrested a couple of times, but somehow I doubt this is his doing anyway. Artie Carroll wasn't in any gangs, he never met anyone he thought was in a gang and as far as I know, he probably thought that gangs were an invention of the news media, 'cause he thought that about a lot of things."

Breath coming in sharp bursts now, Jack took a few more steps toward Castillo. The detective sat watching him, unfazed.

"We went out to the Dixie Kitchen for dinner last night. Kate and I hit it off pretty well. Then I saw her smoking and that killed my interest in her, y'know? 'Cause this is a new world and how can you be that smart and smoke? So I figured I wouldn't go out with her again. 'Cause she smoked! You like that irony?" Jack heard his voice getting shrill, but couldn't help it.

"They drove me back here and dropped me off, and that's the last time I saw them until I saw their pictures on the news this morning," he said, his voice rising nearly to a shout. "And what the hell are you doing here wasting your time with me when you should be out there catching the bastards who did this?"

Castillo watched him impassively, save for the tiniest bit of sympathy in his eyes.

Jack felt as though he were melting inside, all at once. His shoulders sagged and he turned his back on the cop, but he did not cry. "I'm sorry," he said, his own voice sounding like that of a total stranger.

"Me too," Castillo replied.

The detective stood up and crossed the room to stand just inside the door. Jack looked at him, surprised.

"Can I reach you here if I have any more questions?"

Jack nodded.

"I'm sorry for your loss," the detective told him.

Then Jack was alone again.

Eternity.

After Jack knocked on the Carrolls' front door it seemed like forever, an eternity of moments, before he heard footsteps inside. His entire body felt numb and cold and awkward. Conspicuous, as though anyone who saw him ambling up the front walk would think him an intruder.

An intruder upon the grief of Artie's devastated parents.

When Mrs. Carroll opened the front door, Jack flinched. She had a wary cast to her features, likely from too many conversations with reporters that day. But when she saw Jack, she fell apart piece by piece right in front of him. He had hoped that he could bring some tiny comfort to her. His arrival had apparently had the opposite affect.

"Oh, my God," she rasped, little more than a whisper. She held herself there, shaking, in the doorway.

"Mrs. Carroll," Jack ventured gently. "Ellen." His mouth could hardly form the words. There were ghosts in her eyes, tiny hauntings that were not about the death of her son but about the death of all the days she would have spent with him if he had lived, all the smiles she might have seen, the college graduation and the wedding and someday the grandchildren.

"I'm so sorry," he said. He felt as though the wind had been knocked out of him, his chest aching.

Jack began to cry.

He stepped inside the house and tried not to think about the room just up the stairs where all of Artie's things would start to gather dust, waiting for his return. Remembering would only hurt more. The comic books they had read and the girls they had dreamed aloud about. The hamster Artie had gotten when they were eight, and the mazes they had built for it out of wooden blocks.

Guns N' Roses albums when that was all they knew of rock and roll.

Red Sox games on Channel 38 or on the radio, and sometimes in Fenway Park.

They had spent so much time together after Jack's mother died, and Artie had never pressed him to talk about it. With Artie, he didn't need to talk about it. And during all those times, the Carrolls had watched out for Jack just as they had for Artie.

"I'm sorry," he said again.

Mrs. Carroll wrapped her arms around him as though Jack were all that kept her from slipping deep into the pit of her despair. Jack glanced over her shoulder and saw Artie's father standing in the hall that led from the kitchen into the foyer. He was just watching them, his red-rimmed eyes damp but no tears in his eyes. His face was expressionless, as though his mind had abdicated control of his body and gone off to a place where he wouldn't have to hurt so much.

"Look at us," Mrs. Carroll said as she pulled back and wiped her eyes. "A son without a mother and a mother without a son."

Difficult as it had been for him to visit Artie's parents, seeing Molly was worse. Jack drove his battered Cherokee to her mother's run-down house in Dorchester and took a roundabout route so he would not have to pass by the spot where Artie and Kate had been murdered.

Slaughtered.

Part of him felt as though he ought to visit the Nordlings as well, but he had only met Kate a few times and would not have known what to say. He had known Artie's family his whole life and hadn't really *had* to say anything. All the emotions spoke for him.

Jack rapped on Molly's door. He didn't hear her coming and thought at first she might not be home. Then he heard her voice call weakly from within.

"Who is it?"

"It's me, Moll. It's Jack."

When she hauled open the door he was stunned at the change in her. She had always been pale, but now she looked ill, her flesh white and puffy, almost as though she had been killed along with Artie and Kate.

"Oh, Jack," she said, all the pain in her heart expressed in those two words. Then she shook her head, and Jack understood: there were no more words, nothing sufficient to describe what she felt.

Molly stepped away from the door and Jack walked in. He closed the door and glanced around.

"Where's your mom?" he asked tentatively.

She pressed her lips together in a tight white line, a grimace of pain and humiliation. "Out."

Jack swallowed hard. Then he grabbed Molly and gave her a tight squeeze. Mrs. Hatcher was a drunk and probably a lot of worse things than that. He wondered what kind of person could have learned that her daughter had lost two of the people closest to her in the world and then gone about her business as if it nothing had changed. But he didn't speak those thoughts aloud. Molly had enough pain.

"Thank you," she whispered.

Jack said nothing. He had no idea how to respond to that.

"Thanks for coming here. For being here. For . . . for being strong."

Jack laughed at that. When he spoke he was not surprised to hear the hitch in his voice. "Strong? God, Molly, I'm far from that. This is killing me, same as you. I feel all torn up inside, like I'm full of broken glass."

She nodded, eyes closed. Her teeth had caught her lower lip and she gnawed on it for a moment. Then Molly opened her eyes and gazed at him.

"You're just you, Jack. There's nothing you can do. And you are strong. You were always the one we looked to because you were always the grown-up, y'know? The rest of us could be as immature as we wanted to be, but you didn't have a choice. You had to grow up too soon 'cause of your mom dying. Maybe it was selfish of us, but we relied on you for strength. Artie most of all. Sometimes I think half the reason he's . . . half the reason he was such a kid still was 'cause you were mature enough for both of you. He could screw around as much as he wanted and he knew you'd always be there if—"

Molly choked off the last few words. She gasped a

moment as though she had forgotten how to breathe, and then she glanced away.

"But I wasn't there," Jack said weakly. "I wasn't there, Molly."

Her eyes searching his now, Molly reached up to touch his face. "Don't blame yourself, Jack. There's nothing you could've done."

"I know," he agreed, and nodded grimly. "And besides, I'm supposed to be the strong one, right?"

They held each other then. Neither of them spoke for quite some time.

In the ensuing days, Jack spent as much time with Molly as he could. He managed to work on Monday and Tuesday, but in his off hours he would drive his Cherokee out to Dorchester to see her. Usually he would pick her up and take her out to a coffee shop in a better part of town. In each case, he took the long way around, not wanting to go through the neighborhood where the murder had happened.

They talked about Artie mostly, and Kate some as well. They talked about Molly's going to college in the fall and about graduation from high school. Molly stayed out of school those two days. Two things they never talked about were who had done this awful thing and why it had happened.

On Monday afternoon the police told the Carrolls that Artie's remains would be released on Wednesday morning. Funeral arrangements were made accordingly. A wake on Wednesday night, and the funeral first thing on Thursday.

"I know . . . I know it seems quick," Molly told him on the phone Tuesday morning. The pain in her voice was almost more than Jack could bear. "Mrs. Carroll said they wanted . . . that they wanted Artie to complete his journey so the rest of us can begin to heal."

Molly broke down after that, and though he had surprised himself those past days with his ability to comfort her, this time he just could not find the words.

They hung up a few minutes later.

It rained all day Wednesday. The sky was gray and the wind a bitter reminder that summer was still a long way off. The pub was generally closed only on holidays, and on Tuesdays during the winter. But that Wednesday, Bridget's Irish Rose was locked up tight, and as gray inside as it was out.

Bill Cantwell drove them to South Boston for the wake in a fifteen-year-old Oldsmobile that cut like an ocean liner through the storm. Jack didn't have to ask why South Boston. The funeral home was the same one Artie's grandfather was buried out of when the boys were in the seventh grade. Mr. Carroll would bury his son in a grave right next to his own father's.

"How are you holding up?" Courtney asked.

Jack had been watching the rain, his face against the window. Outside it was so dark it should have been night. When he shifted his gaze to his sister, he saw that she had turned around in the front seat. "I'll be all right."

He saw Bill twitch in the driver's seat, as if he might say something. He didn't. The big man kept his hands on the wheel and his eyes on the road, and only moved to scratch at his beard from time to time.

"Hell of a storm," Courtney said, her words like a fishing lure.

Jack knew she was really calling him a liar, telling him she didn't believe him when he said he would be all right. Of course, that was true—he *was* lying. But what else could he have said?

The rain spattered the glass. "I keep thinking about Stevie Ray Vaughn."

Now Bill did look in the rearview mirror at Jack. "The blues guy? Guitar player? The one who died in that helicopter crash?"

Jack just stared at the rain. Listened to it strike the peeling paint on the metal roof, and patter on the window. "Artie loved Stevie Ray," he said, his voice surprisingly strong. "After he . . . died, they released an album of stuff he'd recorded. *The Sky Is Crying*, it's called."

"Like it was crying for him," Courtney said softly.

"Yeah," Jack replied. "I don't really mind the storm. It seems . . . right. It seems just right."

The car was silent after that, except for the splash of puddles against the tires and the rain on the roof and glass. No radio. No talking. Just what remained of Jack Dwyer's family, and his pain, and the crying sky.

Later he would never be able to say why he looked

Christopher Golden

up just then, glanced between the two big front seats and out at the rain-swept road in front of them. He shuddered with a chill from the cold and the damp and gazed out at the street where the headlights cut through the ominous dark of the thunderstorm.

Artie stood in the middle of the road, gray as the sky, the curtain of rain making him seem little more than a phantom.

Before Jack could scream, the car passed right through him.

CHAPTER 4

Eyes wide, mouth slightly open, facial muscles slack, and breathing as though he had just sprinted a few blocks, Jack spent the rest of the ride to South Boston staring at the back of his sister's head. From time to time he glanced over at the back of Bill's head as well, but for the most part he kept his gaze locked on Courtney.

She never turned around. Never gave any indication that she had seen anything out of the ordinary. Neither did Bill.

Jack said not a word.

By the time they were pulling into the lot behind O'Connor Funeral Home and jockeying for a parking space, he had begun to breathe normally again. What he had seen was impossible. Jack knew that, of course. Which left only one conceivable explanation.

I imagined it, he told himself as he climbed out of the

backseat of Bill's car. *Artie's on my mind so much I just . . .
conjured him out of the rain. I miss him so much that my
mind's playing tricks on me, that's all*

Bill got out of the car and walked around to pop
open an umbrella and hold it over Courtney as she
climbed out. The big man looked at Jack's sister with
such affection that Jack wondered if Bill might care for
her more than he let on. The rain sluiced down Jack's
face, and his hair grew damp with the droplets.

"Don't wait for us, Jack," Courtney said. "Go on
ahead; stay dry."

Jack made no reply. He mentally acknowledged the
words but simply could not muster the effort to give his
thoughts voice. Courtney glanced back at him, a tender,
supportive smile on her face. Then her expression changed.

"Hey, little brother," she said, tentatively, "are you all
right?" Though she had to put most of her weight on
her cane, Courtney reached out to lay her hand gently
on his arm. "You're pale."

Jack nodded but still did not speak. It seemed as
though Courtney might say something more, but she
only squeezed his arm and then turned back toward the
funeral home. Jack had seen the sympathy in her eyes,
the love and caring. She thought he was simply over-
come with grief that they were here for the wake of his
best friend. That was part of it, certainly.

The other was the image in his mind of Artie standing in the rain, the storm cutting through him as
though he wasn't there, the car passing through his
body. And then he wasn't there at all.

I'm losing it, Jack thought as he followed Courtney and Bill along the path to the front door of the funeral home. *Get a grip on reality, Jack. Artie's dead. He's gone.*

He felt a bit more stable, more focused, as they climbed the front steps. Courtney maneuvered extremely well with her cane. Though Bill still held the umbrella over her, she refused to let him lend her an arm on the stairs.

"I'm twenty-eight," she told him. "I may have to walk like an old lady, but I won't be treated like one."

Bill blinked as though the words had hurt him. Then one corner of his mouth lifted in a tiny smile, and he watched her with open admiration. Jack followed them in. Careful to keep it away from Courtney, Bill closed the umbrella and shook the rain off in the foyer of the funeral home.

When his sister cast an inquisitive glance in his direction, Jack nodded again to indicate that she should go on in. Nodding seemed to have become the only form of communication of which he was capable. Courtney moved through the hall of the grand old building and into the swarm of mourners buzzing about. Jack closed his eyes to take a breath, but opened them again instantly. In that darkness behind his eyelids lingered a pallid phantom with Artie's face.

"Hey."

A huge hand alighted upon his back and Jack looked up into the soft, wet eyes of Bill Cantwell. With his beard and his rugged features and those soulful eyes, he resembled nothing so much as an enormous grizzly.

"If you need someone to lean on," Bill said, voice low, "you can lean on me."

Jack patted Bill once on the chest of his ill-fitting sport coat. He nodded again and then felt as though that was not enough. "Thanks," he said, voice barely above a rasp. But it was a word, at least. He could speak again.

With Bill backing him up, Jack inserted himself into the crowd of mourners. A great many people—family and friends, people from the neighborhood, and some kids from Emerson College—had come to grieve for Artie Carroll and to sympathize with his parents. There were students and teachers from Boston Catholic, including a great many Jack recognized. One or two had been classmates of his and had graduated with him the previous year. The others were in Kate and Molly's class.

Kate. Friday night they would all be grieving the same way for her.

"Jesus," Jack whispered to himself. He wasn't sure if it was a prayer or not. And if it was, he would not have dared guess exactly why he was praying.

Eyes front, he avoided looking directly at anyone. He felt Bill's solid presence behind him and was grateful for it. It was like having a bodyguard, only it wasn't his body that needed protection from the pain. Along the hall there were two large arches that led into a room so filled with flowers that the scent filled the building.

Jack's palms were sweaty, and he wiped them on his suit jacket. His suit, a gray pinstripe he had bought for a cousin's wedding. That was all it was good for—weddings, wakes, and funerals.

In the room with all the flowers, he lifted his eyes for the first time. Across the room he spotted Mr. and Mrs. Carroll. Artie's mother looked like a scarecrow, hair mussed, flesh as gray as the storm, clothing not hanging on her quite right. There were no tears on her face, not one. Jack had never seen anyone look so hollow. As though they had switched roles since the last time Jack had seen them, Mr. Carroll was the opposite. His cheeks were red, and tears streamed down his face in such a regular flow it was as though he were leaking. Artie's grandmother was there as well. She sat in a chair beside her walker talking animatedly to a younger woman who might have been one of Artie's aunts or cousins.

Jack took all that in seconds after entering the room. But his attention was not on the shattered family at the far side of the room; it was focused on the casket behind them: dark wood inlaid with a lighter, almost reddish wood, gleaming as though a fresh coat of wax had been applied.

Closed.

Of course it's closed, he thought, standing frozen in the middle of the room as mourners milled around him. *Artie was torn apart.*

As he stared at the closed casket, Jack found suddenly that he could move, that the sick feeling in his stomach had been replaced by a dark knowledge that what was to come, the remembrance of his friend, was important.

Around him, people whispered to one another with none of the levity often found at wakes, particularly Irish wakes. No fond stories were being told about the deceased with great amusement, no laughter of relatives, no happy reunions of people who had come together to pay tribute to the dead. Artie had died at nineteen years of age. He had been brutally murdered. There was no place for smiles or laughter here, not even in his memory.

Not yet. Jack knew in a disconnected way that at some point he would think of Artie and laugh about something they had done, some foolish antics or absurd debate. But not yet.

He took a deep breath and strode quickly over to Mrs. Carroll.

Her gray emotionless features altered when he approached. She pressed her lips together as though holding back a cry of anguish and she blinked back tears that threatened. "Jack," she said.

He kissed her cheek and embraced her tightly and said not a word.

She held him away from her and looked into his eyes. "He loved you, Jack. You never let him down. Ever. He would have wanted you to know that."

Jack could not stop the moisture that burned at the corners of his eyes. He squeezed Mrs. Carroll's hands and then moved on to her husband. Though Jack held out a hand to shake, Mr. Carroll pulled him into a hug that was almost painful.

"Come see us again soon, Jack," the man said,

almost choking on the words and his tears. "I think it would help."

"I will," he said, but even as he said it, he feared it might be a lie. He would go see them again sometime, but not soon. He doubted such a visit would help anyone.

Then Mr. Carroll let him go, and Jack found himself in front of the closed coffin with its gleaming wooden surface. He took a deep breath, steeling himself to cross the six feet of carpet that separated him from his best friend's mortal remains. The smell of flowers was overpowering, the splash of color all around the casket too much. Too cheerful.

The smell. He wondered if the tradition of sending flowers to a wake had started because mourners needed something to combat the stench of death. His face twisted into an expression of revulsion at the thought, and he wondered why he had thought such a thing. Then another bizarre thought arrived unbidden: *he's not in there.* With one last breath, he closed his eyes.

Once more, against the darkness of his eyelids, he saw the image of Artie standing in the street, gray thunderclouds above, heavy rain spilling down around him.

It was him, Jack thought now. *Not my imagination. But it had to be. You're just losing it, Jack. That's it. You miss him too much.*

A hand closed on his biceps. Jack started, momentarily frightened. He opened his eyes, heart skipping a few beats, and turned to find Molly standing next to him swathed in black from head to toe. The red hair that usually tumbled around her shoulders was pinned back tightly and her face was white save for the light dash of freckles on her cheeks.

"Hey," she said, a sad, tired smile on her face.

It was the first smile Jack had seen, and he offered it back to her.

"I was waiting for you," Molly went on. She bit her lip, very purposefully did not turn her eyes toward the casket. "I didn't want to go up alone."

Jack swallowed. He reached down and touched her hand, twined his fingers in hers, and side by side they crossed those few feet and knelt on the padded support in front of the casket.

They prayed together in silence and Jack never let go of her hand. He had felt so powerless, so injured, standing there in that room amid the scent of flowers, until Molly came along. She didn't want to say goodbye to Artie alone, and neither did Jack, but together they were strong.

"I thought I saw him earlier tonight."

Molly blinked once, then stared at him. They were perched on a sofa in a sitting room down the hall from the mass of people still moving in and out of the funeral home. Across the room in a small chair that looked as if it might break at any moment, Courtney sat with the head of her cane in both hands and spoke animatedly to Darrin Sannicandro, who had been Jack and Artie's history teacher at Boston Catholic. Jack had said hello to him, but not much more. Since Courtney had been Jack's guardian since their mother's death, she knew Mr. Sannicandro well enough from school events.

They talked about tragedy.

Behind them, Bill Cantwell stood and watched over Courtney. He was their ride, and though he seemed to know no one else in the place, Bill did not rush Courtney to leave. Not for the first time Jack caught himself thinking of Bill as family. It was a definition that fit quite nicely.

While he observed Bill and Courtney and Mr. Sannicandro, Jack felt Molly staring at him.

"What did you say?" she finally prodded him.

Jack shrugged sheepishly. "Nothing. It was just me being whacked. On the way here I was looking out at the storm and I thought I saw him. It was only for a second, but I . . ."

He let his words trail off.

"You miss him," Molly said, simple as that. "I dreamed about him last night. He was . . ." Her voice got lower, and she smiled self-consciously. "We were at his house and he was going through his CDs, organizing them. You know how he did that all the time?"

Jack nodded, remembering.

"I asked him what he was doing." Molly's smile remained, but her eyes were wet again. "He said he was choosing his favorites, 'cause they would only let him take a few."

Jack's chest felt tight.

"That's what he said," Molly repeated. "They only let you take a few. I think he's all right, Jack. I really do."

"I know he is," Jack replied. "It's just the rest of us who are a total mess."

They chuckled together at that, and Jack felt as though a tiny bit of the weight on him had been lifted. Together they leaned back into the sofa and sat quietly side by side and remembered.

They picked up Chinese takeout on the way back to Bridget's and Jack, Bill, and Courtney ate together in the dim light of the pub. Several people came to the door as if the Closed sign and the lack of bright light were not enough to indicate the place was not open for dinner that night. Courtney waved pleasantly to the ones who noticed them, sitting there eating Chinese food from steaming white boxes.

Talk was about anything but Artie or Kate, anything so they didn't have to discuss the funeral the next morning, Kate's wake on Friday, or her funeral on Saturday. Awful as it was, Jack wished he could fast-forward those days, put them behind him. Though they avoided talking about those things, that avoidance was so obvious that it was no comfort at all.

By the time Bill left, it was full dark outside, even beyond the storm clouds. The rain had tapered off a bit, but it still fell in a light sheen that streaked the long windows of the pub.

Courtney locked the doors behind Bill, then went back and sat next to her brother again. He studied her face, the way the sprinkling of freckles over the bridge of her nose always made her seem to be smiling, even when she wasn't.

"Thanks for today," he said.

"For what?" she asked, frowning.

"For everything," he replied. "I . . . needed you there. I don't know what I'd do without you."

"You'll never have to find out, so don't worry about it," Courtney promised.

Neither one of them pointed out how tentative that promise was. The Dwyers knew better than most how unpredictable life was and how easily promises could be shattered.

"I've got some orders to get to," she told him, then stood up, cane in hand. "Do you mind?"

Jack shook his head. "We've got a business to run. Can I help?"

"Shouldn't take too long. Watch some TV, read a book, relax your brain a bit."

"I think I'll stay down here a little longer," he told her. "I like the rain."

Courtney nodded. "Want a beer?"

Surprised, Jack looked at her. "I'm only nineteen."

"You've never had a beer?" Courtney replied doubtfully.

"I'll pass," Jack said. "But thanks for the offer."

After Courtney went upstairs to their apartment above the pub, Jack went to the bar. He tossed out the empty Chinese food containers, washed the forks and spoons they had used, and put them away, then wiped down the table. The rain spattered the windows, and cars roared by on the street outside from time to time. As he was turning their chairs upside down and putting them on top of the table, there was a knock at the door.

Jack glanced at the figure beyond the glass in the door and squinted. With a shake of his head he walked over and peered through the glass at two guys in suits with black umbrellas.

"We're closed!" he called to them.

The guy mouthed something and gestured to the sign that listed Bridget's hours of operation. Jack rolled his eyes and sighed, then lifted one hand and pointed, so the suits could see him, at the hand-printed sign about eighteen inches above the other, the one that said the pub was closed for the day due to a death in the family.

"Can you read?" Jack asked, though he knew the man could not have heard him through the door.

With a scowl, the guy threw up his hands and quickly strode away, umbrella bobbing above him, the other guy in tow.

"Jerk," Jack muttered under his breath.

"Tell me about it."

The voice had come from behind him. Jack spun, eyes darting back and forth, trying to see into the dark corners of the dimly lit room. He felt the words on his lips, wanted to shout "Who the hell is in here?" But he had recognized that voice.

Something moved in the darkness behind the bar.

"Listen, bro, if you're not going to drink that beer Courtney offered you, can I have it?"

Jack could barely make him out; he saw only a

shadow at first. Then suddenly the figure behind the bar seemed to solidify, to take on color and substance.

"Artie," he whispered.

There he was, shaggy blond hair framing his face, Boston Catholic High sweatshirt on. But he wasn't there.

He wasn't there.

Jack closed his eyes, suddenly sick to his stomach. Artie could not be there because Artie was dead. *Unless . . . unless he isn't dead. I never saw the . . . Oh, hell, Jack, you've lost it completely. Artie is dead.*

When he opened his eyes, Artie was still there, wearing that big old familiar goofy grin. Jack shuddered as if his gears were rusty, but he managed to take a step toward the bar. And then another. And then he realized that he could see the bottles of Jack Daniels' and Wild Turkey and Southern Comfort on the shelf behind where Artie was standing—the whiskey bottles, the mirror above them, and Jack's own reflection in the mirror. They were obscured, as if he were looking at them through fog, but they were there.

"I can see through you," Jack whispered.

In truth, he could see *himself* through Artie, in that mirror.

Jack froze in place. His skin prickled all over and his face felt hot, but his hands were as cold as ice. He felt a scream building in his gut, right alongside a surge of nausea. But a quick glance up the stairs reminded him that Courtney was up there. If he screamed she would come down, and that was the last thing he wanted.

"You didn't answer me, Jack," Artie said.

His voice sounded hollow, as if it came from inside a coffee can.

Jack tried to speak, couldn't manage it, then tried again. "You're dead," he said.

Artie's smile disappeared. He looked angry now, and Jack thought, in the dim illumination that came in from the street, that he could just make out long, ragged tears in his face and neck. Then they were gone.

"Come here, Jack," Artie said in that hollow voice, and beckoned him with a finger. "Sit down at the bar and talk to me."

Jack hesitated. Then he did it. He had no idea how he managed to make his legs move, as scared as he was, but he walked over to the bar and sat on a high stool across from his best friend's ghost.

"Look at me, bro," Artie said. "Take a good long look at me. Now do whatever it is you need to do— pinch yourself or whatever it may be—to convince yourself that I'm really here. 'Cause I *am* here."

His translucent skin was yellow, almost as blond as his hair, but Jack was transfixed by his eyes. The rest of Artie's body and his clothes were transparent. So were those blue eyes. But looking through those eyes he could not see the whiskey bottles or the mirror. He saw something else. *Somewhere* else. And suddenly Jack didn't want to look anymore.

"You're a ghost," he whispered.

"You got it in one, amigo," Artie told him. "You're right. I'm dead; not that I want you to remind me of it all the time. I know this has gotta be tough for you, man. I know that. Right now your mind is doing backflips trying to figure out if you're nuts, if I'm really here, and how the heck that can be if I am. Okay, it'd be nice if maybe you were a little glad to see me, bro, 'cause at least we can communicate like this even if, okay, my appetite has changed a little. But I understand, truly I do. It'd be like, okay, I've always believed in conspiracies and you haven't, so it'd be like the CIA walking up to you and saying 'Guess what, Jack? Artie was right. There *were* three shooters in Dallas. The U.S. government *did* import cocaine into this country to undermine urban areas and keep minorities down.' I totally get what your situation is right now. All right, as much as I can, considering I'm on this side. But, y'know, given the chance to trade, bro, I think I'd rather be in your shoes."

Artie. Jack's mind whirled as the patter unfurled, the staccato speechifying he had come to both dread and love so much. *This really is Artie.*

Through the terror and confusion he felt, a tiny smile played on his lips. "Artie?"

"Jack?" Artie mimicked good-naturedly.

Jack shook his head in disbelief.

"You look like crap in that suit, by the way," Artie said. "It's too small for you, it's wrinkled, and it's so not you. That was the best you could do for my wake? What are you gonna wear to the funeral, like, a clown suit or something? Big shoes and all?"

Jack chuckled. "Oh, my God, I'm insane. That's all there is to it. I'm out of my mind."

"You know you're not," Artie told him. "It's me."

"What . . . I mean, am I always going to be able to see you?"

"I don't know," Artie said, and he looked puzzled, the weird space behind his eyes seeming to flash with white light. "But you can see me now. You, and apparently only you, 'cause I tried to talk to some people on the street, but nobody saw me."

"Molly?" Jack asked.

"Not Molly," Artie said quickly. "Never Molly. I'm dead, Jack. As far as she knows that's that. It wouldn't be fair to her to know I'm around, watching and all. She's gotta live."

"But you came to me," Jack said tentatively, mind still spinning. "Not that I'm not glad, but—"

"You weren't my lover, Jack," Artie said. "Not that I don't think you're a superb specimen of the male species. Besides, you were thinking about me so much that I could feel it, like it was pulling on me, and I knew I could talk to you if I just thought about it hard enough. I knew you were the only one I could come to, Jack. I need to tell people about the things that . . ."

A ripple passed through the specter behind the bar and Artie seemed to be in pain. For a millisecond, Jack saw his wounds again, and then they were gone.

"I have to warn people about the things that killed me," the ghost said. "*You* have to warn them, Jack. You have to do something."

"Things?" Jack asked, even more confused, mind still trying to catch up to reality, to make sense of a world where ghosts were real, where he could speak to the dead.

"Things," Artie echoed, nodding. He narrowed those otherworldly eyes and focused on Jack. "Monsters, Jack.

"They're called Prowlers."

C H A P T E R 5

Molly went to Artie's funeral alone. When she woke up that Thursday morning she found her mother sprawled across the sofa in the living room with VH-1 still on the television and several empty beer bottles on the rickety coffee table. Another bottle lay on the carpet on its side; its contents had spilled out to create a foul-smelling stain that would likely never come out. If Molly's mother ever made any effort to get it out. More than likely, Molly herself would try later in the day, or possibly tomorrow, but by then it would be too late. The stain, and the stink, would have sunk into the carpet forever.

Molly couldn't take the time to worry about it this morning. She had to go and watch them bury her boyfriend. When she left the apartment, taking the rusty Dodge Omni without asking, her mother was still unconscious on the sofa.

*　　　*　　　*

It was chilly at the cemetery. Molly wore a navy blue skirt, a white blouse, and a navy blue jacket, an outfit she had bought to wear for college interviews, paid for with money she earned behind the counter at the convenience store two blocks away from her house. It had been robbed twice in the eighteen months she worked there, but fortunately never on her shift.

Though the sun shone brightly down on the marble and granite headstones and on the mourners gathered around the open grave and the casket above it, Molly was cold. She needed a heavier jacket, but did not feel that either her thick winter coat or the leather jacket Artie had bought her for Christmas would have been appropriate. So she clenched her teeth and tried not to shiver, and she studied the faces around her so that she would not have to look at the casket or the grave. She stood with the Carrolls only a few feet away from Father Hughes. The priest's lips moved. Though he was clearly speaking, praying, none of the words made sense to Molly.

Her tears had been flowing since the ceremony at church had started. There was no eulogy—no one who might have delivered one felt capable of doing so without breaking down completely. Molly had wept in silence all through the funeral mass. Now, as those gathered said their last good-byes, her breath hitched and she cried all the harder.

Almost angrily, she wiped at her eyes with a hand-kerchief that a woman—one of Artie's cousins, she thought—had handed her. She let herself feel the cold, let it get into her bones, tried to imagine it freezing her tears to icy streaks on her face. Her breathing slowed, and Molly began to get control of herself. The priest was not done yet, but it was over. There at the edge of Artie's grave, that was the end.

Mrs. Carroll laid a comforting hand on her shoulder, and Molly looked up to see her own resolve reflected on the woman's face. "You can't escape pain," Hal Ulrich, her guidance counselor, had told her one day when they were talking about her mother. "But you can tame it."

Molly knew that was what she had to do, was already doing. Mrs. Carroll seemed to be doing the same thing. Artie's father, on the other hand, was hiding from his pain. His face was emotionless, sculpted in stone, his eyes rimmed red but dry. He might crack at any second.

Then there was Jack.

What is going on in his head? Molly wondered as she glanced over at him. Jack stood with his sister and Bill Cantwell on the opposite side of the grave, amid a crowd of other people, most of whom Molly did not recognize. Jack looked like hell—worse than she imagined she did—as though he had not slept at all the night before. At church, Jack had approached her, spoken softly to her, but he had been skittish. A couple of times he seemed about to tell her something, but then he just shook his head.

At the cemetery, he was worse. Molly kept trying

to catch his eye, but only once had he even noticed her. Instead, Jack gazed off into nothing, eyes not focusing on anyone or anything. Several times she spotted him muttering to himself. Molly told herself he must have been saying a prayer, and hoped she was right.

The priest finished and the mourners gathered even closer around the casket. They passed by, one by one, silently saying their last good-bye to Artie. Many of them pulled a flower or two out of the expensive arrangements that were lined up around the grave site, then dropped them on top of the casket. Molly did not take a flower. She waited until Artie's parents had walked past the grave and started back toward their car, and then she closed her eyes.

Good-bye, Artie, she thought. *I love you. Nobody could ever make me smile like you.*

When she opened her eyes again, Jack was standing in front of her.

"Jack!" she said quickly, heart speeding up. "God, you spooked me."

He laughed at that, but it wasn't a nice laugh. It was a sad, ironic, cynical laugh, at some private joke. Molly did not get the joke and was not at all sure she wanted to.

"Are you all right?" she asked.

Jack winced and suddenly seemed even more tired. "Not even close. I'm also the one who's supposed to be asking you that. Since your mom . . . couldn't make it, why don't you come back to the pub? Courtney and Bill have to open up soon, but I thought maybe you and I could walk a bit, y'know?"

Molly had felt lost ever since she heard that Artie was dead. Now she saw that Jack seemed even more lost. It would be good to spend some time together, to walk off some of their hurt. To tame their pain.

"Sure," she agreed. "Only . . . do you think Courtney would lend me some sweats or something? I don't want to walk around in this."

Jack smiled thinly, his eyes seeming to focus on her for the first time. "Yeah. We'll find you something to wear."

Artie left them alone.

As Jack and Molly walked through Quincy Market, then up to the Common and across to Newbury Street—where they strolled alongside hip young twenty-somethings for whom money was rarely an issue—Jack could not help but look over his shoulder and glance at each street corner. Artie had left him after more than an hour of conversation the night before, fading into an insubstantial mist and then disappearing altogether.

This morning, when he woke, Jack had tried to tell himself that he had, in his grief, imagined the whole episode. But that lasted about thirty seconds. It was crap, and he knew it. He really *had* seen Artie, spoken with him. His best friend was dead, but his spirit lingered in this world. As he dressed and ate breakfast and while Bill drove him and Courtney to church, he had been distracted by the thought that Artie might appear at any time. Courtney had been concerned for him, but Jack had barely registered it.

No Artie at the pub. No Artie in the car. No Artie at the church.

He was waiting for them at the cemetery. As they pulled in behind the other cars in the funeral procession, Jack glanced out at the grave with the tarp-covered dirt and the gleaming casket and saw Artie standing beside the priest, crying for the loss of his life.

Jack felt like a ghost himself, walking up to the grave with Bill and Courtney. His entire body felt numb. He stared at Artie, at this apparition no one else could see, a gossamer specter who wiped phantom tears from his eyes. The mourners had gathered around Artie's family. Molly stood with them and cried endlessly.

The ghost glanced at Jack, composed itself—himself—and smiled sadly before dissipating into thin air. A moment later Artie appeared beside him.

"You okay?" Artie asked in a voice only Jack could hear.

"What the hell do you think?" Jack had muttered in return.

"Don't get snippy with me," Artie replied grimly. "You're not the one who got his face ripped off."

Jack shivered, bile rising in his throat. But then he nodded slowly. "I'm sorry. You're right."

"Don't tell Molly," Artie had warned.

"I said I wouldn't," Jack whispered.

When he glanced up again, Artie was gone and the

priest was saying a final blessing over the grave. As he and Molly returned to the pub and then went for a walk, he kept expecting Artie to appear again, but he didn't. Jack wondered if that was because it pained him too much to see Molly and to know what death had cost him.

For hours they wandered about, Jack only half paying attention. They ate lunch at a small, trendy pizza place on Newbury Street, and looked in the windows of art galleries. Eventually they started back. They were on the Boston Common, just past the entrance to the Park Street Station, when Molly stopped and stared at him.

"What's wrong?" Jack asked.

"Who are you looking for?" Molly demanded.

A chill ran through him, but he frowned. "What? I mean nobody. What do you mean?"

Molly stared at him a moment longer and then glanced away. Her eyes filled with moisture, but she wiped them once and no tears fell.

"Hey," Jack said gently. "Molly, what is it? I'm sorry if I seem distracted, but . . . I keep thinking about Artie."

"Yeah, me too." Molly looked up at him. "I'm glad we did this, y'know? Walking around, just talking about him. And about the future. What now, right? High school graduation and college and life in general. It sounds like it'll be hollow without him, but I know that's not true. Life will go on, right?"

Jack closed the distance between them and pulled

her into an embrace. She hesitated a moment and then wrapped her arms around him.

"It will," Jack promised. "I . . . I've been thinking about my mother a lot lately, because of Artie. Look at me and Courtney, Mol. Life does go on. The hurt will always be there, like a scar, but it becomes part of you."

"I promised myself I wouldn't cry anymore," she whispered, voice tight as she held back the tears.

Jack let up a little bit, held her away from him so he could look into her eyes. "Maybe that's not such a good idea. You can't not feel what you feel."

"I can't cry all the time."

"How 'bout just once in a while?" Jack suggested.

Molly smiled and hugged him again. "You've been so distracted today, as if you're not all here. But I need you here, Jack. With Artie and Kate gone, and with . . . home . . . I need someone I can talk to, someone who understands."

"I do," Jack assured her. "I do."

She whispered then, and her voice sounded like a little girl's. "I thought I saw him, you know. The night he . . . Saturday night. I woke up at two in the morning, and I thought I saw him standing in my bedroom. Creepy, huh? The weirdest thing. Like he was saying good-bye. I know how crazy that sounds . . ."

Jack stiffened. He could picture it in his head, Artie becoming slowly aware of his death and his spiritual state, standing at Molly's bedside, not knowing how to say good-bye. The image broke his heart all over again.

"It doesn't sound so crazy. I think I see him all the time," Jack told her. "I'm sure he's still . . . with us."

Molly sighed and gave him a look as though she thought he was just being nice. "You're sweet," she said.

Then together they walked out of the park and headed back toward Bridget's. A short time later Jack escorted Molly to her mother's car, and they hugged again as they said good-bye, made promises to be there for each other. The next day was Kate's wake, after all, and the grief would have a new layer then.

After she drove away Jack turned back toward the pub and found Artie hovering, immaterial and translucent, right behind him.

"Oh, Jesus, Artie," Jack snapped, heart hammering in his chest. "Don't sneak up on me like that."

"I can't actually help it," Artie told him, smiling mischievously. "But I'll see what I can do."

Jack stood there, trying to figure out what to say next. Artie's smile disappeared and was replaced by an echo of his earlier sadness. It felt like a kind of betrayal to Jack that he could think of nothing to say, but he was at a total loss.

"Casual conversation's a bit difficult with ghosts, huh?" Artie asked.

"You could say that," Jack agreed, though he managed a small chuckle.

"I got the feeling last night that you didn't believe me about the Prowlers."

Jack shuffled his feet.

"It's all right. I'm glad you don't think I'm a figment of your imagination. But listen, I figured you needed proof, so I thought we should get some. I've met some . . . people here, in the Ghostlands. Other victims. They've started to keep track of the Prowlers. If you're going to help me, you've got to believe in them. And to believe, you'll need to see them, to really see them."

"How do I do that?" Jack asked, dumbfounded. He was aware of the traffic going by, of people glancing at him apparently talking to himself in the middle of the street.

"I'm going to guide you. And we're going to find a Prowler."

Atop the bell tower, Owen Tanzer crouched and looked out over Copley Square. The wind ruffled his hair and carried a myriad of scents to him. He gazed down upon the people milling about far below. Even in what little light the stars and sliver moon provided, he could pick out each person and judge him with the gaze of a predator.

A group of young women celebrated something. Couples of all ages moved along in a variety of paths; several of them pushed children in strollers or wore babies in packs strapped over their shoulders. Two loud men exited an expensive bar puffing on cigars. Cars and taxis roared by loudly, exhaling rancid fumes. Dozens went in and out of the mall on the far side of the green that stretched below. Several homeless people lingered in the shadows around the distant steps of the Boston Public Library.

Prowlers moved among them, unnoticed.

Tanzer closed his eyes and sniffed the air again, the odors of the city below painting vivid pictures upon his mind. This tower had been Eric Carver's home, when Carver had still thought he could continue to pass for human, to be on his own instead of part of a pack. Now the tower was the pack's lair, and Tanzer controlled it all with fang and claw. In the rooms below, the members of the pack rutted and slept and ate and argued. He allowed them human pastimes as well: television, books, films. Tanzer worried that these entertainments might lull his pack into believing themselves human, and so he constantly reminded them of their true nature. They walked the streets like humans. Here in the lair, they could reveal their true selves, and Tanzer encouraged them to do so.

On the tower's roof, however, he retained his human appearance just in case he was spotted. They would not be able to remain in Boston any longer than they had any other city, but he did not want to hasten their exodus any more than necessary. For that reason, only two of the pack were allowed to lead a hunt each night, and even then, their groups had to hunt in different locations, away from the lair.

The lair must be protected at all costs.

The Prowlers who slipped through the darkness in the square and other places in the area were guards, sentinels put in place to watch for anyone who might have more than a passing interest in the lair, including police, journalists, and members of other packs. Tanzer's pack had been forced to eliminate all three from time to time. Atlanta. Detroit. Philadelphia. Not Boston, though. Not yet.

In Boston they were just getting started.

The pack moved from city to city, found a lair, and began to hunt. But that was only one of the functions of the pack—the short-term outlook. Tanzer's long-term plans were more ambitious. As they traveled, the pack grew. In small towns and remote areas on the road they found smaller packs of three or four, sometimes just families. In the large cities they found mostly rogues and pretenders, those who needed to be brought back to the wild, like Carver.

By ones and twos and fives the pack grew, until it was the largest pack of Prowlers in America since before the Civil War. At the moment there were fifty-seven, if Tanzer counted himself. Fifty-seven Prowlers roaming the narrow alleys and parks and posh neighborhoods of Boston.

Crouched on the stone parapet atop the deserted bell tower, thoughts only slightly interrupted by the rumble of a large truck rolling by, Tanzer sniffed the air again and relished the aroma that drifted up to him.

Fear.

By his count, the pack had slain thirty-two people since their arrival in Boston. Homeless people, prostitutes, a would-be car thief, young runaways, two taxi drivers, several couples starry-eyed with romance, a baby whose young mother left it on the steps of a church in the North End, and a handful of others. Some had been properly disposed of. Others were left where they died. The police were the only ones who could have put it all together, but they seemed so in love with gang violence as an answer that they had not yet come poking around the lair.

But the fear was there. The police had linked several of the killings, and the media was rife with stories. Newspapers wondered if a serial murderer was on the loose. Others accepted the authorities' talk of gang war as an explanation. But the message to the people of Boston was clear: There was something abroad after dark of late, something to fear.

Tanzer laughed to himself, a low snuffling sound, deep in his throat. He stroked the three white parallel scars on his face, a gift from his father once upon a time, so very long ago. As the wind whistled across the roof, he sniffed the air again.

There.

He lowered his chin, thick lips curling back from his sharp teeth as he sniffed again, his gaze focusing upon two men who moved along the sidewalk as though they owned it. One was tall and broad across the shoulders, with muscles rippling beneath an expensive Italian suit. Perhaps thirty. But Tanzer's attention was on the other man. He was older by fifteen or twenty years, shorter, smaller, almost too thin. And yet he walked two paces ahead of his companion and it was clear he was in control. He walked like a man used to being obeyed, used to being feared. He walked like a dangerous man.

Finally, here was one worth the hunt.

Tanzer had the scent.

He grabbed hold of the parapet and swung off the roof and into the belfry. The enormous bell was flaked with rust and stood ponderous and silent in the dark alcove at the top of the tower. It had apparently been so for years. Tanzer went around it and loped to the door and bounded down the seven stories to the ground. There were members of the pack on every floor. Two females, Vanessa and Dori, were on the landing at the fifth floor, watching him with expectant, flashing eyes as he leaped from the sixth step to the landing, muscles rippling.

"You go to hunt?" Dori asked.

Vanessa took a step toward him. "May we join you?"

Tanzer pulled up short, glaring at the females. They had been in the pack that merged with Owen's in Philadelphia. With a lightning-fast blow, he struck out at Vanessa. Her nose twisted, and blood spouted from both nostrils as she went down.

"Unless I ask for your company, I hunt alone," Tanzer snarled.

With a roar he bounded off the landing and halfway to the fourth floor. He grabbed hold of the banister halfway down and threw himself over, completely bypassing the next landing.

Jasmine stood on the third floor waiting for him. "They should know better," his mate said, eyes downcast, every inch of her body speaking to him. Her stance revealed her respect, love, and obedience, but it also revealed her lust for him.

"They should," Tanzer agreed. "Next time they will. The pack must hunt in groups, but not its leader. Only I may choose to hunt alone."

"They would usurp my place at your side if they could," Jasmine said. She stepped closer to him and nuzzled her head under his chin, rubbing her body against his.

"If they could. But they cannot," he assured her.

Jasmine wanted him to ask her to come along on the hunt. Tanzer sensed it. But she would not ask. She knew the ways of the pack.

He sensed something else then. It hit him all at once as he inhaled deeply and took in the odors of the pack. Violence below. Bloodlust and fury.

"A challenge?" he asked.

"If Carver is courageous enough," Jasmine told him.

"Carver?" Tanzer asked, surprised. He took another whiff of the air and confirmed it. "Interesting. This I'd like to see."

He stood up straight, body still humming with the thrill of the hunt. It could wait, though, for a few moments. More slowly, he walked down the stairs with Jasmine at his side. His right hand reached around her and came to rest on the back of her neck, and he stroked her there, the way she liked. Her hair was dark red, dyed that savage color, and her eyes were burnt orange, there in the shadow of the stairs. She looked up at him and he thought of copper.

Long before they reached the first floor, Tanzer heard the shouting.

"I've given this place over to the pack," Eric Carver snarled. "It is our lair now. But the things inside, they're mine. Unless Tanzer takes them away, they belong to me. He left me my room and my bed, and you trashed it."

Tanzer smiled appreciatively. The pretender actually sounded dangerous. All this time hiding behind the mask of humanity had not dulled him as much as Tanzer had feared.

He held Jasmine's hand as they reached the bottom of the steps. They turned from the foyer into a large parlor on the right. In the center of the room, Carver squared off against Ghirardi, the leader of a small band they had picked up in Michigan, just before arriving in Detroit. Ghirardi was thick-necked and strong, but stupid. Though Tanzer brought new members into his pack most often by explaining his vision for the future, sometimes he had to do so by force. Ghirardi and his clan were one example. Tanzer had won the right to lead them by defeating Ghirardi in combat. It had taken him seventeen seconds.

Though he had been no match for Tanzer, Ghirardi was brutal. Carver was a pretender, and too used to playing human. He was angry, though, so he had the edge there. Ghirardi saw only that Carver was smaller, thinner, and seemed more civilized, so he did not take him seriously.

Tanzer knew just from watching the way Carver moved that underestimating him was a mistake.

As the two beasts faced each other, Ghirardi let his control of his form slip a little. The human disguise began to peel back, revealing the Prowler within. Fur and fangs and claws erupted from the thin skin, and then Ghirardi was gnashing his teeth and snapping at the air between them.

"I took your bed," Ghirardi growled. "Tanzer didn't take it, but he didn't say no one else could. You want to take it back, you're more than welcome to try."

The parlor was filled with beautiful furniture. There were vases and paintings and a small reproduction of *The Thinker* on a baby grand piano, its top propped up and the strings exposed. For the most part, the pack had left Carver's things alone. They were treasures, art and other items to be appreciated, by a human or a Prowler. Though Carver was the lowest member of the pack, they had let him be—all of them except Ghirardi. Tanzer wondered if the others were simply deferring, in almost human fashion, to the Prowler who had provided their lair, or if they sensed the same thing in Carver that he did. Carver was not brave. That was true. But backed into a corner, he would be savage.

Four other members of the pack were in the large room when Tanzer and Jasmine entered and joined them in watching Carver and Ghirardi circle each other. From their scent alone, Tanzer knew the others expected blood, wanted it. Two were from Ghirardi's clan and they were tensed to spring, to act should their former leader need help.

Tanzer narrowed his gaze and snarled to let them know they were not to interfere. A challenge was a challenge.

Carver snarled and advanced a single step toward Ghirardi. "You'll stay out of there or I'll kill you."

"So kill me." Ghirardi crouched expectantly. He laughed, but it came out a low, mocking growl.

Carver nodded slowly, almost to himself. At Tanzer's side, Jasmine tensed. She would never interfere, but they all reacted this way to a fight among them. Seeing violence made them feel more like killing.

"No killing," Tanzer said, his tone low but firm, the voice he had used to inspire them to follow him. For it was he that they followed. Without him, they would fight among themselves and destroy what he had built. Tanzer would not allow that. "The pack has its rules," he reminded them. "There can be a challenge, even injuries, but no killing unless we're dealing with a traitor to the pack. You both know that."

"Fine. I'll just cripple him," Ghirardi snarled. He scratched idly at his furry snout. "Then you'll have to kill him before we move on from here anyway." He focused his red eyes on Carver. "And I'll still get his bed. Then I'll start breaking one pretty thing at a time."

Carver changed so quickly that Tanzer almost missed it. His true form did not so much as erupt from the human guise as flow into it. Many Prowlers left shed skin behind when they changed, but Carver's transformation was instant and total. The beast emerged from the human disguise their kind had learned to manifest millennia ago. Where before, Carver's features had been human, they were now purely Prowler. He flexed his long talons and gnashed his teeth as he lunged for Ghirardi. The other Prowler lashed out and raked his talons across Carver's chest, tearing his shirt and the furred flesh.

Carver struck back. His reflexes were quick and he fought smart and dirty. He raked his talons across Ghirardi's face, scratching one of the beast's eyes. Tanzer stiffened as he watched, wondering if Ghirardi would lose the eye. Blood flowed. Ghirardi howled, loud enough that Tanzer snarled under his breath, a signal for them both to take care not to be so loud that it would arouse suspicion in passersby. Ghirardi brought an arm up to wipe away the blood, then tried to blink it away as he lunged, half-blind, for his challenger.

Swift and decisive, as though it had been his plan all along, Carver backpedaled, stepped out of the way and grabbed a high-backed chair. With feral strength and brutality, he lifted the chair and brought it down hard on Ghirardi's head. The chair shattered, and Ghirardi went down.

"Mine," Carver snarled.

Ghirardi shook his head, blood streaming from his eye and snout, obviously reeling from the blow. He roared loudly and lunged at Carver again. Once more, the other dodged. Ghirardi was stronger, possibly just as quick, and he certainly had greater endurance—you could beat Ghirardi's thick skull for hours and not put him out.

But Carver was smarter and stunningly vicious, and

Tanzer quickly began to realize that, unlike any of the others in the pack, even in his natural, bestial form Carver did not completely lose the human thought processes he had developed. In combat, Prowlers regressed to their most feral, most primitive state. It was talons and gnashing teeth, and that was that. But Carver had used the chair to his advantage.

As he watched them, Tanzer wondered if the thing he most disdained in Carver might not be his greatest strength.

Ghirardi lunged again. Carver's talons flashed out and he grabbed Ghirardi by what remained of the beast's shirt and by tufts of fur. With a small, savage roar of his own, Carver propelled Ghirardi along, using the other's momentum against him. Muscles rippled beneath Carver's fur as he slammed Ghirardi into the open top of the piano. He knocked out the wooden prop stick and slammed the heavy piano lid down on top of Ghirardi; once, twice, five, six times.

Ghirardi lashed out with his feet, struggling to be free. He was tired, but as Tanzer had expected, even the nastiest beating would not put him down. Carver must have understood that now. And yet Tanzer saw no hesitation in his eyes.

With a sudden lurch, Carver reached out and grabbed a lamp off a small table. He whipped off the shade, baring the gleaming light, then broke the bulb off in the socket. Ghirardi thrust himself up, tossing the lid of the piano up, breaking it off its hinges to shatter a vase and other knickknacks on a shelf behind it.

He turned toward Carver.

Carver jammed the broken lamp into Ghirardi's chest, slamming him back into the piano. There was a crackle and the smell of burning fur as electricity from the broken bulb in the socket passed into Ghirardi's body. The big animal jerked several times, chuffing noises of pain coming from his snout. Then he collapsed in a heap on the floor.

His eyes fluttered, and he stared up at Carver with hatred, but Ghirardi was too weak to move as Carver knelt over him and took the soft furry flesh of his throat between his teeth.

From fifty-seventh in the hierarchy of the pack, vicious Eric Carver had just risen to twenty-fourth.

Tanzer smiled.

He walked over to Carver, who jumped with surprise, perhaps expecting another attack, but then leaned his head to one side to bare his own throat to Tanzer.

Owen studied him. Then reached out to take Jasmine's hand.

"I'm going hunting, Carver," he said. "Change your clothes and come along."

C H A P T E R 6

The lights flickered as the subway train rattled around a turn in the tunnel, brakes screeching with that harsh buzzsaw-through-metal squeal that Jack always thought sounded as if the train was scraping the walls as it passed. A pale girl decked out in all black with her hair dyed darker than her clothes sat beside him with something pounding into her ears from a Walkman turned up so loud that Jack heard every jangling note. With her black hair teased up into spikes and body jewelry punched through her eyebrows, ears, nostrils, top lip, and, one might imagine, just about anywhere else she could poke something sharp through, she drew plenty of attention and stares from other passengers on the Green Line train.

Jack was glad.

If they were looking at the girl, that meant they weren't looking at him. Never in his life had he felt so out of place, so much like an impostor. No one seemed to notice him, which made the experience all the more surreal. The men and women in business suits with their cell phones, the kids in street clothes, the grandmothers with shopping bags—they were all moving through a world he no longer lived in. He watched them like a voyeur, envying them in a way, but also feeling strangely superior, as though their ignorance made them somehow less than he was.

Ironic, considering that he would have paid a great deal to be ignorant again. He'd heard it said that ignorance was bliss, but he had never understood that statement until now.

Huddled against the wall and the dirty window beside him, Jack looked out into the darkness of the tunnel beyond. He could still see the reflections of the commuters who were jammed in all around him. Still felt out of place. For in the window he also saw Artie's reflection. His best friend's ghost stood leaning against the door between the cars. A woman in an elegant suit, attractive and without much makeup, stood to his left. To his right, an unshaven blue-collar type in a hooded zip-up sweatshirt that barely covered his prodigious gut.

There wasn't enough room between them for Artie's ghost, but he stood there just the same. Where their bodies crossed, at hips and elbows and, in the case of the unshaven man, the entire right side of his upper torso, Artie was simply not there. Their bodies blocked his out as though portions of him had been rubbed out with an eraser, leaving only a kind of mist around both of the people with whom he shared space.

As Jack watched the three of them, two living commuters and a dead one, the elegant businesswoman shuddered and hugged herself as though she felt cold, though it was more than warm enough on the train. Artie shot her a withering, irritated glance and waved her away with a flick of his wrist, the way he would an annoying insect.

The woman shivered again and glanced over at the obese man with a frown, as though he had bothered her in some way.

Jack turned away from the window and glared at Artie.

The ghost gave him a phantom, innocent smile and shrugged his shoulders. "What the hell do you want me to do?" he asked. "She's bugging me. Just because I'm dead, I'm not supposed to react?"

Artie stepped away from the back wall of the train car, pushed his hands through his shaggy hair, and passed right through a pair of rough-looking punks in baggy pants and high-tops to stand in front of Jack with his hands on his hips.

Jack stared at him, then glanced around nervously at the people around him and wouldn't look at Artie again.

"Bro, come on!" Artie cried. "Give me a break here, all right? I mean, okay, this takes a little getting used to, right? But you think it's easy for me? Okay, I now have the ability to see any woman naked, and that's not a bad thing. But—hello!—I can't do a damn thing about it because I'm *dead*."

In spite of himself, Jack chuckled softly and quickly put a hand up to hide his smirk. The Goth chick with the Walkman glanced at him, but only for a second. Then she scowled and went back to glaring at the people in suits.

"Oh, so me being dead is funny to you?" Artie said. "Oh, that's nice, Jack. Really nice. You're a bud."

Jack fixed him with a frustrated glare. Artie had been pretty quiet on the train so far, mainly because Jack had told him to. The last thing he wanted was a bunch of people to see him talking to himself on the T.

"What?" Artie snapped. Then he grinned. "Oh, right, the silent treatment. Listen, I've got access to the secrets of the universe over here, man. All these spirits wandering around, they know things, right? Kennedy? Three shooters. I told you, Jack. I can find out all kinds of things now, but it's too late for me to do anything about it."

Though he had been clowning only a moment before, Artie's voice now took on an air of profound despair. Jack's heart ached for him.

"Too late," Artie repeated.

"Not necessarily," Jack said quietly.

The Goth chick gave him a hard look. Jack rolled his eyes as he looked out the window. How she could hear anything with the noise crashing into her eardrums from the little headphones was a mystery to him.

"Problem?" the girl demanded angrily.

"You have no idea," Jack told her.

With a grunt, she shifted in her seat and turned away.

"I think she likes you, bro!" Artie crowed. Then he dropped to his knees on the floor, half-dissolved into one of the high-topped punks, and leaned right through the Goth girl to kiss Jack on the cheek.

The pale, tough girl shuddered suddenly. Jack felt something cold brush against his flesh, and he understood how she felt. He did not respond, however. After a moment he glanced over at Artie again. The ghost was grinning, his body even more transparent somehow. A white-haired lady with big shopping bags on her lap frowned at him as though she had caught him staring at her. Which was probably exactly what she thought.

Jack looked away.

He heard Artie snickering and could not stop a smirk from returning to his lips. A moment later the train slowed for a stop. The Goth girl gave Jack a sneer as she got up and pushed past people to be one of the first off the train. Commuters swarmed out of the car as others pushed on board without waiting. Jack could not help but turn and watch in fascination as the people going both ways passed through Artie. Each time someone moved through him, a puff of mist rose around his spectral form, like the chalk dust that flew off when they had clapped erasers together as kids at St. Matthew's Elementary.

Artie clowned as the commuters boarded, as the

flesh-and-blood world, the real world, made contact with the intangible essence which was all that remained of him. He wasn't a person anymore. He was a thought. An idea. A memory with a voice.

As he remembered all they had shared, and watched Artie playing the fool—mugging next to newly boarding commuters, pretending to trip or tickle them, kissing a gorgeous woman who stood out from the crowd—Jack felt the tragedy of his friend's death even more keenly. In a way, it hurt more to see him this way than to imagine him as nothing but a corpse in a coffin next to his grandfather's. It hurt to know for certain that his mind still existed, could understand all that had happened to him, and all that he had lost.

Artie glanced at him with those eyes, windows into the darkness of the afterlife, and Jack looked away, hoping to hide his pain. For his bitter thoughts about Artie's existence as a phantom of himself had given way to thoughts of another who had died. Thoughts of Jack's own mother.

Where is she now?

"Hey."

The whisper came from right beside him. Jack started and looked at the businessman who had sat down beside him, only to see Artie's transparent face emerge from the side of the man's head. The ghost was no longer smiling.

"It's okay," Artie whispered. "Really. I'll be all right. I'm still here, right? Or maybe not here, exactly, but I'm still. Understand? I'm still. That's better than not being anything at all, which had always been my fear, y'know? Plus I can still see people, can still talk to you. Maybe you won't miss me as much this way, right?"

Jack sighed. The businessman shifted uncomfortably, obviously aware of Jack seemingly staring at the side of his head. To avoid a confrontation with the guy, Jack turned away and looked back out the window. He could see in the reflection that Artie had stood up again.

"And maybe it makes you miss me more," Artie said softly. "I thought it was just me, feeling that way. I'm sorry, Jack. Maybe . . . maybe I shouldn't have come to you at all. I could have just gone on, y'know? But I didn't want to go without making sure someone knew what had really happened, before I told someone that *they* were out there. I should've just . . . gone."

The train squealed as it pulled into Kenmore Station. Jack got up and stepped around the businessman to join the crowd pushing to get off. He glanced around to see where Artie was, then looked out onto the platform and saw that the ghost had already gotten off the train.

Through the wall, of course, he realized. Why would he bother with the door?

Together they went with the flow of people up to the traffic-clogged intersection of Kenmore Square. Buses were lined up at the big station in the middle of the street, and Boston University students crowded the sidewalks. Artie was quiet as Jack crossed the street and headed up toward Fenway Park. On a game night, there would have been no room at all on the sidewalk, but the Red Sox were still down at camp in Fort Myers,

Florida. Few people were headed toward the ballpark tonight.

"Artie," Jack said, keeping his voice low. "I'm glad you came back."

The ghost stopped walking suddenly, but drifted another few inches. That was when Jack realized that Artie did not have to walk at all, but merely went through the motions for the sake of illusion. Though whether the illusion was for his sake or Artie's, Jack did not know.

"You don't have to say that," Artie told him. "It wasn't fair of me, I know. I died. You didn't. I shouldn't have interfered with you just living your life."

"You're my best friend."

"I was," Artie corrected.

"You still are," Jack said, lowering his voice to a whisper as a pair of middle-aged women passed by hand in hand. "Look, we could talk about all the things we've lost, but at least we can still talk. Still communicate. I don't really understand how, but—"

"Unfinished business," Artie interrupted.

"Huh?"

Artie shrugged, bounding around with the nervous energy he had always had when he was alive. "I don't know all the rules, Jack. There *is* somewhere to go for me, I know that much. Kate went on to wherever she was meant to be. But I chose to stay behind because of the Prowlers. I can't go without making sure someone stops them, someone does *something*. Think about it, bro: it's like the biggest conspiracy in the history of the world, and it cost me my life. How could I have walked away from that?"

Jack smiled affectionately. "You couldn't have."

Without a word, they fell into step side by side again.

"Exactly. So I stayed here in the Ghostlands, and I talked to some of the other . . . spirits . . . and I learned how to focus myself—my energy, I guess—so that you could see me."

"Ghostlands," Jack said. "You mentioned that once before. What is it exactly?"

"Just here," Artie told him. "All around you. It's the world within the world, or outside it, maybe, the one you can't see, where the dead linger with humanity if they can't bear to leave or if they have something they need to do. You'd be surprised how many of us there are."

Jack's throat felt dry. He glanced at Artie out of the corner of his eye, and through his friend's body he could see a neon Budweiser sign glowing in the window of a sports bar.

"Is . . . is my mother there?" he asked. Jack shoved his hands in his pockets.

Artie glanced at him as they walked. "I don't know, Jack. I'm sorry. My guess is that if you never saw her, she probably went on. And, hey, you and Courtney have done great things with the pub, and you've turned out okay, so maybe she didn't have any reason to stay."

Jack nodded slowly, didn't meet Artie's gaze. "I thought I saw her once. I never told anyone. It was in the restaurant, about two years after she died. Place was hopping, I was busing tables, and I looked up and saw this woman standing just inside the front door and, God, it looked just like her."

"Maybe it *was* her," Artie suggested. "Maybe she checked on you guys and saw that you were going to be okay and went on."

For a minute or so they walked along in silence. At the corner of Yawkey Way, in the shadow of Fenway Park, Jack stopped again and looked at Artie. Looked into the infinite space behind the eyes of a ghost.

"I want her to be happy," Jack said, his voice choked with emotion. "To be in heaven, or whatever. But I never got to say good-bye to her. I'll never know if she's proud of me. When I find someone I want to marry she won't be there."

Artie reached out and laid a spectral hand on his shoulder, and for just a moment Jack imagined he could feel the pressure of his friend's comforting grip. Then it was gone. It had all been in his mind. Artie couldn't touch him. Not really.

"If she's still here, and I ever see her, I'll tell her," Artie promised.

Jack nodded, filled with too much emotion to speak. After a moment he cleared his throat and looked at Artie. "I've gotta be honest with you, buddy. I'm standing here talking to a ghost. Freaky as that is, I've accepted it. And I want to take down the bastards who did this to you and Kate. But werewolves—"

"They're not werewolves, bro. I told you that. They're Prowlers. These things have been around since the beginning of time. They can *look* human, but they were never human beings. They started out as animals, and that's what they'll always be. Word I hear is that human advancements pushed them into the shadows and the unsettled places of the world, the fringes of human society. They're splintered, scattered. Not too many of them left.

"Now suddenly they're making a comeback. At least this group is," Artie explained. "And you don't just have to believe me, Jack. 'Cause I'm going to show you one."

"Yeah, what's up with that?" Jack asked. "How can you guide me to one of these things? Do they leave some kind of trail for you to follow?"

"No," Artie replied, "but I asked for help. In the Ghostlands, we stick together."

Artie gestured up the street toward the arched entrances to Fenway Park with their high metal gates. In front of the second entrance there lingered a quartet of ghosts.

"Jesus!" Jack shouted, heart thudding in his chest.

"You can see them?" Artie asked, his voice revealing his surprise.

Jack nodded as he stared at them—a middle-aged priest, an elderly couple, and a woman in a nurse's uniform. He could see through them all, and there in the darkness they seemed even less tangible, even more like illusions than Artie.

He blinked, looked at the nurse again. "I recognize her," he said.

"Corinne Berdinka," Artie told him. "The Prowlers

got her in the parking lot right outside the hospital where she worked. The others, too."

"God," Jack whispered. He shook his head. "How come I can see them?"

"I don't know," Artie confessed. "Maybe they want you to. Or maybe because we've had so much contact, you're just getting used to looking at the world on another level. Maybe it's like being able to see ultraviolet light or hear a dog whistle. Maybe you're starting to be able to see the Ghostlands."

A chill ran through Jack. He looked at the other ghosts and then at Artie. "I-I'm sorry, man, but I don't think I want to see all the dead in the Ghostlands. I don't know if I could handle that."

Artie glanced away, unwilling to meet Jack's eyes. "It may be too late for what you want."

Jack took a deep breath and then let it out slowly. Part of him wanted to run, but he could never do that. Not after what had happened to Artie. Not after what these things, these Prowlers, did to him. He glanced at the other ghosts lingering in front of the metal gate just up the block. The priest raised his right hand and blessed Jack with the sign of the cross.

He shivered, and all of the fear he had been suppressing rushed into him. His stomach roiled with nausea and he felt short of breath. Jack scratched at the back of his neck and shifted from foot to foot. He was scared, frightened, by all of it, by the ghosts— even Artie's—and by these animals that were hunting and killing people, these ancient beasts that had apparently been outsmarting humans since the beginning of time.

No, he corrected himself. *Not outsmarting us. Hiding from us.* And if they really had been hiding all this time, lurking in the shadows, maybe they were afraid, too. Maybe it was time to bring them out of the shadows. Maybe it was their turn to be hunted.

"All right," he said under his breath. "Where's this monster you want me to see?"

Artie pointed. "Right in there."

Jack chuckled in disbelief. "In Fenway Park? You've gotta be kidding."

"Maybe she's a baseball fan."

Carver watched Owen Tanzer in awe. The pack leader made a great deal of noise about how they were invisible because they could look human. *Maybe some of us,* he wanted to say. *But you're about as inconspicuous as a guy walking into an abortion clinic with a pair of AK-47s and plastic explosives strapped to his chest.*

As they moved through the trendy crowd on Newbury Street, people literally gawked at Tanzer. Those who weren't smart enough to be afraid of him. The rest just sort of glanced and then looked away, intimidated by the enormous, dangerous-looking man with the scars on his face. And Jasmine wasn't exactly one to blend in, either. Not only was she beautiful, but her hair was dyed such a deep, unnatural red that people could not help but look at her.

Carver had been converted. At first Tanzer had taken

over his life by force, but he had quickly come to accept his talk of returning to the wild, of joining the packs around the world, of becoming a nation of Prowlers, treating human civilization like a game preserve. It sounded very sweet to him. Tanzer was powerful, smart, and charismatic. But he did not understand humans the way Carver did. Carver, after all, blended in.

On the other hand, he had never been able to hunt prey like Tanzer. The pack leader had caught a scent from the top of the tower nearly fifteen minutes before they actually walked out of the building. Tanzer had picked up that scent without any trouble and been able to follow it despite the car exhaust fumes and the smells from nearby restaurants and the people crisscrossing through the city.

With Jasmine and Carver in tow, Tanzer had stalked his prey over to Newbury Street and down to the Capitol Grill, where the three of them had waited outside for more than an hour. Carver would have left, but Tanzer wouldn't hear of it. Once he decided upon his prey, he would not be deterred. So they waited. In order not to be noticed they visited a handful of stores along the street, always checking the scent at the Capitol Grill before going on to another.

Finally the man had emerged. He was an older man, gray-haired but sophisticated, with an aura of power about him. He might have been a highly paid lawyer or a politician, but Carver got one look at the beefy thug following two steps behind him and thought, *Organized crime.*

He mentioned this thought to Tanzer, who only looked at him and shook his head sadly. "Humans," Tanzer had said. "They're humans. This one has a swagger about him, an arrogance that cries out for a challenge. He's about to get it."

Carver had laughed at that.

Now, as he and his pack mates followed the prey and his bodyguard, he knew that he had given himself over completely to Tanzer's dream. For once they killed this man, the press and the police and the criminals would be in an uproar, and the clock would have begun to tick on their remaining time in Boston.

Looks like I'll have to give my two-week notice at the firm, he thought, amused.

The prey walked back the way he had come, cutting over from Newbury to Copley Square, apparently for pleasure. A few blocks past Carver's home, the lair of the pack, there was a parking garage. The prey went in.

"Perfect," Tanzer whispered.

Carver wanted to speak up. Jasmine beat him to it. She touched Tanzer on the shoulder, and he turned to look at her with love in his yellow-and-green eyes. People moved around them on the sidewalk.

"So close to the lair?" Jasmine asked, her voice a low growl.

"It's my prey," Tanzer replied, as though that explained everything.

And, Carver realized, it did. Tanzer was the pack

leader. Once he chose his prey, he would not give it up.

"We should follow the car," Jasmine said. "There are only three of us, but we can do it. To protect the pack."

Tanzer's lip curled back, revealing sharp fangs. His true nature was revealing itself. He did not want to wait. Carver realized that he felt the same way.

Jasmine stepped back, as though she feared what he might do, but Tanzer grabbed her arm and pulled her close, kissed her deeply. He glanced around, apparently to be sure no one was close enough to hear.

"They are humans," Tanzer said, his voice little more than a rumble in his chest. "We are Prowlers. We have nothing to fear from our prey. If they get too close, we move. We have an entire world upon which to hunt, Jasmine.

"An entire world."

Tanzer turned from them and went into the parking garage at a fast clip. He disappeared into the shadows. After only the slightest hesitation, Jasmine followed, Carver right behind her.

They had been behind Tanzer only by seconds. Yet by the time they caught up with him, the prey was dead, blood and gore spattered across the hood of a silver Lexus. His bodyguard lay on the pavement between two cars, his neck snapped. Tanzer had revealed the beast within him, and muscles rippled beneath his fur as his talons tore open his prey's belly to get to the sweeter organs. As Carver and Jasmine watched, he sniffed the air, then dipped his snout into the dead man's guts.

"What if someone comes?" Carver asked Jasmine, nervous but excited.

"Then we kill them too," she said.

Only seconds.

And the humans had not made a sound.

CHAPTER 7

For years Boston city officials and representatives of the Red Sox and Major League Baseball had talked about tearing down Fenway Park and putting up a new stadium. The prospect was bittersweet. Fenway was the grand old dame of American ballparks, harking back to an earlier age when fans older than age seven could still believe that baseball was about the game and not the money. But beneath the bleachers, the park itself was a warren of cracked concrete and stagnant beer smell, and when it rained, puddles formed *inside*, in front of the concession stands. How all that water got in was anybody's guess.

Jack knew it was only a matter of time. Eventually, and probably very soon, a new Fenway would become fact and the original just a memory. A little piece of what made Boston unique would die.

But as he crept as quietly as possible through the

wide, drafty walkways beneath the bleachers, Jack felt certain that long after it was gone, the ghost of Fenway Park would remain, and the spirit of old-time baseball would linger.

It was dark down there, but enough moonlight and starlight streamed in from the entrances and the stairwells that led up into the stands for him to see. Barely. The stale smell of beer and popcorn filled his nostrils, and the silence—the utter lack of noise that usually came from the fans and the announcers out on the field—seemed to echo in the concrete shadows.

"If I get arrested," Jack whispered, "I'm gonna be pretty pissed at you."

Beside him, Artie's ghost smirked and shook his California surfer boy hair. "What're you gonna do, Jack? Kill me?"

Jack had no answer for that one.

"Not that this is what you want to hear, Artie went on, "but I can guarantee that getting busted for trespassing is, like, totally the last thing you should be worried about at the moment. All you'd have to do is tell people you did it on a dare, or that you're just an overzealous fan or whatever. 'Course that's not gonna happen."

"Why not?" Jack asked, his voice a little too loud.

Artie held a single ghostly finger to his spectral lips and shushed him. "You haven't noticed any security guards yet, have you?"

"Not a one," Jack agreed in a low whisper. "That's pretty much my point, though, Artie. I'm bound to run into one of them."

"No. You won't. They're not down here."

"Well, where are they?"

"Out on the field."

"On the—" Jack frowned, then felt his facial muscles go slack. "And the . . . the Prowlers?"

Artie pointed toward the stairs that led up and outside. A kind of chilling electricity ran across Jack's skin, a frozen prickling that had nothing to do with the weather. Jack wet his lips with his tongue and found that his whole mouth was suddenly dry. He glanced from Artie to the stairs and then back to the ghost. Finally he started to walk slowly toward the stairs.

"Not that way."

Jack turned suddenly at the sound of the soft female voice, so filled with sadness. It was the ghost of Corinne Berdinka, still in her nurse's uniform. He studied her more closely now and saw that, like Artie, she was a gossamer thing, completely transparent. Behind her eyes lay the endless void of somewhere else.

Maybe that's the Ghostlands, Jack thought. *When I look into their eyes, maybe that's what I'm seeing.*

"What's wrong, Corinne?" Artie asked.

The phantoms lingered there, not quite standing and not quite hovering. They regarded one another carefully, and then Artie glanced over at Jack.

"They want you to have the best view. And the safest. If you aren't careful, you'll end up joining us on this side."

Jack watched the ghosts as they lingered side by side, not quite touching, and tried to figure out what they reminded him of. It came to him after a brief moment, as his mind flashed on the many wildlife documentaries he had seen on television over the years. Groups of giraffe or tigers or elephants would stand around a watering hole or near their chosen territory and it was clear that they were part of a herd, part of a tribe.

Once upon a time Artie had been his best friend, but they weren't members of the same tribe anymore. Jack still shared a connection to his dead friend, but Artie had other allegiances now. Even as this thought crossed Jack's mind he noticed movement farther along the row of concessions and bathrooms in the depths of Fenway Park, and saw the spectral priest appear. The other ghosts seemed to sense him and turned to see him raise his left hand in a beckoning gesture.

"Down here," Artie told Jack. "Looks like Father Pinsky's found a place he figures you won't be noticed."

"Yeah," Jack muttered sadly. "Thank the padre for me."

He padded softly after the spirits, noticing how as they moved through shadows and light they sometimes became invisible to him. Even as he made this observation, a scream tore through Fenway Park from out on the field; a single, piercing shriek of pain and terror. The melancholy that Jack had been feeling whenever he saw Artie's ghost dissipated in an instant.

The scream chased away the melancholy with a dizzying suddenness and the world around him turned inside out. What had been dreamlike was now hyper-real. Jack's senses were attuned to the smallest sounds, from distant car horns to the drip of water from a ceiling pipe. The cold concrete tunnels beneath the bleachers now looked like enormous tombs. Fenway was nothing but catacombs now, catacombs where the dead walked.

"Come on, Jack. They're almost done. It's important that you see this. That you believe," Artie said, his voice barely above a whisper, though supposedly the Prowlers could not have heard him in any case.

I believe, Jack wanted to tell him. *Can we just go?*

He said nothing, though. He was afraid to speak now. With that scream, the possibility that it was all true—ghosts, Prowlers, murder, and savagery—hit him full force. Though he had accepted all he had seen thus far, in the back of his mind there had remained the hope that this was all some extended hallucination brought on by grief. The fact that no one else could see or hear these ghosts made it simple to perpetuate that hope.

But that scream . . . anyone could have heard that scream.

The horror of the past week had suddenly shattered the barrier between Jack Dwyer's mind and the rest of the world. And out there in the tangible, three-dimensional, hard-edged world . . . it could kill.

"Hurry or you'll miss them," Artie urged him. He toyed with the zipper on his sweatshirt, just as he had always done when he was alive. "If they come back this way—"

"Got it," Jack interrupted. "Let's move."

With more stealth than he ever would have imagined he possessed, Jack moved past another line of concession stands beside Artie and Corinne's ghosts. He had no idea where the spirits of the elderly couple had gone. They might still have been there, but invisible to him. He didn't ask about them. They were already dead, so the Prowlers couldn't hurt them.

As Jack reached the phantom priest, the specter dissipated. He shuddered, unnerved by the disappearing act.

The Ghostlands were all around him. The inhabitants wished him well, which was nice, but they wouldn't be a hell of a lot of help to him if he got into a jam.

"Up there," Corinne whispered, behind him.

He glanced at Artie's face, could see a Coca-Cola sign on the wall through his friend's features, then turned and walked gingerly up the steps. At the top, outside now, with the bleachers of Fenway Park rising all around him, Jack crouched behind a row of seats and looked down at the field. The backstop was in front of him, as was the large net that stretched above the seats to stop foul balls from striking the fans.

He was almost directly behind home plate, one section up from the field.

There were no more screams, but he could hear snarling. Jack stared down at the field through the netting and the wire mesh backstop, and he could see them out there. He counted four corpses—the security guards. Five enormous beasts were tearing at the dead men with long fangs and thick, powerful talons. Not one of them looked the same as any other, either in size or in color. Their fur was silver, brown, gray, black, even a golden color whose brightness reflected the moon. Most were crouched on all fours, tearing at the flesh of the bloody cadavers, ears perked for any disturbance.

One walked upright, though slightly crouched. It seemed to be standing back and observing the others, but to Jack the main significance was that it was standing on two feet.

They must have come in through the same tear in the fence that he had entered. The Prowlers may very well have made that hole, solely for the purpose of hunting. No animal could have done that. They must have stalked the security guards and herded them down onto the field for the slaughter. Efficient and brutal.

As Jack watched, the Prowler closest to him—right about where the shortstop would stand—glanced up into the stands, almost as though it could see him. Jack froze.

Oh, God, no. I'm not here. I am so not here. He wanted to look around for Artie, but he did not dare move even an inch. Instead, he concentrated on feeling the wind on his face and hands. Which way was it blowing?

Off the field. That was good. So the wind had not carried his scent to them. At least not yet.

The one who had looked at him, a beast with golden fur now spattered with red blood, turned its attention back to its captured prey. It clamped its jaws onto the dead man's upper thigh, right through the pants of his guard's uniform, and tore with such ferocious power that the fabric shredded and flesh ripped.

Artie, Jack thought. *That's what they did to Artie.*

Something changed in him. Something snapped. Through the terror and the revulsion, the awe and disbelief, a dangerous calm descended over him. He still felt all of the other emotions, but now new ones began to blossom within him.

Hatred. Fury.

Monsters, he thought as he crawled on hands and knees back to the stairs. Father Pinsky and Corinne were gone, but Artie remained. Silently he led Jack back to the tear in the fence. Not until Jack had walked back over the bridge and into Kenmore Square did Artie speak to him.

"I'm sorry, but you had to see that."

"I know. I wouldn't have believed you if I hadn't seen it myself."

Jack sprinted across the square, dodging traffic and other pedestrians, though there were fewer people on the street now. A bus honked at him, but he ignored it. He bought a cup of coffee and descended into the T station, Artie's ghost in tow.

They stood next to each other as they waited for a train. Jack sipped the coffee and found it almost undrinkable. Almost. He shuddered at the taste, but it did warm him. It was not terribly cold that night, but he needed to be warmed.

People gathered around.

Jack's gaze darted about, and he examined all the strange faces around him, searching for one that did not look exactly right. He was on guard now, and thought he probably always would be. If they could pass for humans, could look like regular people on the street, then every stranger had to be suspect.

Anyone might be a monster.

He closed his eyes tightly and heard the scream from the park again, saw the intelligent yellow eyes look up toward him from the infield. As he heard the screech of metal on metal made by the approaching train, he felt a cold spot form on his upper arm. *Artie*, he knew, but he did not open his eyes.

"What are you going to do now?" Artie asked.

Jack chuckled dryly, darkly. "What you should always do with monsters. I'm going to kill them."

The train pulled in and he opened his eyes to find that Artie was gone and a number of people close by were giving him odd, fearful looks.

They're wondering if I'm a monster, he thought. He glanced at a few of the people and shook his head sadly. *You have no idea,* he thought. *No idea.*

Dori loped toward the opening she had torn in the metal to enter Fenway Park with the others falling in close behind her. Her stomach felt heavy, and she was deeply content with the results of her hunt. The news would be spectacular in the morning, the media would take the story of the guards' murder and turn it into a tale about blasphemy, about the stain such an act of violence put on the church of professional sports.

Delicious. She loved to make the news. The pack had lasted seven months in Atlanta. That had been the longest. She was beginning to wonder if Boston would earn a record for their shortest stay in any city. At first, Tanzer had insisted on keeping to the fringes, but once Ghirardi had killed the priest, all bets were off. As far as she was concerned, the more colorful the better.

She stood aside, stretched, and let her bones pop and her flesh fold and flow out to cover her true form, her true face. They had left their clothes hidden in a cubbyhole near the gate. Once dressed, she stood aside and let the others slip out before her.

It was only as she pushed through the opening torn in the metal mesh that she caught the scent.

Dori sniffed the air.

Human. Male. Frightened.

The scent had not been there when they went in, she was certain of it.

An aging Prowler named Vernon, whose hair when he was hiding beneath the mask of humanity was as silver as his fur, trotted back to where she had paused.

"What is it?" Vernon asked.

"Go back to the lair," Dori told him, her voice a low growl. "I want to check something out."

Vernon loped away.

Dori sniffed the air again and began to track the scent.

* * *

It was long after closing that Jack returned to Bridget's Irish Rose. The chairs were up on tables and the floor had been mopped. The fans still turned lazily overhead, more for atmosphere than temperature at this time of year. At the bar, in front of the long mirror, Bill Cantwell poured two fingers of Chivas Regal for his only customer, who also happened to be his boss. Courtney shifted on her stool, smiled at Bill, and sipped tentatively at the whiskey.

Jack watched all of this through the frosted window. He stood on the street corner and pressed his face against the cool glass, and his heart at last began to slow to a normal beat.

Normal.

All right, it was true he'd never seen Courtney drink Chivas Regal before, and her conversation with Bill seemed surprisingly intimate—a closeness that fed into Jack's recent suspicion that the two were slowly becoming more than friends and co-workers. Still, the quiet of the pub, the relaxed, tired smiles of the two of them, that was normal.

This was home.

And what had Robert Frost said about home—that it is the place where, when you go there, they have to take you in . . . no matter how crazy they think you are.

A sound carried across the street, a tinkling of metal. Jack started nervously and turned to search the night for its source. A dog. Its metal tag clinked as it trotted by, roaming far from its home. It was a big animal, a German shepherd, and any other time Jack would have noticed it with a certain amount of trepidation. Dogs were unpredictable. Tonight, though, he silently urged it to move along, to go on home, get off the street.

It was an animal, after all.

And there were predators about.

With a sigh, Jack steadied his nerves, dug out his keys, and opened the door to the pub.

Courtney and Bill glanced over and smiled as he locked the doors behind him. Then his sister got a clear look at his face.

"Jack, what's wrong?"

Courtney fell silent. Jack figured she did not know how to put into words the things she saw on his face and in his eyes.

That made two of them.

"Jack?" Bill echoed.

A tight knot of anxiety and leftover fear formed in his stomach. He felt . . . not nauseated but hungry, as if his belly were empty and dried out, tight as a drum.

Without a word, he hugged Courtney as she sat on the stool. His foot bumped her cane, and it slid to the floor with a clatter, but she made no move to retrieve it. Instead, she hugged him back, then held him away from her and studied his eyes. "What is it?"

Jack swallowed hard, smiled, and shook his head. Then he glanced at Bill.

"Court's already got a drink. You might want to pour one for yourself," he said, and chuckled. The little laugh sounded a bit unhinged to him, but Jack wasn't surprised. That was how he felt. "Bartender, beer thyself."

Whatever Courtney had seen in Jack's eyes, Bill obviously saw it too, for he poured himself a stiff shot of Chivas and topped off Courtney's. He tipped the bottle toward Jack, who shook his head to indicate that he wouldn't be drinking. Bill left the bottle on the bar, just in case.

"Something tells me beer's not going to cut it," Bill said.

"Talk to me, Jack," Courtney urged. "You've got me worried."

"I don't think what I've got to tell you is going to make you feel much better," he said, his low voice carrying across the dimly lit pub. He wondered again about his mother's spirit. She had moved on, or so he believed, but he wished she were there watching over them, even if he could not see her.

Courtney took a sip of her drink. "Well?" she asked.

Jack told them.

By the time he finished, Bill and Courtney had killed half a bottle of Chivas.

"Prowlers?" Courtney said in wonder, her face slack. "Ghosts, Jack? You know how it sounds."

Jack nodded. "Look at me, Courtney."

She did, stepping awkwardly away from the stool. She leaned on him, sister and brother face-to-face. Nobody in the world knew Jack the way Courtney did.

"I *saw* them," he said. "For real."

"Oh, my God," she whispered.

After a moment they both turned toward Bill. He had paled considerably, and yet Jack was surprised to see that his expression was one of concern, maybe even fear, but not disbelief.

"Bill?" Courtney prodded.

He did not look at Courtney, though. Instead, Bill locked eyes with Jack. "This isn't the first time I've heard of these things."

"What?" Jack muttered. "Where—"

"I was on the road on a vacation the year before I started playing pro ball. In a bar north of Sedona, Arizona, I heard a couple of guys talking about a local girl who'd been murdered. One of them was convinced it was these Prowlers, these monsters. Gave me the creeps. I didn't hang around there very long."

Courtney scoffed. "Bill, come on. I'm not saying I don't believe Jack saw something awful, maybe even talked to Artie's ghost. I've got a pretty rich imagination, and I've seen an odd thing or two myself from time to time. Maybe there really are monsters out there, I don't know. But a drunk in a bar? He might as well have blamed that Mexican goat-sucker thing, what is it? El Chupacabras."

"And maybe these things are the reason for the existence of legends, like El Chupacabras and werewolves and whatever else." Bill tossed back a shot of Chivas, then poured another before gazing steadily at Jack again. "I've known you a long time, Jack. You've pulled a few pranks in your time, but I know this isn't one of 'em. Like your sister, I'm not about to doubt you on this. But I've got another reason to believe you.

"The guy in the bar. The one who talked about the Prowlers? He was the town sheriff."

CHAPTER 8

Kate Nordling was buried during a rainstorm on Saturday, in a grave her parents had bought for themselves. The cemetery was in the wealthy town of Newton, but other than the fact that the cars in the procession were more expensive, Jack thought Kate's funeral was a lot like Artie's. Students, teachers, family—all grieving, all now missing a part of their lives.

One main difference was the presence of the media. Artie's murder had been news, but not the kind that brought swarms of reporters and cameramen.

In the previous forty-eight hours, however, everything had changed. The morning newscasts had been boiling over with reports of the slaughter in Fenway Park on Thursday, and that was only part of the story. In a parking garage in downtown Boston, mafia boss Francesco Rizzo and an associate had been murdered. Police were downplaying Rizzo's murder as mob related, but the reporters had their noses to the ground, and they knew something didn't smell right. Jack had seen two separate television news reports that morning in which the reporter had wondered aloud if the two cases were related—and if they were connected to several other area murders in recent weeks..

"God, I hate all the media," Molly muttered angrily.

Jack had a protective arm around her, and with the other hand he held up the large black umbrella that protected them from the rain.

"I know what you mean," he said as he glanced about. "It's all rain and umbrellas. What do they think they're going to get on film here?"

Molly stiffened and gazed up at Jack. "Who cares about the rain?" she whispered. "What are they doing here? This is . . . I mean, Kate's family shouldn't have to deal with this. It's private."

"Absolutely," Jack agreed.

Though she did not seem satisfied with his response, Molly sighed and turned her attention back to the graveside service. Jack was glad. All morning he had been waiting for Artie to appear, but there was no sign of him or of any other ghosts. If Artie was right, and he had begun to be able to see the Ghostlands, it was apparently an ability that came and went unexpectedly. Jack would have been greatly relieved if that had turned out to be true. He thought he might go more than a little crazy if he was surrounded by ghosts all the time.

You are *surrounded by them all the time*, he thought. *You just can't always see them.*

The idea chilled him. He stood in the middle of the cemetery and glanced around at the names engraved on the stones nearby. Boer. Slikowski. Farchand. O'Rourke. Geary.

Are you here? he thought. Then he glanced at the casket beside Kate's grave. *Are you here, Kate? I'm sorry if I was a jerk. I'm sorry for what happened to you.*

Jack shivered and closed his eyes tightly. If any of the ghosts were there, he did not want to see them. Not right now. He did not know if just thinking of them, calling out to them in his mind, would draw their attention, but that was something he did not want to do.

"Hey," Molly whispered. "Are you all right?"

He nodded. Rain dripped onto his shoulder from the edge of the umbrella, but he wanted to make sure Molly did not get wet, so he ignored it. *Let the rain fall,* he thought, and remembered a song that went something like that.

Let the rain fall.

"I've just had enough of churches and cemeteries for a while," he replied softly.

Molly had an arm around his waist and she squeezed him tight. "Me too, Jack. Me too."

Her usually unruly red hair was pulled tight in a bun, and a few stray strands blew across her face in the moist breeze. Her face was so pale that some of her freckles seemed to have faded, but Jack was sure it was just the gray day. The sun would bring them out again, he knew. Molly had always been a pretty girl. It occurred to Jack as he looked at her that while she was merely pretty most of the time, when she was truly happy, smiling or laughing—or when she was in emotional torment—she was gorgeous.

Molly seemed to have somehow risen above all the pain of Artie's and Kate's murders. Though tired, she looked almost angelic.

Jack had always thought Artie was lucky to have her, lucky she put up with him. Now Molly would go on without him. Eventually she would meet someone new, have another boyfriend, never knowing that Artie was there, nearby, able to watch her at any time.

Much as he grieved for the pain Molly was in, he felt far worse for Artie. *You should go on, man,* he thought.

The answer came back unbidden from the back of his own mind: Artie had not yet gone on. Could not go on until he found a way to stop the Prowlers. Now it was up to Jack to help him with that.

The reporters crowded around like hunting dogs on a scent. They knew the story was here, but they did not know what the truth of it was. They could not, Jack thought, have begun to imagine what the truth was. It had occurred to him more than once that the police must have linked all of these crimes and been downplaying their conclusion in order to avoid causing a panic. But that was just guesswork. Maybe the police knew, maybe they didn't.

Kate's parents cried for her, but they did not know. Molly.

Jack wished he could tell her, but Artie would never

forgive him. And he had all eternity to haunt Jack about it if he wanted to.

Only Courtney and Bill knew, and they were only half convinced. Jack was pretty much on his own. But he had seen the monsters, and he knew he had to figure something out, find some way to stop them. If that meant going to the police, that was what he would have to do. And hope they didn't lock him up in an asylum somewhere.

Even when it was over, it wasn't over.

When the priest had said his final words and blessed Kate for the last time, and the mourners had walked stone-faced past the media vultures and back to their cars, that was only the beginning of the day of grieving. It was a tradition Molly had never understood, but the Nordlings invited everyone—everyone without a camera, at least—back to their home.

But even though Molly didn't understand it, she went. Kate's parents would have been hurt if she had not. Jack had been hesitant about it—he had never even met Kate's parents—but Molly told him she wanted him to go, and he agreed. They rode over in Jack's eight-year-old Jeep Cherokee, neither of them speaking much. As he had so often lately, Jack seemed distracted, glancing out the window and in the rearview mirror every few seconds.

Once inside the Nordlings' home, though, Jack disappeared. Molly spotted him from time to time, speaking to one of his old Boston Catholic High School teachers or to some kid he knew from his four years there. But for the most part, he seemed to linger on the periphery.

By the time Molly caught up to him, they had been at the Nordlings for nearly three hours. It was after four in the afternoon when she found him standing in a corner of the kitchen, drinking Sprite from a plastic cup and trying to appear unobtrusive.

"You're avoiding me."

Jack blinked, obviously a bit taken aback. The clock on the wall ticked steadily. The chatter from the other mourners had diminished as the afternoon wore on, but there were still a great many people in the living room and dining room. In the kitchen, the detritus from the various foods that had been provided had built up; casserole dishes and trays and glasses covered the table and most of the counter space.

"I haven't been avoiding you," he replied, his voice flat.

Molly flinched. A twinge of sadness touched her heart. She glanced around to be sure no one was nearby, then she moved in closer to him, taking one of his hands in hers. "Jack, talk to me," she said, heart aching. She searched his warm brown eyes, saw how tired he was. But there was more than pain and exhaustion there. Molly thought she saw confusion as well.

"I don't know what to say," he confessed, an ache in his voice.

A bone-deep melancholy swept over Molly, a sadness completely unlike the grief she felt because of what had happened to Artie and Kate. Every emotion was raw, and each one was frayed to the breaking point. With all she had already lost, she needed Jack to lean on. She knew he needed her as well, though maybe not as much.

Stray locks of her red hair had escaped, and Molly brushed them away from her face. She gazed up into Jack's eyes. "We're all that's left, Jack," she said, clutching his hand even more tightly.

Mrs. Gerritson, the biology teacher from B. C. High, popped quickly into the kitchen to slide a stack of dirty dessert dishes onto the counter. She glanced apologetically, at them. obviously realizing she had interrupted something. Molly waited until the woman had slipped out to speak.

She let go of Jack's hand and leaned against the refrigerator beside him. It hummed against her back.

"I had other friends, Jack," Molly said. She nodded as if to reassure herself of that. "But while I was with Artie, I drifted away from them. I spent so much time with my boyfriend that they moved on without me. I guess it happens. The only one I stayed really close to was Kate, and she's . . ."

Molly bit her lip and stared down at the tile floor. Jack laid one of his large, strong hands on her shoulder for comfort, and Molly leaned into him, grateful for the support.

"With all the time we spent together, you and I and Artie, well . . ." She turned to face him again but could not lift her eyes. She was not used to opening her heart, particularly when it was so raw. When she continued, she did not look up. "You're about the best friend I have, I think. It's just you and me now, and you've been so quiet and stuff, I just . . . The funerals are over. Without Artie, there's nothing keeping us together. Not school, not anything. I don't know if I can handle it if you let our friendship go, y'know?"

"Oh, Jesus, Molly no." His voice cracked with emotion.

Molly finally raised her eyes to Jack's face and saw nothing but pain and horror there.

Then he smiled. Her friend smiled, and Molly knew it was going to be all right.

"I'm sorry, Moll," he said quickly. "I had no idea you were thinking all that stuff. What a jerk, huh? God, I've been so wrapped up in my own head with all this . . . and other stuff I've had on my mind." Jack hugged her tight enough to cut off her breathing.

Molly felt as though ice was shattering all over her, including her mouth, which stretched into what felt like its first smile of the day.

"I'm not going anywhere," Jack told her. "Nowhere. You got it? You're stuck with me now. Somebody's got to play big brother and keep an eye on you."

"You've always done that," Molly told him. As she held on to him, her eyes fell upon the collection of magnets scattered across the face of the refrigerator. Most of them were Kate's. Molly had been with her when she bought a number of them, including a set featuring the Powerpuff Girls. Bubbles, Blossom . . .

She could never remember that last one.

With a deep breath, Molly pulled away from Jack and stared up at him again. "Know what? I don't think I can cry anymore. I need a break from tears and hurting and all of it."

"What do you want to do?" Jack asked.

"Feel like going to the movies?"

Boston had fewer than its share of movie theaters. There were mutliplexes at Copley Place and in Kenmore Square, but not many beyond that, except for the Capitol. Located right on Tremont Street across from Boston Common, the Capitol Theater was a faded movie palace that specialized in foreign films, independent cinema, and little weekend festivals. They had an all-nighter every Friday night, and the marquee announced that the following week it would be Eastwood spaghetti westerns.

Jack loved westerns.

"Look at that," Molly said as they walked up Tremont and she spotted the marquee. "You'll be in heaven next week."

Her voice was tight, a bit forced, and he knew they were both thinking the same thing, that if Artie were alive it would have been guys' night out. But they had agreed that they needed a little time off from hurting so much, so Jack did not put a voice to his thoughts.

"If Courtney will let me take next Friday off," Jack replied. "This week I've pretty much left her hanging."

Molly bumped him as they walked along the cracked concrete sidewalk. "I'm sure she doesn't mind, Jack. It isn't like you're calling in sick or something. We should go."

Jack gave her a sidelong glance. "You don't even like Clint Eastwood."

"I don't mind him. Maybe I need to see more of his movies."

With a laugh, Jack shook his head. "All right. Let me talk to Courtney. And I appreciate your sacrifice."

As they walked up to the box office, Molly gave a little laugh as well. They had driven back from Newton, left Jack's Jeep in one of the few parking spaces that were reserved for the pub, and walked up to the Capitol. They hadn't bothered to get dinner after all the food they'd eaten at the Nordlings', but all their travel had taken time, and it was after six o'clock. Now, at the box office, they stared at the movie times and tried to figure out their next move.

"Quite a dilemma," Molly muttered.

Jack agreed. The latest George Clooney flick, a supernatural thriller that had gotten excellent reviews, had been out of the first-run theaters since before Christmas, but the Capitol had it now. The problem was, it had started twenty minutes earlier and the next showing wasn't until a quarter to eight. Their other option was a kung fu comedy Jackie Chan had made in China about a dozen years ago.

"The dubbing is probably really, really awful," Molly said.

"But it starts in ten minutes," Jack replied. "And we could use a laugh."

And maybe I'm not in the mood for a supernatural thriller, with or without George Clooney.

Which was how they found themselves sitting in the darkened theater a short time later, a big tub of popcorn on Jack's lap, laughing out loud at some of Jackie Chan's antics. The film was a bizarre mix of elements. One minute it was played for laughs, and the next it was all-out action with some real suspense. And Chan's acrobatics were extraordinary. Jack had never really been a fan, but he had only seen one or two of the man's American films. This was something else entirely.

Molly laughed right along with him. Though she had said she didn't want any popcorn, she raided his bucket throughout the movie. They sipped watered-down sodas and once in a while leaned over to mutter something to each other. A couple of times they were shushed by a couple sitting behind them, a thirtyish guy with a goatee and square glasses and a diminutive woman whose pale face and black hair made her look a bit Goth without any obvious effort to do so. Jack wanted to tell them off. There were only about twenty other people in the theater—it was a pretty early showing—and they could have sat anywhere else in the theater. But he knew it was rude to talk during the film, so he kept his mouth shut.

From time to time during the film his attention was drawn to a girl who sat alone in the front row. He had spotted her when she walked into the theater just a few minutes after he and Molly had. Her face was full and round, and her eyes were almost impossibly large. Her raven-black hair was lustrous and she was all curves. When she had first come in, their eyes met; then she glanced at Molly and moved on, down to the front row.

Half a dozen times, when he had glanced at her, the girl was turned slightly to look back at him, almost as if she could feel his eyes on her.

Jack was glad to be there with Molly. It was important for both of them, and he cared for her deeply. But he could not suppress a tiny twinge of regret that he had not run across the startling girl with the huge eyes at another time.

Molly leaned over to him. "I'm really glad we did this," she said, her voice low.

"Me too."

The guy shushed them again. Jack rolled his eyes, smiled to himself and tossed some popcorn at Molly, just to cause trouble. Molly stifled a laugh and glared at him, her eyes flicking toward the seats behind them. Jack pretended to throw some more popcorn at her, but then ate it instead.

On screen the action was heating up. Jackie Chan was infiltrating the headquarters of a gang of drug traffickers he had already humiliated with various household appliances and a garden hose, but now he was set to take them down once and for all. The beautiful female cop who had become his sidekick carried a gun, but Jackie just had Jackie. No need for guns when he could taunt a guy to death with a flyswatter or beat him unconscious with a rake.

Even as these thoughts raced through Jack's head, the action erupted onscreen. Jack shifted in his seat to get more comfortable. As he did so, he glanced again at the girl in the front row.

Artie was standing beside her.

Jack started, spilling a little popcorn. Molly looked at him with concern, but he reassured her with a sheepish grin. *Just me being a goof,* he tried to communicate to her.

Then he looked at Artie again. The ghost seemed even more translucent than ever, there in the already spectral glow of the movie screen. Artie's body was almost black because there was only darkness behind him, but he stood tall enough that his head and shoulders were in front of the screen, and through them, Jack could still see the movie playing. He could barely make out Artie's facial features, but he knew his dead friend was looking at him.

Jack wanted to speak, to say something to Artie, but that might have sent the couple behind him into a rage, and besides, he didn't want Molly to think he was nuts.

Fortunately, Artie spoke first.

"You gotta get outta here, bro. Now. Seriously."

Jack glanced at Molly. She hadn't heard anything. Nobody shushed Artie. It was true, then. No one else could see or hear him.

"You're not listening, Jack. Take Molly and get out of here right now. They're here, don't you get it? They must have gotten your scent at Fenway or something, and they've been tracking you. I just heard about it a few minutes ago and I came as quick as I could, but if you don't get out of here, there'll be no one left to stop these things."

Artie began to walk toward Jack through the rows of seats, his insubstantial legs swirling into mist as he passed through metal and cloth. As he drew closer, Jack could see his face better, could see the fear etched there, and the pinpoint holes of his eyes, windows into another world, into the Ghostlands.

He stopped two rows away.

Jack fidgeted, unsure what to do. Could he drag Molly out of there without explaining why they had to go?

Right through Artie, he noticed the girl in the front row start to fidget as well. She did not glance at Jack this time, but she tilted her head back slightly and began to sniff the air where Artie had been standing, as if she could smell him, knew he had been there. She frowned.

Slowly, she turned to look at Jack.

Jesus, he thought fearfully, as he tried to keep his face from revealing his sudden terror.

"Dammit, Jack, get out of here!" Artie screamed.

The girl looked back up at the screen. Jack nodded quickly to Artie and leaned over to Molly. He took her arm and when she glanced at him, he gestured with a jerk of his head that they needed to go.

"What's wrong?" she asked. "Are you—"

Jack put a finger to his lips, but Molly was not going

to leave without knowing why. He could not have blamed her. There were maybe ten minutes left in the movie. But Artie was right. The last thing he wanted was to walk out of there with Prowlers following. In the back of his mind he saw the security guards being torn apart in Fenway Park, heard the sounds of it again, and tried to block it all out.

"We've gotta go right now," he told her in the quietest whisper he could manage. He looked to Artie for support—though it wasn't as though Molly could have heard him. Artie was gone.

Molly still wasn't getting it. She opened her mouth to argue. Jack glanced for a microsecond at the girl in the front row, the girl who had sniffed the air, and then back at Molly. He leaned in again.

"Do you want to end up like Artie and Kate?" he asked.

Her face blanched, all color seeping out of it until she was as pale as death. Silently Jack put his popcorn tub on the floor of the theater, took one more look at the girl—*She's not a girl*, his mind screamed—in the front row, and then stood up to lead Molly out of the theater.

"Aw, come on!" snapped the guy behind them, whose view of the screen was blocked for a moment by their sudden departure.

No! Jack thought in alarm. It was too late. The guy's voice had drawn the wrong kind of attention. As Molly stepped out into the aisle with him, Jack peered down at the front of the theater and saw that the girl with the huge eyes was staring back at him.

He knew she wasn't what she appeared to be. When she met his eyes, she must have seen that he knew, because she smiled. Her teeth seemed impossibly long, remarkably bright, there in the dark of the theater.

"Hurry," Jack muttered, and he put a hand on Molly's back to hustle her up the aisle.

Just before they left the theater, he glanced back one final time.

The girl from the front row was gone.

On the other side of the theater, two other people had gotten up from their seats and were moving up the aisle.

Jack's heart started to beat wildly.

"Go!" he shouted at Molly.

They ran through the lobby. The concession stand guy and the ticket taker looked at them as though they were lunatics, but said nothing. When they burst out the door and onto the sidewalk, Molly was shouting at him.

"Jack, you're scaring me!" she said, her voice edged with panic. "What are you talking about, end up like—"

He grabbed her arms, spun her around to look at him, gazed deep into her eyes to make sure she knew how serious he was. "Haven't you been watching the news? The things that killed Artie and Kate have killed a lot of other people. Right now they're after us!"

Back in the lobby, he spotted two guys coming out of the Jackie Chan film early. Still no sign of the girl, but he knew she was there. Somewhere nearby, stalking them. Night had fallen and cars sped by on Tremont Street, but there weren't too many people walking around—enough for there to be witnesses, but not enough to keep them from dying.

Molly threw up her hands. "How do you—"

"Run!" he shouted.

He pulled her into the street. A cab slammed on its brakes, tires squealing, and the driver leaned on his horn. A couple of other drivers also beeped, but Jack and Molly ran across Tremont to the edge of the park. He didn't bother turning around to see if they were being followed. The Prowlers were there, Jack knew.

We're being hunted.

CHAPTER 9

Most of Boston Common was abandoned after dark. Basic logic dictated that the winding paths, out of sight of the street, weren't safe after the sun went down. But at the fringes of the Common a number of people were still about, particularly by the Park Street Station, which jutted out of the Common where Park Street met Tremont as if it had simply erupted there one night. No pretzel or flower vendors at this hour, but several homeless people were meandering about, and one ragged-looking man was standing in front of the T station entrance, coin-filled cup in hand.

Jack brushed past him without slowing down, knocking his cup to the concrete. The man screamed obscenities at him and threw a punch meant to hit Molly, but he was too slow. The coins jangled as they rolled around on the ground, but by then Molly and Jack were inside the station.

"Wait, Jack!" Molly shouted.

He pulled her by the hand, but Molly stood her ground and forced him to turn.

"Not now, Molly!" he snapped.

"Yes, now! What the hell's going on? What did you mean about Artie and Kate. I don't—"

Outside, beyond the doors, the homeless guy who knelt on the ground picking up coins started shouting at someone else. Jack stared through the glass doors to the station and locked eyes with one of the two men who had rushed out of the movie. He had perfect hair and sideburns, a ratty leather jacket, and eyes like the burning-ember tips of cigarettes. Jack barely noticed his partner, a broad-shouldered bald man with a face chiseled in stone.

Those ember eyes terrified him.

"Oh, God," he whispered.

"Jack?" Molly asked, more afraid than angry now.

That was good. He wanted her afraid. Even as she said his name, she glanced back at the doors to see what he was staring at, what had spooked him. She saw them.

"Them?" she asked. "Are they—"

When the man with ember eyes reached out to open the door to the T station, Jack grabbed Molly's hand again, screamed at her, and hauled her toward the turnstiles. They had no tokens. Without a moment's pause Jack grabbed Molly around the waist and practically tossed her over the turnstile, then leaped over after her.

He ran, and she ran with him.

"Jack?" she asked, her voice pleading as they fled down the escalator.

Up above, a pair of MBTA workers shouted after them, warning that they were going to call the cops. Jack prayed that it was not just an idle threat. He did not look back to see how close the Prowlers were. He did not want to know.

"Go, go, go!" he urged Molly on.

"I'm going!" she snapped at him.

"Run faster if you want to live," he warned.

She said nothing after that. She vaulted the last five steps to the bottom of the escalator, and he followed suit. Then they were sprinting past the people who seemed to be sleepwalking through the labyrinthine station.

Jack glanced over his shoulder. The two men walked quickly after them, but did not run. They seemed to be slipping in between people as though everyone else were standing still . . . either that, or by some instinct, nobody would get near them.

Several T lines went through Park Street. Jack and Molly went through the Red Line station and ducked down the stairs to the Green Line. Molly did not ask again what was going on. Both of them were breathing hard. Jack felt his heart clench in his chest just as the rest of his body did, ready to defend himself and Molly if necessary.

Perhaps a dozen people stood waiting for the Green Line train to come through. Jack pulled Molly behind a square concrete pillar and put a finger to his lips. He could hear the shrieking of brakes coming from the subway tunnel, could feel the hot blast of air pushed along through the tunnel in front of the train. It was coming.

So were the Prowlers. He could almost feel them coming, but did not dare peek out to see. From behind the pillar, he could see three people sitting on a bench waiting for a train. It took him a moment to realize one of them was a ghost.

The phantom appeared to have once been a homeless woman. When Jack spotted her, she glanced at him and her eyes widened in surprise. Apparently she had not expected to be seen. Then she held a finger up to shush him the way he had done to Molly, and pointed back the way Jack had come.

The Prowlers. She knew what they were, or at least knew Jack was running from them.

"They haven't found you yet," a low voice whispered behind him.

Jack grunted and turned quickly to see the ghost of Father Pinsky close behind him. He flinched, startled by the nearness of the spirit. Even Artie had not come that close to him. Jack could see that Father Pinsky's eyes, like Artie's, were windows to some other world, a place of dark fire and sparkling stars.

"All the scents down here have them confused," the preist said. "The train's coming. Wait for it. Just wait."

"Thanks," Jack whispered.

Then he glanced over to find Molly staring at him as though he'd lost his mind. Jack opened his mouth to explain, then shook his head. "Long story," he murmured.

The train screeched and hissed its way into the station, and the doors opened. Molly moved, but Jack held her back.

"Hold on. Give it a minute. Hang on. Hang on," he urged her. People got off the train and others got on. In the final moment before the doors would have closed, Jack put a hand on Molly's shoulder and went for it. "Now!"

They sprinted the ten feet to the train door even as a bell jangled and the doors started to close. With inches to spare, they slipped through.

The doors opened again. The driver had apparently triggered them again to make sure Jack and Molly did not get hurt. People glared at them, but Jack ignored them. He poked his head out the door and quickly saw the man with ember eyes and his muscle-bound sidekick board the train three cars back.

"Did they get on?" Molly demanded.

Jack nodded grimly. "We're trapped here now. We've got to get off." He glanced around wildly, ignoring the increasingly strange stares from other passengers.

Then Molly reached up and grabbed his face. She pinched his mouth and chin in her hand and turned his head so he would look at her. Her greenish eyes had darkened with anger or fear or exertion, and her hair was even more unruly than usual. With her other hand, she held on to a metal pole in the middle of the car. She let go of his face and beckoned with one finger so he would lean in toward her.

"No more," she whispered to him. "I'm scared, Jack, and I'm sad, and I'm worried about you. Who the hell are those guys?"

"You have to trust me," he whispered back.

"I do," she replied firmly. "But you have to trust *me*, too."

Jack glanced at the door at the other end of their car. No one was supposed to move between cars while the train was in motion, but somehow he doubted the Prowlers were going to obey the rules.

Nearly overwhelmed with the urgency of the moment, knowing what would happen if the creatures caught up to them, Jack almost snapped at her. But then he peered into Molly's eyes and saw how much she needed to know. He also saw the strength there, and the courage.

He had to trust her.

"Artie and Kate and a whole lot of other people were hunted and killed, but not by people," he whispered, staring deep into Molly's eyes. "They're monsters, Molly. Called Prowlers."

She shook her head, her rejection of his words so fundamental it did not even make it to her lips. The expression in her eyes said it all.

Jack took her hand and squeezed it gently. "You don't have to believe it, but believe *me*. Those two guys are after us. If we don't do something—"

"Like what?" she demanded.

The people nearest them had started to edge away as they overheard Jack's insane ramblings. That was good, he thought. It gave them space to move. Others stared openly at them as well, but Jack ignored them. He glanced around the train again and was suddenly struck by how many more people were on board than he had thought when they jumped on.

Ghosts. He knew it almost before the word formed in his mind. Quickly, he looked around again and realized there were seven or eight ghosts on board the train, just in that car alone. All of them were looking at him. More than that, though, they were really seeing him, as if he had become one of them. For just a moment it seemed as though a mist had formed inside the subway car, as though he were seeing everything around him through a rolling fog.

The spirits took on flesh and weight and color.

With a start, Jack saw that Molly had suddenly become transparent, as insubstantial as Artie. He was terrified that if he tried to touch her, Molly would be insubstantial as well.

This is it, he thought. *I'm seeing the Ghostlands. I'm . . . part of it.*

"Am I dead?" he wondered out loud.

A hand gripped his shoulder. Jack turned, ready to fight, but it was Artie.

In the flesh. He appeared just as healthy as he had on the night he died.

"You're not dead, bro. Maybe something in between life and death if we can see you like this, if I can lay hands on you. But if you don't move your ass, you're going to be dead for real. You can't run away, Jack. I don't want you to kill anyone but if you let these things live they'll find you again. They could track your scent to friggin' Albuquerque and back. You gotta take 'em out."

"*Artie* . . ." Jack said, and even his voice sounded different to him. Hollow. Haunted.

His head rocked back as if he'd been slapped and he blinked to find that the world had inverted itself again. The ghosts were still there, but they were transparent, true phantoms.

Molly was flesh and blood again and in his face. "What's happening to you?" she demanded, her voice tight, as though she might snap at any moment.

"Later," he said quickly.

His eyes darted around. The ghosts down at the far end of the car started shouting at him, and he saw that one of them was Corinne Berdinka. He focused on her face, on her eyes, and saw terror there. The Prowlers were moving fast. They were coming through. Time had run out.

"This way," Jack said, and he darted past a couple of other passengers who swore loudly at him.

Molly seemed about to argue, but she looked at him again, searched his eyes for something and must have found it, because she went along with him.

"Go through to the next car, but not far in," he told her. "Stand inside the glass and let them see you."

"We're not supposed to—"

"Go!"

He shoved Molly ahead of him, and she hauled open

the heavy metal door, then pushed through and shoved open the door to the next car. Jack followed her, but he stopped between the cars. The screech of metal and brakes filled his ears, and he was buffeted by the wind produced by the speed of the train. Chains rattled below where the two cars were coupled together, and Jack stood with a foot on either side of the narrow breach beneath him. As the train turned, he fought to keep his balance, hands pressed against the outside of the train on either side.

From inside the train, he would not be visible.

All of that had transpired in less than a minute. The train was moving between stations at top speed now. Fourteen seconds ticked by before the door to his right was hauled open again. The bald, muscle-bound guy stepped into the breach. His eyes were focused straight ahead, and Jack knew what he was staring at: Molly. If she had done as Jack asked, she would be standing right there—bait. And this guy, this creature, wanted to do to her what he'd done to Artie.

Then, in the heartbeat before the Prowler would have seen him, Jack saw its nose and mouth push out slightly, the skin stretching as if something else lurked beneath it, something with a snout and long, glistening fangs, and all he could think about was the story of Little Red Riding Hood and the wolf disguised as her grandmother.

Why couldn't Red see the truth?

Because it looked like her grandmother, Jack thought.

His stomach convulsed. The Prowler noticed him in

its peripheral vision. Fingers gripping a tiny lip of metal, his only way to brace himself, Jack crouched slightly and shot his right leg out in a straight, hard kick that knocked the creature back out of the breach. It scrabbled for a handhold and found none, then roared in defiance before it tumbled into the two-foot space between the train and the hard concrete wall. Bones snapped as the train dragged the beast a moment. Then it fell to the tracks, hit the third rail, and sparks of electricity burst off it.

Jack reached for the door leading into the next car. He was too late. The man with the ember eyes came into the space between cars behind him. His grin was filled with razor-sharp teeth, and his hands no longer looked human.

"Well done," he snarled. "For all the good it did you."

Molly saw it all.

For just an instant, she was horrified at what Jack had done. Her mind raced with the terrible possibilities, recoiled from the one that disturbed her the most: that he had just murdered a man at random. But why, then, had the man come through between the cars?

Even as these things occurred to her, the other man stepped into the breach between trains. He grabbed Jack by the collar and grinned, and in that one simple moment, Molly really *saw* him—his teeth and his hands and his eyes—and knew that she had to act. Jack had said they were monsters. Maybe she wouldn't go so far as to believe that. But they were killers. That much she now understood.

Her red hair tumbled in front of her face as she jammed her hand into her purse and rooted around for the touch of metal, for the stun gun her mother had given her the previous year on her birthday. The only intelligent gift her mother had bought her since the dance lessons she'd had when she turned nine.

"What the hell are those two doing?"

"Somebody's gettin' his ass kicked, looks like."

Molly ignored the voices around her. Beyond the door, the guy with the sideburns slammed Jack's head against the glass, and it splintered into a spiderweb pattern of cracks. She shoved past a guy in torn denim with piercings all over his face, and grabbed the door handle.

"You're not supposed to—"

She hauled the door open.

The monster snarled and she saw the teeth, and for just a second, she really did believe.

"Jack, get down!" she shouted.

He ducked.

Molly rammed the Taser into the guy's chest, silently thanked her mom, and fired. Electricity surged through him, and the guy was shocked backward, slammed into the door of the other subway car, and fell.

And changed.

He should have been completely incapacitated for at least half a minute, possibly even knocked unconscious.

His body bucked with the electrical charge but he managed to climb to his knees above the gap between the two trains.

And he changed.

As if his skin were being sucked inside him through every pore, even as another body burst from underneath, his body transformed completely in a matter of seconds. The shock of the Taser stun had flicked a switch inside him, knocked out whatever focus he must have had to use to maintain the illusion of humanity.

Teeth extended from a long, curved jaw; his body seemed to grow larger, and sinewy muscles rippled beneath thick fur; fingers had become claws with razor-sharp talons.

Monster, Molly thought. It was the only word in her mind.

Then the thing focused on her with its blazing eyes like burning cinders, and it began to growl.

"Jack, get in here!" she shouted.

He was gingerly touching the back of his head, and she saw that there was blood on his fingers from his injuries. The train started to slow as it came into Government Center—she could not believe how fast her world had changed, turned upside-down between one T stop and the next—and she grabbed Jack and pushed him through the door behind her.

She stunned the thing again.

It howled.

"Run!" she yelled.

Jack was surrounded by other people who had seen

what happened, had seen the thing attack and then seen it change. Some of them were moving as fast as they could, getting off the train. Others were crowding around Jack and Molly, trying to get a better look, not even realizing the danger they were in.

With a muttered curse, Molly stunned the guy closest to her. He went stiff and fell to the floor of the car.

"Get the hell out of my way or be next!" she shouted.

People moved. Some took off, running ahead of her. Molly and Jack got off the train and ran into the Government Center station. It was busier than Park Street, plenty of people around, not to mention the vendors down there, underground. The passengers who had already gotten off the train pointed at them and yelled or just whispered to one another. Next to a newsstand a twenty-something guy had been playing an electric guitar that was plugged into a portable amp. He stopped singing right in the middle of an old Bonnie Raitt song.

"What the hell are they?" she asked.

"They're called Prowlers," Jack told her.

So now she had a name for them.

Molly and Jack ran toward the stairs.

Someone screamed.

She turned around and saw the beast, the savage monster, make a shaky leap onto the platform from between two cars. Molly's heart raced even faster. Her throat felt dry. The thing had taken two Taser blasts and was barely fazed.

"We're dead," she whispered. "Run, Jack. Come on!"

But Jack wasn't with her. She had a moment to fear that the thing had gotten him, that he had been injured and she had been so concerned with her own safety that she had left him behind. Then she saw him.

Despite the blows he'd taken to the head, Jack ran over to the kid playing guitar. The guy was staring in horror at the Prowler, which was now loping along the train platform toward them. The young guy didn't balk when Jack ripped his electric guitar out of his hands. Its cable popped out of the amp as Jack hefted it.

The Prowler froze, then wobbled a bit on its feet as it regarded Jack.

Then it lunged.

Jack held on to the neck of the guitar with both hands and swung the instrument around with all his strength. It struck the Prowler's head with a resounding crack, and the thing went down hard on the platform, its head smashing against the concrete. Several people screamed, others gasped. The guitar had shattered.

But so had the monster's skull.

Molly ran to Jack. Without a word she threw her arms around him. He let the remains of the guitar slip from his hand. The kid who'd been playing it stared at his ruined instrument but said not a word.

"Sssh, we're okay," Jack said.

Only then did Molly realize she was crying. The horror and fear had caught up to her, and she wiped at her eyes now, trying to get control of herself. Her mind whirled with the impossibility of what had happened.

But it *had* happened.

Shouts rang through the station. They looked up to see MBTA police running across the platform toward them, toward the dead creature that lay on the floor.

Jack stiffened. "We've gotta go."

"But we've got to tell the police—"

"There was another one," he said quickly. "A girl. At the movies. I saw her and knew she was one. She's gotta be around somewhere. Once they've got your scent, they don't stop hunting."

"How do you know that?" Molly asked, shaking her head.

"I just know."

Jack grabbed her hand and together they ran for the stairs. The MBTA cops called out for them to stop, but they were more interested in the creature on the platform. The police pursued them too, but Jack and Molly had a long head start.

With Molly in front of him, Jack hustled up the stairs. He glanced behind him for the cops, and for the female Prowler that had been at the theater. Artie's words had stayed with him, about the creatures getting his scent. He could not shake the feeling that it wasn't over.

Thoughts of Artie brought back a clear, chilling memory of the moment he had truly seen the Ghostlands, but he blocked it out. It was possible that thinking of it could make him see it again, and he didn't want that, not even if the dead could help him.

Before they reached the top of the stairs, Jack heard sirens.

"The police," Molly said. She glanced back at him as they hurried toward the exit. "We've got to stop and talk to them, Jack. They've got to be told about these monsters."

"They'll figure it out quick enough," he told her, mind racing. "I'm more worried about staying alive."

A moment later they reached the top of the stairs and walked swiftly out of Government Center Station into the the ugly sea of concrete that was City Hall Plaza. Boston's City Hall looked like a parking garage with a broad cement no-man's-land around it. They had to cross that expanse in order to get home. Other people were around, spectators drawn by the police sirens.

A cop car bumped up onto the cement not far away.

Jack took Molly's hand and led her away from the T station, away from the arriving cops, away from everything. Sirens filled the air, but he kept his back to them.

They hadn't gone a hundred yards before he saw the girl.

The beautiful girl with the oval face and the enormous eyes. Her smile was suggestive and mocking at the same time. She stood just ahead of them. A handful of other people were walking around—couples hand in hand, a trio of guys obviously heading for the T after spending some time at a bar. They checked the girl out as they passed, but there were no catcalls, no comments. It was almost as if they knew better.

Jack froze, pulled Molly's hand so that she came to a stop beside him. With a grunt of surprise, Molly shot him a fearful look.

"That's her," Jack said.

Molly pulled the stun gun out of her coat pocket, where she had stashed it on their run up the stairs.

"My name's Dori," the girl said. "Thanks for the chase. A good hunt always helps me work up my appetite."

Then, there in the middle of City Hall Plaza, she changed.

It took only a few moments. The drunk guys shouted something and ran toward the T station. A twenty-something couple coming up behind the Prowler stopped short before taking off in the other direction.

Dori crouched before them, ready to spring. She growled and began to advance.

"Get ready to split up," Jack whispered to Molly. "You go right, I'll go left. And use that Taser."

With a high, ululating cry, Dori charged them.

The night exploded with gunfire.

Dori's body danced under the onslaught of bullets, blood splashed over the concrete wasteland, and then the Prowler's corpse dropped to the ground in front of them.

Jack looked up in astonishment as the police moved in.

From the top of the steps that led out of City Hall Plaza and toward Quincy Market, Jasmine watched in disgust and frustration as Dori was cut down, slaughtered there on the concrete. The police surrounded the two humans who had been her chosen prey.

Police. Dozens of witnesses. Prey who had survived.

Boston was no longer safe for them.

Tanzer would not be pleased.

CHAPTER 10

The cops let Jack and Molly walk away.

Despite all they'd been through that night, it was that one thing that disturbed Jack more than anything else. After all that had happened on the train, in the station, and right there in City Hall Plaza a hundred yards from the mayor's office—after dozens of eyewitnesses had seen a Prowler in the flesh and the police had shot one to death—the cops had let them walk away.

Bridget's Irish Rose was still buzzing with pub business downstairs—the restaurant was closed—but Courtney and Bill left work behind the minute Jack and Molly came in and began to tell them what had happened. Molly looked like hell, pale and wide-eyed, hair even wilder than usual. She appeared afraid it would start again at any minute.

Jack understood. Though he tried to remain calm, he felt the same way. Every shadow suddenly seemed alive to him. Every strange face seemed impermanent, as if at any moment it might change, might become monstrous and savage. It was chilling.

Now the four of them sat around the kitchen table in the upstairs apartment, trying to understand.

"I don't get it," Courtney said, shaking her head. She glanced at Jack, then looked to Bill as though she thought he might have the answer. "How could the police just let them walk away after all that?"

Big Bill stroked his beard and studied Jack. His eyes did not move at all. He was focused only on Jack. "You tried to tell them what happened?" he asked.

Jack sighed and nodded slowly. He glanced at the moon-and-stars clock on the wall—quarter past ten—then at the Superman cookie jar on the counter. His mother had bought it a couple of months before she died, and it showed the wear of time. Superman's nose was chipped, and there was a fleck of paint missing from the *S* on his chest.

"They weren't listening," Jack explained. "I mean *really* weren't listening. This one cop, in uniform but obviously outranking these other guys, he comes over and makes sure we're okay, takes our names and addresses and stuff, then tells us to go home."

"All the people . . ." Molly chimed in, the three words drifting across the kitchen like the scent of something cooking, lingering in the air.

Courtney reached across the floral-patterned table-cloth and laid a hand on hers. "Molly? You all right?"

"Not even close," Molly replied.

But Jack saw that her eyes were suddenly a bit more focused, and that was good. That was very good.

"What were you saying?" he asked.

Molly nodded, as if to herself. "All the people came up from the subway. And those drunk guys? They all saw it. But one of the cops said something to me, like 'Wow, did you ever see wolves come down into the city like this before?' Then he went on about how they had a moose stomping around Melrose a couple of years ago and a bear the year before that, and more and more deer finding their way into the city. When any moron could just look at the thing on the ground and know it was no wolf."

"Hunh," Bill grunted. He took a long swig from the bottle of Sam Adams in front of him.

"What's 'hunh'?" Jack asked. Though his own mind was already turning it all over, like the tumblers of a lock.

Courtney let go of Molly's hand and sat back in her chair, also watching Bill.

The bartender shrugged. "Well, you said they hustled the monster out of there pretty quick, right? The cops sent you on your way in a couple of minutes, and you said the Prowler's body was gone before that, right?"

"There were no chalk lines and no crime scene photographers," Jack told him, "but there wouldn't be, if the cops really believed these things were animals."

"That's the *if* that concerns me," Bill replied.

"Oh, man," Jack muttered. He leaned his elbows on

the table and lowered his face into his hands. When he looked up, he saw that Molly and Courtney were both staring at Bill.

Courtney tapped her fingers on the table. "I see where you're going. A handful of people got a good look. The cops hurried to make sure the dead Prowlers were out of there quick, and talked to the witnesses so that they would start to question what they'd seen, question if it really was wolves."

She looked at Jack. "You tried to talk to the police, and they brushed you off."

Jack nodded. "Like they see this kind of thing every damn day."

"Maybe they do," Bill offered.

The words resonated in Jack's head, and he shivered. He glanced at Molly and saw from her expression and the way she shuddered that what Bill had said was sinking in for her as well. It was impossible, but it was devastatingly simple.

"The cops know," Jack said, voicing the thought they all shared. "This isn't the first Prowler they've seen. They've already connected all these murders together and come up with Prowlers as an answer. If the monsters have killed before, there have to be other reports from other police departments. Maybe some of them are thought of as crazy, like UFO sightings or something. But after a while . . ."

"Yeah," Molly whispered. "After a while, when you see it happening in your own town, maybe right in front of you, you don't have any choice but to admit that those who claimed that werewolves or whatever were killing people in their towns may have been on to something."

Courtney got up so quickly that her chair squeaked on the linoleum. They all watched as she grabbed her cane, went to the cabinet above the sink where they kept the goodies, and came back with a bag of Chips Ahoy. The corners of Jack's mouth twitched up in just a hint of a smile. His sister always resorted to chocolate in a crisis.

"And they just hide the information from us?" Courtney gazed at each of them in turn, anger burning in her eyes. "Why? Because they don't want to cause a panic or they don't want people to laugh at them. The mayor doesn't want anyone thinking he believes in this crap, even though they've got corpses now. The dead bodies of actual monsters are sitting in the city morgue."

With a scowl of disgust, Courtney shook her head. She reached for the cookies, but there was no pleasure on her face as she did so.

"Actually, I'd guess they'll dispose of the bodies. Cremate them or something," Bill suggested.

Molly hugged herself and shuddered, though it was warm enough in the apartment. "If they know all this, why are the Prowlers still out there? Why haven't the police stopped them?"

The clock ticked louder on the wall. Jack noticed a tiny spray of green spots on one wall and had no idea where they had come from. Paint or something, from a project of Courtney's, no doubt. He had a can of Coke on the table that had been sitting there getting warm and flat. Now he snaked a hand out, picked it up, and took a sip. He rolled the soda around in his mouth for a moment and contemplated what it was doing to his teeth.

"The cops don't know where the Prowlers are," he said.

"I hope that's it," Bill replied.

Everyone looked at Jack. He nodded quickly and set the soda can down again. "I'm sure of it," he said. " I met that guy, Jason Castillo. The homicide detective. He's on Artie and Kate's murder case, and I think he really cares about this. If there's a conspiracy here, it isn't that the cops are protecting these things. They don't know where the Prowlers are hiding."

"They don't have to hide," Molly said. "They look like us. Like people. They could be anywhere. Driving a city bus, reading a newspaper on a park bench, teaching high school. Right? They don't even have to be all together."

"I guess," Bill said hesitantly. "But from what you've all said, I'm getting the feeling that we're dealing with a pack. If so, they'll stay together like any group of animals. They'll have one lair that they share."

Jack took another sip of warm Coke and sat up a little straighter. "Then we have to find this lair. And we've gotta kill them."

"How do you propose we do that, little brother?" Courtney asked, looking doubtful.

With a deep breath, Jack looked at each of them in turn. When he glanced at Molly, he reached out and held her hand tightly in his own. They had shared a horrifying experience, but now there was strength between them, and reassurance.

He looked back at his sister. "I'm working on it."

Molly could not sleep.

With all that had happened, she did not want to go home. Did not want to be alone, and being around her mother was an awful lot like being alone. They had no reason to suspect that there were other Prowlers hunting them, but Molly felt safer with Courtney and Jack. Never mind how late it was when their conversation finally wore itself out.

Bill and Jack had gone downstairs to close up, put up the chairs, and say good night to the few staffers who had hung around after closing. Then Bill had gone home.

Courtney gave Molly a pair of warm sweatpants and a Harvard University T-shirt to sleep in, and made up the pull-out sofa in the living room. When they turned in for the night, neither Jack nor Courtney shut off the light in the hallway, and Molly was glad. The last thing she wanted was to lie there in the dark.

Lie there and think about Artie. Now that she had seen the monsters that had killed him—Oh, my God, how could such things exist in secret in the modern world? But they did. They did. And now that she had seen them, she could imagine all too well the terror and panic her poor, sweet Artie had felt in the last seconds before the Prowlers tore him apart, viciously ripped into him.

Molly lay on her side on the pull-out bed and kept her eyes on the light in the hall, never even glancing at the shadows pooling around her. Her eyes began to fill with tears, her soul tormented with thoughts of Artie's final moments. And yet, even as the first of those tears slid sideways down her face to dampen the pillowcase, a change began to flow through her.

Grief gave way to hate, sorrow to anger.

Something had to be done. Molly had no idea what she could do to help the police locate the lair of the Prowlers, even with help from the Dwyers and Big Bill Cantwell. But she knew it would be impossible to keep her mind on anything else until she knew they had been found and destroyed.

At length, she forced herself to close her eyes. Though being in Jack's home made it almost impossible for her to get her mind off all that had happened, Molly felt safe with him and Courtney. Jack had always exuded a kind of easy self-confidence that she found almost intimidating in a guy. Not arrogant, not cocky, just himself, and that was enough. With all his babbling and sweetness and self-deprecating humor, Artie had always been much more her kind of guy. Artie had needed her.

Molly had the idea that since his mother had died, Jack Dwyer never needed anyone except his older sister. Jack was good, decent to the bone, but maybe because of how hard he had worked, he never had the sweetness Artie did.

Still, Molly thanked God for Jack. And for Courtney. Here in their home, she felt more like she was with family than she ever did with her mother.

Mom. As she finally began to drift off to sleep, Molly realized she would have to find a way to warn her mother, tell her to be extra careful, particularly in the dives she hung out in. Her mother would ignore her, Molly knew that. But she had to try.

Sleep came on while she struggled with the bitterness of that thought.

Then, in those first moments of sleep, a voice. A whisper.

"You saved our asses."

Molly opened her eyes. She peered at the light in the hall. The voice had come from Jack's room. Who the hell was he talking to on the phone this late at night? she wondered. He kept talking, but Molly only heard small snippets of his whispers.

"She doesn't know . . . didn't say a word." There was a long break when she thought he must have been listening to his caller. Then he went on, a little louder: "We'll get them, man. I swear to you."

Jack lowered his voice again. Molly swept back the sheets and swung her legs out of bed. It wasn't as though she wanted to eavesdrop, but Jack woke her just when she had finally been able to drift off. Now he was being all mysterious, and the way she figured it, she was in this thing too. She wanted to know what was going on.

As she walked out into the hall toward his bedroom door, which was open just a crack, she could hear him much more clearly.

"I know you hate guns. You've never been quiet about your opinions. But if I can get one, I'll use it. These things aren't human, man. They never were. You know that. The 'no guns' rule can't possibly count with them. But, hey, look, I'll be more than happy to let the cops take care of things, as long as they do it soon. Then there's . . . What? . . . No, I'm not going up against these things without something more than a baseball bat."

Molly held her breath. *I know you hate guns.* When Jack spoke those words, and as she listened to the way he spoke to whoever was on the phone with him, she had a terrible, confusing moment where he seemed to be speaking to Artie. It was just the thing Jack would have said to him, if Artie had still been alive.

Blinking, she shook the chilling thought from her mind and knocked softly on the door.

"Jack?"

The door was open a couple of inches but it was dark within. The light from the hall barely reached inside. She heard the sheets rustle, but nothing more. Jack did not say good-bye to anyone, nor did she hear the familiar plastic clack of the phone being returned to its cradle.

Jack came to the door.

He wore a white T-shirt and ragged blue Champion shorts, and his large form filled the doorway. Though obviously tired, he seemed wide awake, if a bit flustered. His chin was covered with dark stubble, and he scratched at it as he looked down at her.

"Hey, Mol. What's up? Can't sleep?"

Her gaze skittered over to Jack's bed and to the phone on his nightstand. She shrugged. "I just . . . I heard you talking. About all this, y'know? And yeah, I couldn't sleep and . . . Was it Bill? On the phone, I mean."

Jack hesitated, then he smiled softly. "Yeah. Bill. Just kinda making a game plan."

But even as he spoke, he glanced back into his darkened bedroom as if there were something there that he didn't want her to see. Molly chuckled at the very thought of such a thing. Jack was probably just uncomfortable with the idea of her in his bedroom, and she couldn't blame him. It was a little awkward.

"Hey," she said softly. She reached out and took his hand, held it tight until he met her gaze. "You saved my life today."

Jack smiled, suddenly himself again, the guy she had known most of her life. The one they had all looked up to.

"And you saved *my* life. I'd say we're even."

Molly hugged him close, laid her head on his chest, and sighed deeply. "I couldn't get through this without you, Jack."

He kissed the top of her head. "Same here."

At twenty past two in the morning, Tanzer went looking for Eric Carver. He found the lawyer on the seventh floor of his church-tower home, in a small but comfortable room he had asked the pack to stay out of. Carver called it the library. The only furnishings in the room were three fat leather chairs, several standing lamps, two large plants that needed trimming, and the books. Floor-to-ceiling shelves on every wall were filled with them: law books, history books, and hard-cover mystery novels, Tanzer had perused these shelves for several minutes one afternoon, but he had seen little of interest there aside from the history books.

History had value. There were lessons there.

When he slipped into the library this night he found Carver sitting in one of the leather chairs with a book on his lap, one finger holding his place. He had paused in his reading and was now sitting forward and staring out one of the large arched windows at the lights of Copley Square. Even this late at night, Boston was a city that glittered. Tanzer was sad that they were going to have to leave so soon. Another week or two at most. Just long enough to research their relocation.

"Eric?"

Carver started and turned to blink in surprise. "Owen. I'm sorry, I didn't hear you come in."

A smile played at the edge's of Tanzer's mouth. "Of course not."

Without bothering to mark the page, Carver closed his book and left it on the arm of his chair as he stood. "What can I do for you?"

"I want your opinion."

"I'm sorry?" Carver stared at him as if he had not heard correctly.

"Your opinion, Eric." Tanzer walked farther into the room, then casually dropped into a leather chair. He crossed his arms and stroked his chin with one hand, looking up at Carver thoughtfully. "We'll be moving on soon. I would have liked to go to New York City next, but things are heating up for us in the Northeast. I'm considering Minneapolis or New Orleans as alternatives. Your thoughts?"

With pleasure, Tanzer noted the thought that Carver gave his question. From his seat he watched the lawyer pace. After a minute or two of contemplation, Carver turned to him. "Why ask me? I'm not exactly up there in the hierarchy of the pack."

Tanzer frowned. "Why ask you? Because you're intelligent, Eric. You have a clever mind, and there aren't enough of those among us. Where do you think we should go next?"

Carver shrugged with both shoulders and eyebrows. "I wouldn't choose either of those cities, to be honest. If I wanted a hunting ground where I'd be unlikely to be discovered, where I could find plenty of people on the fringes of society and lots of places to hide, I'd go to Los Angeles."

"Interesting," Tanzer replied. "I had thought to work our way across the country, but there is no reason we cannot start at the edges and work our way to the middle. Los Angeles it is."

The lawyer opened his mouth slightly in surprise.

Tanzer thought he looked a bit foolish, a bit too human, but he had learned not to underestimate Carver. Perhaps he was too human, but that flaw was easily balanced out by his virtues.

"I'll want you to work with me on the planning," Tanzer told him.

Carver quickly nodded his agreement. "Yeah. Of course. Whatever you need."

Tanzer sniffed the air. Something had changed. With a silent snarl he sprang from the chair and paced back and forth. He went toward the entrance to the room and sniffed again, felt his nostrils flare in recognition.

He was not at all surprised when Ghirardi suddenly appeared in the doorway.

"Tanzer," Ghirardi said nervously. "Jasmine's back. Something has happened."

"What?" Tanzer asked, eyes narrowed, smelling the fear off Ghirardi. "What has happened?"

"It's something about Dori. She just . . . Jasmine told me to come get you."

"Did she?" Tanzer demanded. He moved closer to Ghirardi, who backed up out of the library into the hall. "Or did you volunteer? Did you think I would not smell you, standing out there listening to this conversation? If your curiosity is not satisfied, Ghirardi, we'll be moving away from Boston in a week or two. Things are heating up for us."

Ghirardi's expression hardened; his lips set in a tight line.

Tanzer growled, a low thunder building in his chest. "You have something you want to say?"

"I like Boston," Ghirardi snapped. "And the only reason we have to haul our asses out of here now is 'cause you killed that mobster, and 'cause Dori and her crew painted Fenway Park with blood. It's like announcing we're here, screaming to come and get us. A couple of stupid moves, and now we're done here."

A ripple went through Tanzer's entire body, a shudder of furious energy, an urge to strike. His nostrils flared, and he stepped even closer to Ghirardi. His human guise began to give way, just a little. "Did you just call me stupid?"

Ghirardi's eyes went wide and his mouth dropped open. A long breath seeped out of him as though he had sprung a leak. "No, no. That's not what I said." He shook his head back and forth vigorously. "All I meant was—"

Tanzer's flesh made a kind of crinkling sound as he moved, and his right hand lashed out, gripped Ghirardi's face and slammed his head against the wall. He was all Prowler now, thick lips curled back from fangs.

"No, no . . ." Ghirardi muttered in terror.

At the last moment he knew he had to fight and he began to transform.

Tanzer ripped his throat out.

Blood splashed on the carpet.

He let Ghirardi's body slump to the floor, then turned to see Carver walk up behind him. Tanzer shuddered as he concentrated, forced his body to change again, forced the growth of skin and the recession of fur, the restructuring of bone. He hated the false face of humanity, but the ability to transform themselves had always been useful for his species.

Carver stood beside him and glanced down at the rug.

"Sorry about that," Tanzer said.

"We're moving," Carver replied. "I can't really worry about a little stain, now, can I?"

Together they walked down the stairs.

Jasmine met them on her way up. Her eyes were wild, nostrils flaring. She could barely keep her facade in place, keep the Prowler hidden. That was unusual for her, and Tanzer was distressed to see it.

"What's happened?" he demanded.

Jasmine went to Tanzer, pulled him close, and held him there, her chest heaving with anger and frustration. Her whole body quivered with barely suppressed energy, the need to lash out. She took a few moments to calm herself, and Tanzer waited patiently.

"It's Dori," Jasmine finally said. She pulled back and looked up into his eyes. "She took Brackett and Axel and went hunting. They're all dead. The cops did Dori, but a couple of civilians took out her two boy toys."

Tanzer twitched. "The bodies?"

"The cops took them away. Fast, too, as if they were eager to hide them."

"And the humans who killed Brackett and Axel? Do they still live?"

Jasmine nodded. "They do. But I tracked them to their lair, so I know where to find them."

CHAPTER 11

The window in the living room was open just a few inches. Molly burrowed beneath the sheet and cotton blankets on the pull-out sofa bed and sighed with pleasure. She had come awake slowly, aware of the deliciously cool breeze that fluttered the curtains and caressed her exposed face before she had truly risen from her dream-laden sleep. Pleasant dreams, despite all that she had experienced the night before. But they were gone upon waking as if that breeze from the window had carried them away.

For several minutes she lay there, enjoying the warmth of the covers in contrast to the chill of the air. Then the scent of fresh coffee began to permeate Courtney and Jack's apartment, and Molly finally opened her eyes.

Sun streamed in through the windows to form odd geometric shapes on the floor. Though cool, the morning looked as though it was going to be perfect, the kind of early spring day that would bring people into Quincy Market in droves. Sunday or not, the lunch crowd was going to be heavy at Bridget's Irish Rose today. Molly had been around the place enough to know that.

In the sweats and T-shirt Courtney had lent her, Molly reluctantly got out of bed and went into the kitchen, lured by the aroma of coffee. Jack was nowhere to be seen, but she found Courtney sitting at the table with a fresh cup in her hand and the fat sections of the *Sunday Globe* spread out across the table. She had obviously already showered and dressed for work, her sandy blond hair gently pulled back with a pair of barettes.

After the events of the last twenty-four hours, it was a scene so surprisingly normal that it startled Molly just a bit. Then relief spread through her. The world had been forever altered for her last night, but this morning she saw that it had not changed completely.

"Morning," she rasped sleepily.

Courtney glanced up and smiled. "I thought you might be in a coma. Another hour or so and I would have had to call a doctor."

Molly frowned, then glanced at the moon-and-stars clock. "It's just after nine o'clock. Okay, I'm definitely not the early bird, but not bad for a Sunday."

With what appeared to be a bit of surprise, Courtney looked at the clock as well. Then she shrugged. "Guess we're used to getting up early.

There's always something to be done running this place. And you looked so comfy. Chalk it up to my envy talking. Cup of coffee?"

"If I want to see ten o'clock, I'd better," Molly replied. When Courtney began to rise, she waved the woman away. "No, no. Sit. Let me get it. I know my way around in here by now."

Courtney went back to her paper and Molly poured herself a cup of coffee before slipping into a wooden chair at the table. They sat together in silence a few minutes, and Molly observed Courtney in her natural element. She read the Travel section and the Arts section, but she paid special attention to local news.

"Anything?" Molly asked.

"Nothing," Courtney replied. "Not a single word."

A tiny fist of fear and suspicion grew in Molly's gut. It was almost inconceivable to her that the fight with the "wolves" from the previous day, despite all the witnesses, had not made it into the paper. The police had done a truly spectacular job of covering it up. She only hoped they were as thorough in trying to put a stop to the carnage.

Those thoughts led to others, and Molly was forced to grapple with her fear. How many more Prowlers were there? Were she and Jack still in danger? She supposed that until she was certain the creatures had been destroyed, those fears would linger. The only choice she had was to go on with her life, try to be alert, and hope for the best. The alternative—living each moment as if the creatures were stalking her, hiding away from the world—was crippling even to imagine. Molly could not imagine living like that.

She wasn't built that way.

On the other hand, there was no shame in being careful.

After another contemplative sip of coffee, she looked at Courtney again. "Where's Jack?" she asked.

His sister raised her eyebrows as she glanced up from her paper. "Hmm? Oh, he's off at the fish market. We've got to have fresh fish. I've been sort of handling it this week, with everything that's happened, and he said it's his turn."

Molly nodded. "You guys do an amazing job of running the place. I know it isn't easy, but you make it *look* easy."

"Well, Jack has taken on more responsibility the last couple of years. That's been a relief, and Bill is always a big help. He pretty much runs the bar, takes care of scheduling, all that. But we can never seem to find enough reliable people who aren't going to bail on us when school starts or when that job at Starbuck's they've been waiting for comes through."

Molly chuckled at Courtney's sarcasm. "Good help is hard to find," she said.

"You're not kidding. Even here," Courtney added. She gestured toward Molly's coffee mug with an expression of regret. "I've got English muffins, half a dozen kinds of cereal, fruit, juice, and three-day-old bagels to choose from, but I'm sorry to say you'll have to help yourself. I wish I could make you a real breakfast but

I've got to get downstairs and take an inventory, see what we can run as specials today."

Still sleepy, Molly pushed her hands through her tangled hair and swept it back away from her face.

"That's okay," she said. "I should probably be getting home anyway."

As Molly lifted her coffee mug to her lips again, Courtney shot her an inquisitive look. "Why?"

Molly glanced at her in surprise. "Huh?"

Courtney shrugged. "Just what I said. Why?" Her gaze wandered a bit, as though she was suddenly uncomfortable with the conversation. "I don't want to get presumptuous on you, Molly, so stop me if I do. Just tell me to shut up and I will. But what the hell do you want to go home for?"

"That's a terrible thing to say!"

"Yeah, it is," Courtney agreed. She grabbed her cane where it leaned against a chair and took her empty coffee cup over to the sink. With a sigh she rinsed out the mug and put it into the dishwasher. Then she turned to regard Molly again, her expression tender and sad.

"It is a terrible thing to say. But it's also true. Maybe you never think about it because you figure until you leave for college you don't have any options. But I think you've been through enough. You live in a neighborhood I'd be afraid to walk a dog through, with a mother who barely knows if you're there or not. You've just lost two people you really cared about to unimaginable violence, and you've seen some things that must have made you start questioning the whole world. I know these monsters have my mind spinning, wondering what else is out there, realizing I don't know half as much about life as I thought I did."

Molly stared at the floor, unwilling to meet Courtney's gaze. "Yeah. Thanks for laying that out for me. What am I supposed to do about it?"

Courtney hobbled to the table and leaned on her cane as she bent to lift Molly's chin, forcing her to look up.

"Stay here," Courtney told her. Then, as if embarrassed by the sentiment, she turned away, leaving Molly staring at her back in astonishment.

"Here?"

"You've got a problem with my place?" Courtney asked. She turned and gave Molly a hard look. "I don't invite people into my life on a regular basis. I'd guess you know that, hanging around with Jack all these years. I like you, Molly. My mother would have said you were 'good people.' It's awful what happened to Artie, and I guess I feel like now's the time for us to circle the wagons, you know? Stick together. All I'm trying to say is if you don't want to go home, nobody here's going to say you have to. This family has never really followed the rules about what family's supposed to be."

Molly stared in disbelief. Her mind raced with the possibilities. Her mother would not object. Though it saddened her to admit that to herself, she knew it was true. If anything, she would be relieved not to have to factor Molly into her life anymore—if she ever really had. Her mother had been looking forward to her going away to college as much as Molly had.

"I don't know what to say. I wouldn't stay without paying you something. I'd get a job."

"Like hell," Courtney snapped, a frown creasing her forehead. "I told you I need all the decent help I can get. You live at Bridget's, you work at Bridget's. At least until you take off for college."

Molly hesitated, but only for a moment. "I'm trying to think of some reason why I shouldn't say yes."

"That's pretty silly," Courtney told her.

"Yeah, isn't it?"

Amazed at the sudden turn her life had taken, Molly stood up and hugged Courtney. She remembered how safe she had felt the night before, how in spite of the danger from the Prowlers, she had felt a kind of power in the fact that she had these people gathered around her, a family by design rather than by birth.

"Thank you so much," she whispered to Courtney, her voice breaking as she fought to keep from crying.

"It'll be our pleasure."

Molly froze. She stood back and gazed into Courtney's eyes. "Jack," she said. "What about . . . I mean, don't you think you should check with him before you do something like this?"

"Him? Nah, he's a guy. They never say no to having a gorgeous girl around." Courtney paused a second, then laughed. "I talked to him this morning, told him I was going to ask you to stay. He liked the idea. I got the circling-the-wagons metaphor from him, to be honest. He's into westerns."

"I think I need more coffee," Molly said, still stunned by this development.

"Fine. But don't take too long. Jack'll take you back to your house to get some things and talk to your mother. Then, as long as she's cool with it, you're all mine. Or didn't I mention that you're working tonight?"

As Jack sat in his Jeep outside Molly's house—or her mother's house now—he turned everything over in his head. Things were happening too fast. The murders, the ghosts, and now his real life, everything he counted on to help him get through the rest of it, was changing as well. It was all right, though. When Courtney had first mentioned asking Molly to move in, he was a little weirded out. But the more he thought about it, the more it seemed like a great idea.

They all had to stick together now.

The day had warmed up to more than sixty degrees and sunny, a perfect gem of a day. The pub would be hopping, and after all the shifts he had missed the past week, he wanted to get back there. But it was more important at the moment to let Molly get her life squared away. Jack knew that inside that dingy apartment, she and her mother were likely having it out.

He hoped they were fighting about it, at least a little. At least enough to make Molly feel that her mother gave a damn. A rusted tricycle lay on its side on the sidewalk next to Jack's Jeep, near a couple of putrid-smelling trash cans. There was no trash pickup on

Sunday, but there the cans were just the same. He kept the passenger window rolled up and tried to ignore the stench. Though he could not have seen anything going on inside, he watched the front door of the Hatchers' building and the windows of the apartment for signs of life. There were none.

When Artie appeared in the seat beside him, Jack let out a yell of surprise and his heart skipped a couple of beats.

"Dammit, Artie. Don't do that!"

The ghost ignored him. Instead, Artie leaned forward and looked out through the windshield at the front of the Hatchers' place.

"Molly's moving in with you, huh?"

Jack frowned, then shook his head, holding up a hand. "Whoa. Whoa, bud. It isn't like that."

Artie narrowed his gaze, but he seemed more sad than angry. "You sure?"

"Totally. Completely sure." Jack stared at him. For once, though he could see through the phantom, he focused on Artie's haunting eyes. "I wouldn't do that to you."

With a slow, deliberate movement, Artie drew closer to Jack, pushed his face up so their noses were maybe half a foot apart.

"I'm dead, Jack."

Flustered, Jack drew back a little. "Hell, Artie, I know that."

"We've all been watching you. Keeping tabs. I heard this morning that she was going to move in, and I was mad at first. And afraid of what might happen. You know what I'm saying, bro?" Artie asked, and searched Jack's eyes. "But the more I thought about it, the more it made me realize that I'm dead."

Jack swallowed, shook his head slowly, but could not think of a single thing to say.

"You're my best friend, Jack. I love you. Nothing can take that away. But Molly, she won't be alone forever. Maybe not even for very long. She's gonna have a new boyfriend eventually."

"That won't mean she doesn't love you," Jack said quickly.

Artie smiled. "She loved me. Past tense, man. Get it through your head, 'cause I'm trying to. You and me, we may be able to talk. You can see me, but in every way that counts, bro, I am past tense. I *was*. She *loved* me. One of these days she'll love someone else. I kinda got to thinking, when I heard she was moving in, that maybe it'd be good if that was you."

Jack held up both hands. "Artie, no man. I'd never do that to you. I love Molly, but not, y'know . . ."

"Okay," Artie said. "All right, Jack. But just know that if that's where it goes, if that's where all this takes you, I'm cool with that. At least I'll know that she's with someone who'll treat her right and really love her. It'd be a hell of a lot worse to see her end up with some jerk. I don't think I could stand that."

"I won't let that happen," Jack promised.

Again, a thin, sad smile appeared on Artie's face. "I hope that's true, bro. I really do."

Jack's mind spun with what Artie had said. In the back of his mind, he had always been attracted to Molly, cared for her deeply, but she had always been Artie's girl, and even thinking about her like that had been off limits. Still was, as far as he was concerned.

"Here she comes," Artie said.

Molly's face was red with emotion as she appeared on the front steps with a large suitcase in one hand. Jack wasn't sure how to read that, and he thought it would be best to let her talk if she wanted to, but not to press her. Besides, he had enough on his mind already.

His hand closed around the door handle.

"Wait," Artie said.

Jack glanced at him, saw that there was something else on Artie's mind. The spirit was troubled.

"We've been following the Prowlers. Hunting them, I guess. They sense us, a little bit, but they can't see us and they sure can't hurt us anymore," Artie explained. "We've found the lair. We're going to lead you to it. Then we'll have to talk about what's next."

Alarmed, Jack stared at him. "Right now? With Molly in the car?"

"Right now," Artie replied. "She's in it now, Jack. I don't want her to know I'm here. Not ever. We talked about that. But she's a part of this, and it's too late to erase that or to start worrying about it. You've got to finish this before the Prowlers move on and start again elsewhere. And they will, you know. Soon."

"Just tell me where and I'll call the cops," Jack told him.

"Are you sure you can trust the cops?"

Before Jack could answer, Molly started walking across the street toward the Jeep. He jumped out of the Jeep and went to take the suitcase from her hand. "You all right?" he asked.

"I've been better. You know what's amazing? My mother was worried about how things would look, me moving in with a guy. It's not even ironic. It's just twisted. How can a woman who lives in this dump and drinks as much as she does and brings home guys whose names she doesn't even know care at all about how something is going to *look?*"

Inside, Jack cringed at the pain in Molly's voice. He rested a hand on her shoulder.

"I'm sorry."

"Don't be," she said firmly. "You and Courtney are saving me from this."

Jack smiled at that and so did Molly. He put her suitcase in the back, and they climbed into the Jeep. When he started the engine and went to pull away from the curb, he saw the ghost of Corinne Berdinka standing in the middle of the street, pointing.

Without hesitation, he followed her guidance.

"We have to make a little detour," he told Molly without looking at her.

"No problem. Where are we going?"

Jack swallowed hard; his throat was dry. "To the Prowlers' lair."

He felt her eyes boring into him as she turned in her seat. "You know where they are?" Molly demanded.

Up ahead, Father Pinksy's ghost had appeared. There were more of them as well. They lined the street like spectators at the Boston Marathon.

"No," he muttered. "No, I don't know. I . . . It's hard to explain."

"How can we go to the lair if you don't know where it is?" Molly asked, sounding confused now. "Are you feeling all right?"

"No. Can't say I am," he replied honestly.

"I don't understand."

Jack sighed. He blinked and rubbed his eyes, keeping one hand on the wheel as he drove. There were so many of them. They couldn't all have been victims of the Prowlers. But they were all ghosts lingering in this world, in the Ghostlands.

The world inverted for him again. Suddenly the buildings they passed, the Jeep he was driving, even Molly there on the seat beside him—all of it became insubstantial and transparent. Reality as a photographic negative.

And the ghosts were real. Full color. Three-dimensional.

I'm there with them. In the Ghostlands. But Molly hasn't noticed, so I don't look any different to her. I'm there and here. Alive and . . . dead? Between worlds.

"Jack, watch the road!" Molly snapped.

He blinked, but the Ghostlands remained more real to him than the street beneath his tires. Still, he managed to give the wheel a tug to one side, to remain on the phantom road.

"What's going on with you?" she demanded

"They're leading us to the Prowlers' lair," he explained.

"Who? Who are *they*?"

"The dead ones. The ghosts." He heard his voice, but it was dull and distant, as though it remained in one world while he straddled two.

Molly stared at him but said nothing for the rest of the ride. From time to time, Jack saw Artie along the roadside, as though he were skipping ahead across vast distances. The Ghostlands did not share the geography of the real world.

Finally, as they pulled into Copley Square in front of the Boston Public Library, Jack blinked again and the world flexed and rolled about him, and he was back. Molly was flesh and blood and staring at him as though he had gone completely out of his mind. He was sure she would really have thought that, too, had it not been for what had happened the day before.

"We're here," Jack told her.

"Which building?" she asked.

He looked around, spotted Artie in front of an old church on the far corner. The ghost was pointing at the bell tower that rose up into the skyline.

"There," Jack said, and he pointed at the tower as well.

"You're kidding."

"No, I'm not."

For several moments, all was silence in the car. Jack guided the Jeep through the square, and then they headed across town toward the waterfront and Bridget's.

"So now what?" Molly asked at length. "The cops?"

"We've got to think about it. We don't know how many there are. We can't be sure whether the cops could get them all or if they'd just be slaughtered. Let's talk to Courtney and Bill, try to make sense of this."

"Do they know?" Molly asked sharply.

Jack frowned and shot her a quick sidelong glance. "Do they know what?"

"About the ghosts. That you see ghosts?"

He shook his head. "No one does. I know you probably think—"

"No," Molly said. "It explains a lot."

Jack kept his eyes on the road, waiting for her to ask about Artie. She never did. Eventually he figured that she didn't ask because she didn't want to know the answer.

Shortly after dusk Jasmine lingered in the thickening shadows of an alley across the street from Bridget's Irish Rose Pub and cursed her luck. She had been here before, of course. The scent of the girl with the wild red hair was familiar to her, and the guy with her was also familiar. Just over a week earlier she had seen them both with the girl she thought of as Vanilla, the girl who had become her prey. There had been another boy as well, with shaggy blond hair. She and other members of the pack had killed them, but this was where the hunt had begun.

Now somehow the redhead and the solid, muscular boy who seemed always to be in her company had not only discovered the truth but had managed to kill two Prowlers in the process and cause the death of a third, Dori.

Just bad luck, Jasmine thought.

But she would never tell Tanzer that. Better that her man never know that all of this had begun with a hunt—her hunt. And once Jasmine had seen to it that these two were dead, there would be no chance of Tanzer's ever discovering that link. She had purposely chosen members of the pack who had not been with her that night so none of them would recognize the scent of either of the targets.

Still, a shudder of anxiety passed through Jasmine. Her heart would not be settled, her mind would not be calmed, until the two young humans were dead.

"Are we supposed to wait here until they close? It could be hours, Jasmine."

With a deep, dangerous frown, she turned toward Carver. He leaned against an alley wall, shockingly different in appearance from the day they had first met. Where once he had worn only the most expensive suits in the finest fabrics, now he was comfortable in denim and leather and wool. Thick stubble covered his chin.

Jasmine gave him a cruel smile. "I've never been very patient," she announced. Her gaze took in the other two, lurking in the dark behind him. Maynard and Cornelius. Both of them wanted her; each wished that he were the alpha of the pack so that he could make her his mate. But neither was foolish enough to challenge Tanzer, nor was either of them very intelligent. She had picked them because they would do exactly as they were told.

But Carver had come along at Tanzer's request. Owen was making arrangements for the pack to move and had left it to her to tie up these loose ends. No one killed a member of the pack and lived; it was as simple as that.

Not quite so simple for Jasmine, however. She had other reasons for wanting the two young humans dead.

"So we just go in, locate the targets you described, and kill them?" Carver asked, his brow furrowed with concern. "There are a lot of customers in there. We won't have time to kill them all, and that means witnesses."

Jasmine shrugged and leaned against the wall, her back arched, her body drawing Maynard and Cornelius's attention.

Carver glanced at her smooth, leather-clad form, but then his gaze returned to her eyes. "It's going to be very messy," he said.

"I like it messy," Jasmine told him. "We're leaving Boston tomorrow, Eric. What difference does it make if there are surviving witnesses? Who'll believe them, once we're gone? The *Fortean Times* and a bunch of paranoid Internet freaks who keep telling the world our secret. Their plan is undermined by the simple fact that nobody believes them. Nobody wants to. That disbelief will control the outcome here as well. If you can do this quickly and quietly without alerting the people who are having dinner and drinks, all the better. If not . . . as long as you kill our prey, and as long as we're gone before the police arrive, I don't care what you do."

Carver smiled and shook his head in amusement.

"What?" Jasmine demanded.

"Nothing," he replied. "Just . . . I never even imagined there'd come a day when I'd have this much freedom. Instead of hiding in the shadows and striking in silence . . ."

His words trailed off. Jasmine understood, though. Carver had been buried deep in his human persona, more a serial killer than a true Prowler. Now he had let the beast emerge from within him, and he was exulting in it. Jasmine reached up and trailed her fingers across his cheek.

"Enjoy," she whispered.

As long as Tanzer never finds out that all this trouble started with me, Jasmine thought. Not that she could reasonably be blamed. There was no way anyone could have foreseen this. But Tanzer might not care about reason.

Farther down the alley, Maynard grunted and stood up straight. "You're not coming in?"

Jasmine shook her head. "No. Consider me backup. Now then, why don't you boys go and kill something?"

CHAPTER 12

Jack hustled out of the kitchen carrying a tray of salads. The two couples at table seventeen were engaged in animated conversation and barely seemed to notice when he slid their salads in front of them. Just before he turned away, one of the women—a tall brunette with sad eyes—glanced up at him and offered the slightest smile.

"Thanks," she said in a small voice that seemed incongruous, considering her stature.

"Anytime."

The pub was about three-quarters full, which was not at all bad for after eight o'clock on a Sunday night. The weather had obviously inspired people to stay out later than usual on the night before the work week began again. It might not have been the best time to break Molly in to the job, but he knew it could have been a hell of a lot worse. And she seemed to be doing just fine, all things considered. Another of the wait-resses, a thirty-something single mom named Elaine who'd been with them for two years, was training Molly.

Jack glanced around but did not see either Elaine or Molly. They were probably back in the kitchen, he rea-soned.

He was about to return there to see if he could be of any more help, but first he shot a quick look up at the front. Neither of the regular hostesses was on tonight, so he had been performing that function, among oth-ers, since about five o'clock. Even as he glanced up, the heavy door was pulled open and a young couple came in.

They were sparklingly good-looking, maybe thirty. Just from a quick glance it was clear that both of them worked out regularly. He had brown hair, a deep tan despite the time of year, a thousand-watt smile that said he was used to getting what he asked for, and his khakis and shirt looked as if they'd been ironed with him still in them. The pleats on his pants were sharp enough to cut someone. She wore an almost identical uniform, save for the bristly olive-green sweater pulled over her blouse. No one could possibly have mistaken her for a man, however. Her long blond hair was swept back over her shoulders, and her blue eyes gleamed even from across the restaurant. She was also tan, and her skin radiated with a health that came from plenty of free time and exercise.

They couldn't have been more out of place.

While Bridget's got all kinds of customers, most of them were tourists or locals or hard-core Irish who wouldn't have dreamed of going anywhere else. Most were middle class folks at best, but the couple who had just walked in the front door looked like they had been unwrapped on Christmas morning and were fresh from the plastic packaging. Ken and Barbie. Walking wealth.

Jack did not have a problem with wealthy people as a rule, but on those rare occasions when those who could have bought and sold the Four Seasons or Morton's found themselves at Bridget's Irish Rose Pub, they often had an air about them that said they were slumming.

Ken and Barbie had that air.

Look, honey, he expected her to say at any moment. *Isn't this quaint? An Irish place. Let's get a Guinness and shepherd's pie, oh, can we?*

But they were customers and at Bridget's they all got the same hospitality until they proved they didn't deserve it. So when Jack walked up to Ken and Barbie where they waited by the front door, he put on the nicest smile he could muster.

"Can I help you folks?"

Ken grinned. Lots of teeth. A Tom Cruise grin. "I'm beyond help," he said warmly. "My wife could use a steak, though. Red meat cravings."

Surprised, Jack blinked. Then he laughed softly to himself. "Right this way," he told them as he grabbed a pair of menus. As he led them to a table he marveled at how completely wrong he'd read them. *That'll teach you to judge just from appearance,* he thought.

The couple kidded each other about their appetites as they passed through the middle of the restaurant, surrounded by brass and oak.

"Nice place," Ken said suddenly.

"Thanks," Jack said.

"I don't guess you're Bridget," Barbie said.

"No. That was my mom. She passed ten years ago."

Genuine sympathy etched the woman's face. "I'm so sorry."

"I appreciate it," he told her. Then he gestured around the restaurant. "It's still her place, though."

Neither of them seemed at all aloof the way wealthy people normally acted. And if Barbie had really dragged him out because she was in the mood for a steak, all the better. Most women who had that trophy-wife, all-day-at-the-gym look would never confess to a desire for a thick steak, let alone joke about it with their husbands.

Ken and Barbie slid into a booth and Jack laid the menus on the table. "I'm Jack Dwyer. Your waitress will be with you in just a minute. In the meantime, if you need anything, give me a shout."

"We'll do that, Jack. Thanks." Ken shot him another grin, then leaned over to kiss his wife's cheek even as he reached for a menu.

There were no more customers waiting to be seated so Jack headed back toward the kitchen. He spotted Molly dropping entrées off at table seventeen and adjusted his course toward her. Her hair was pinned up in a way that was both planned and haphazard at the same time. Earlier in the evening she had seemed pretty harried, but he could tell that she had calmed down some.

When she moved away from table seventeen he fell into step behind her.

"How's it going?"

"Good," she said happily. "Really good, actually. I haven't had anyone be rude to me in two hours, and I think I'm getting this. Of course, it could just be exhaustion setting in."

"Wait'll you have to wake up early tomorrow morning and go to the market with me."

Molly's mouth formed a perfect little O of surprise. "I'm sleeping in tomorrow, buddy."

"We'll see," Jack taunted her.

When Molly laughed, he realized that despite the frenzy of the new job she was more relaxed than he had seen her in a while. This would be good for all of them, he thought. He really wanted her to be happy.

At that thought, however, he remembered what Artie had said about the two of them, and he felt guilty. A sudden awkwardness overcame him, and Molly noticed it.

"What's wrong?" she asked, eyes darting around, obviously worried that some new danger had presented itself.

"Nothing," he assured her. "Just . . . It's good to have you here, Moll."

"Hey," she said tenderly. Then again, "Hey." She embraced him for just a moment. "I don't know what I'd do without you."

"Probably get fired for hugging the boss," he whispered.

Molly feigned insult and whacked his arm. "All right, all right. I'm getting back to work. Are you this tough with all your new recruits?"

"Nope, just you," Jack told her, and he laughed a little, though more to cover his own discomfort than anything else.

Even as his laughter died, Jack noticed something in his peripheral vision. He glanced toward the bar. Amid the small throng of people waiting for drinks or sipping what they already had, and behind a couple of dockworkers engaged in conversation with a scruffy guy who seemed more college professor than laborer, he saw a black suit and a white Roman collar. A priest.

The ghost of Father Pinsky stared across the pub at Jack. The priest closed his eyes and crossed himself.

"Oh, shit," Jack muttered.

Molly had begun to turn toward the kitchen but she stopped and stared at him.

"Jack? What's wrong?"

Her voice had a desperate quality to it, but also a kind of resignation, as though she had known it was only a matter of time before the terror began again. Molly had known it was not over. So had Jack. But he wished it could have stayed away a little longer.

When Molly spoke again, it was in a whisper, right beside him. "Is it the ghosts, Jack?"

"One of them," he said, muscles tense, his entire

body on alert now as he kept his eyes on the praying ghost. "A priest."

Father Pinsky stared meaningfully at Jack, then slowly pointed at the three men in front of him at the bar. The one who looked like a college professor frowned and glanced around as if he had sensed something. He batted at the priest's ghostly form as though Father Pinsky were a mosquito buzzing around his head.

The ghost recoiled. These creatures had killed him. He was dead, they could no longer harm him, and yet he was still afraid of them.

"Are the monsters here?" Molly whispered.

Big Bill Cantwell suddenly appeared behind her. Seeing him there reminded Jack just how big the bartender actually was.

"Yeah. They're here," Bill said grimly.

"How did you know?" Jack asked.

He glanced back at the priest. There were other ghosts there now. Phantoms he had never seen before. One of them, he was fairly certain, was the mafia guy who'd been mauled a couple of nights earlier.

"They've had you and Molly scoped out since they walked in," Bill replied. "And they just don't look right. Take this."

In the space that separated Jack from Bill, a gun suddenly appeared. It was an M9 Beretta, typically used by the U.S. infantry. It held fifteen rounds in the clip. Four years earlier, Bill had taken Jack to a firing range half a dozen times to learn to use the weapon—over Artie's vehement protests—but Jack had not seen it since. Learning to use it had been a matter of curiosity, something he'd mentioned to Bill just once: "What's it like to fire a gun?"

"Jesus, Bill," Jack whispered. "We've got a lot of customers in here. I . . . we can't afford to have anyone get hurt."

The burly bartender nervously ran a hand across his bearded chin and glanced past Jack. "I don't think that's up to us. Do you?"

Molly stared at both of them, then stepped in closer. Her voice was barely a whisper. "What are you going to do?"

Bill made no attempt to answer. He looked to Jack.

One deep breath and Jack turned to her. "Go back into the kitchen. Tell Courtney what's up. Then I want you to stay back there. If they're here, they're after both of us."

"My stun gun is in my purse, in the back office."

Molly frowned as she said it, a great many things passing between them without words. Chief among them was this clear message: she was not going to hide in the kitchen. And Jack knew his sister wouldn't either.

Jack nodded. "Go tell Courtney. Both of you keep a distance, give yourselves room to fight or run or whatever."

"We should call the police," Molly argued. "If the cops show up, the Prowlers will be gone."

"But they won't stay gone," Jack responded.

"You're not thinking—"

"Maybe not," he snapped. "Maybe not. But I don't like that the cops are hiding this thing. Maybe costing people's lives by trying not to scare us. Well, hell, we *should* be scared. If people knew, you can damn well bet these bastards would've been caught sooner. Maybe even before Artie and Kate . . ."

"This could ruin your business, everything you and Courtney have worked for," Molly told him, her eyes pleading. "We know where they are. Just call the cops and be done with it."

Jack gently touched her cheek, but there was cold iron in his gut and his jaw was set. "They come into my place, Moll. My place. Trying to kill me. Kill you. Who knows what else? After what they did to Artie I want justice. I don't know if the cops can give them that. Now I just want to tear 'em down."

Bill grunted, a kind of fire in his eyes. "They think they're untouchable."

Molly stared at Jack a moment. Her throat worked as she swallowed hard. Then she nodded. "All right, then. Let's touch them."

"Bill?" Jack asked.

"It's your place."

With a nod, Jack untucked his cotton shirt with the pub's logo on the breast, then tucked the Beretta into the waistband of his pants against the small of his back. He turned as he did it so no one would notice but he need not have worried. The only people gazing in their direction were Ken and Barbie, who seemed troubled and a bit annoyed that no one had waited on them yet.

Molly headed for the kitchen. Jack called after her.

"Molly? Tell Jacqui to wait on those people at table six."

She blinked, gave him a bemused sort of look, and went through the swinging doors.

Jack shot Bill a hard look. "Why don't you get back to work?"

The big man nodded. He headed for the bar with a bit more speed than usual. Jack watched him go, then surveyed the restaurant. An older couple had paid their bill and were going out the door, the man moving with that odd shuffle some elderly people used. Conversations combined into a kind of white noise static, cut occasionally by a high female laugh. At the bar now there were four or five regulars glued to ESPN on the TV bolted to the rear wall.

Bill made his way behind the bar. A couple of guys called out to him good-naturedly as he relieved Silvester, a skinny Croatian kid who worked as a waiter and sometimes covered the bar for Bill. The guy was as out of place at Bridget's as Molly would have been serving cocktails at a Chinese buffet, but everyone loved him, even the old school Boston Irish.

The three animals at the bar stood in a clutch, holding pints of beer and shooting furtive glances around the restaurant. The thick-necked pair Jack had mistaken for dockworkers looked as if they were there to start a fight, but the other guy—the one in the soft brown leather jacket and the celebrity stubble—he pulled off his disguise fine. His eyes tracked the pub from time to time, but because of his smile and the easy way he held himself, he wasn't obvious.

Jack did see the beast in his face, though. Something about the eyes and the general structure of his features.

As if he sensed Jack's eyes on him, the celebrity glanced over. For a heartbeat, his gaze locked with Jack's. He smiled, then averted his eyes. Jack did not look away, but he saw Bill reach under the bar, grab something, and hold it out of view, just below the long oak bar. Silvester had been shooed away, sent back to the kitchen most likely.

Behind him, Jack sensed someone approaching. He took a quick glance over his shoulder and saw Courtney and Molly moving up on him. Molly had a hand in her pocket, grasping something. Her Taser.

With a tiny smile that was devoid of all humor or amusement, Jack strode across the restaurant and up the two steps into the bar area. A half-wall topped by brass railings separated it from the main restaurant. Molly and Courtney had moved toward the front door.

The ghosts were gone. Or perhaps Jack's focus was so much on the here and now that he could not see them.

The regulars greeted Jack. He nodded at them but did not respond. Tension rippled off him, and several of the regulars snapped to attention as though he had asked for backup. He knew he should tell them to take off, but didn't. Backup couldn't hurt, particularly now that he'd drawn attention to himself. One of the two thick-necks eyed him as he stepped up behind the other two.

Jack took a steadying breath, then tapped the celebrity on the shoulder. Feeling the cold weight of the gun against his back, he let his right hand dangle at his side and shook it out.

The celebrity cast him a sidelong glance. Jack realized that he'd made a mistake in sizing the guy up from a distance. Next to the pair of Neanderthals he'd come in with, he looked skinny. He was thin, true, but bigger than Jack had thought and he moved as if he were coiled up tight, ready to spring.

"Something I can do for you?" the Prowler asked, his tone light and amused.

"You've made a mistake."

The celebrity frowned. "I don't follow you."

"I think you do. You and the other animals shouldn't have come here. Not just here, as in my place, Bridget's. But here, as in Boston. You shouldn't have killed my friends."

The Prowler's nostrils flared. His eyes narrowed and his lip curled up and suddenly he appeared a great deal more like a beast, though he still wore a human face.

Then he smiled, said one word. "Messy."

As if his voice had triggered it, all three of them changed. The celebrity was smooth, the flesh seeming to recede back into him as bones popped and fur bristled and slavering jaws extended. The other two were cruder, shredding their skin as their true features tore through from beneath.

Jack could smell them now, the animal stink of the Prowlers. He almost gagged it was so strong. Beasts, that's all they were. Fangs and claws and instincts, like bears or wolves or tigers. But Prowlers could also think, and that made them the most dangerous animal of all.

Across the room, a waitress named Missy Keane—who had just happened to be watching the men at the bar—shrieked in terror.

"What the hell?" shouted Tommy Herlihy, one of the regulars just down the bar.

Jack stepped back, whipped the Beretta out from behind his back.

The three Prowlers moved simultaneously. One of them leaped up on top of the bar. Tommy Herlihy reached for it—either drunk or braver than Jack had given him credit for—and was slapped away with a long talon that tore furrows in his cheek. Tommy cried out in pain as his friends caught him, but nobody heard Tommy's shout.

Glass shattered. People screamed and ran for the door. He heard Molly and Courtney urging them on, shouting for them all to leave, to run. Jack tried not to wonder if any of them would ever come back.

All this happened in two seconds, as Jack was drawing the Beretta from behind his back. The thinner Prowler, who had looked like a celebrity in his human face, lunged at Jack and batted the gun out of his hand. It hit the floor, drove a divot up out of the hardwood, and slid away.. The creature grabbed Jack by the throat and lifted him one-handed off the floor. Jack coughed, choking, and grabbed the thing's powerful hands.

"Messy," it said again, its voice a growl, nothing more.

Right about then, Bill brought up the shotgun and blew a hole in the chest of the Prowler standing on the bar. Gore spattered onto the bar and over into the restaurant, and then Bill was flying over the oak top with a leap that Jack would have thought impossible for a man his size.

The beast holding Jack turned slightly, alarmed by the shotgun blast. Its arms were so much longer than Jack's that Jack could not have reached it with his hands. Instead he used the power of the Prowler's grip against it and swung his right leg up in a snap-kick to its sternum. Something cracked when the kick landed. The Prowler grunted and dropped Jack.

"Don't move!" Bill screamed at the thing. "On your knees!" He leveled the shotgun at it, and the beast began to comply.

"Jack!"

The scream was Molly's. Jack spun to see the third Prowler—how could he have forgotten the third one?—going for Molly. The moment seemed to freeze in time. From his vantage point up at the bar he could see the entire restaurant, a nasty bit of wide-screen. Missy Keane was gone, either out to the back or out the front door with some of the customers. The folks at table seventeen were gone, and most of the tables were deserted, people having run out the door or rushed to the back of the restaurant. A group that stood with their backs to the swinging kitchen doors included some of the waiters, such as Bud Trainor and Kiera Dunphy, and the Ken and Barbie couple.

From the kitchen, Kiera's brother Tim and a couple of other cooks had shoved their way through people, carrying the biggest knives they could find.

Nobody was close enough to help Molly.

Molly had screamed his name.

Adrenaline pumping through him, Jack ran the three steps to where the Beretta lay on the hardwood floor. It had just stopped spinning, so quickly had everything happened. He snapped it up in his right hand and turned to see the Prowler slash out at Molly. Even as it did so, it leaped back, accompanied by the crackle of electricity and the odor of singed fur.

The Taser! She stunned it.

But the beast was barely dazed. Though it was more cautious, it began to move in on her again. Jack could barely see Molly past the Prowler, but he knew he had to take the shot and hope its body would stop the bullets, that they wouldn't pass through. He leveled the Beretta two-handed and took aim.

Courtney stepped in the way.

With a swing worthy of Fenway she cracked her cane across the back of the beast's head. It grunted at first. And then it roared. The Prowler turned and slashed her across the chest. Courtney screamed as she went down, blood seeping through the tears in her clothing.

But she was out of the way.

"Molly, get down!" Jack shouted. He leveled the Beretta and pumped four rounds into the Prowler as it turned toward Molly again. The beast went down in a bloody heap.

"No!" Bill screamed. "Courtney!"

Tim Dunphy and the other cooks came running up. They were all staring at the dead monsters, at Courtney's blood where Molly crouched over her, at Bill who still had the shotgun leveled at the surviving creature.

"Tim," Jack snapped. "Tim!"

Dunphy blinked, then focused on him.

"Get everyone out of here—staff, customers. Tell them we owe 'em a dinner once we get the place cleaned up, but get them out of here."

Dunphy nodded.

"Ambulance is on the way," a voice called.

Jack looked up to see the customer he'd thought of as Ken waving a cell phone. He shot a hard look at Bill and the Prowler they'd left breathing, and he cursed under his breath. "Go," he told Tim.

As Dunphy started hustling the customers and staff out the door, Jack went over to check on his sister, his mind whirling. If an ambulance was on the way, thanks to Ken and Barbie, there'd be cops on the way as well. And he didn't want cops yet. Not yet.

The last of the customers pushed out the door. Jack took a quick glance at Bill, who had the growling monster down on its knees up at the bar.

"Hey," Jack said to Courtney. "You all right?"

His sister was sitting up, her back against the wall, which he took as a good sign. Her face was pale and sickly-looking as if she might throw up, but she smiled wanly. "Could you take a look?" Courtney asked, voice edgy and hesitant. She gestured at Molly. "Neither one of us could bring ourselves to do it."

Jack nodded grimly. He lifted away a torn bit of her blood-soaked shirt. He grimaced at first when he saw the three wounds on Courtney's chest, just below her bra. But then he narrowed his gaze and studied them. Not her belly, but her chest. Ribs and sternum would have protected her insides for the most part. The third and bottom wounds looked relatively deep, but the other one was superficial. *Thank God*, Jack thought. *I couldn't survive if I lost you too.*

"I think you're—"

"You okay, Courtney? Jack, what's the story?" Bill called to them.

Jack turned to him and his eyes went wide with alarm. Bill had allowed his concern for Courtney to distract him. As the bartender focused on Courtney, the Prowler on the floor surged up at him. It grabbed the barrel of the shotgun just as it discharged, blowing out an ornate chandelier. The shotgun clattered to the floor, useless.

Jack lifted the Beretta, but he couldn't take a shot without possibly hitting Bill. He moved closer.

"Back off, you son of a bitch!" Bill shouted as he grappled with the Prowler. "You don't want to do this."

"Oh, but I do," the Prowler snarled.

It slashed at Bill's neck, trying to tear his throat out, but got mostly shoulder and arm instead. The pain must have been excruciating. Bill let out a feral cry as he staggered back, clutching his shoulder. He shook his head, trying to throw off the pain, Jack thought.

"Back off, Bill!" Jack shouted, Beretta now leveled at the Prowler. "I've got him. And we need him alive."

The Prowler glanced at Jack, but only for a moment, as if the weapon did not concern him at all.

"No, Jack," Bill snarled. "Put the gun away. This cocky little bastard is all mine."

His voice changed. A low, guttural snarl. A growl.

Then his body changed as well. With a fluid ripple and a pop of bones shifting in place, with hair bristling out all over his body and needle-sharp teeth glistening in a long, vicious snout, Bill transformed.

Bill Cantwell was a Prowler.

CHAPTER 13

In a handful of days, slipping away even now, the world as Jack Dwyer had always known it was destroyed. Or, more accurately, the world had been peeled back like the layers of an onion to reveal the truth beneath, and it was enough to make him cry.

Prowlers—monsters from the darkest edge of human imagination—roamed the world. Ghosts lingered on the periphery of every moment, existing in their own parallel realm, the Ghostlands, a kind of spectral curtain superimposed over the world of the living. Jack could see them, even speak to them. His best friend had been violently murdered and yet remained to advise him and exhort him to action.

It had all seemed a nightmare to him until this very moment.

Jack stared in horror at the two creatures, the two Prowlers, tearing and battering at each other in the middle of Bridget's Irish Rose Pub. His horror stemmed not from their mere presence, which was terrible enough, nor from the devastation as one struck the other hard enough to send it flying into a table and chairs, shattering the furniture. His horror was closer to home.

One of the monsters was his friend.

"Bill?" Jack whispered.

Behind him, he heard Courtney and Molly cry out in surprise and horror. On Courtney's part, he thought there was probably some grief in there as well, for Jack believed his sister loved Bill.

After that, it all happened too fast for him to feel more than the shock that filled him now.

It was simple enough to tell the two beasts apart. Size alone would have done it, for Bill was much larger than his opponent, but there were other differences as well. Bill had gray-and-silver fur, much bushier than the sleek reddish brown of the attacker.

God, what are you thinking? he asked himself. *This can't be!*

But it was.

Jack held the nine millimeter Beretta steady in his hand, aiming at both of them, but unable to fire.

Monsters, he told himself. *They're monsters.*

But one of them was Bill.

The one he'd thought of as the celebrity lunged across the middle of the restaurant with extraordinary speed, claws slashing air and then slashing Bill. Blood spattered the floor. The celebrity was faster than Bill, but suddenly that did not matter. His attack had brought him in too close. Bill reached out, grabbed him by the throat and the front of the shirt and jacket that still hung on his monstrous body, then drove the Prowler's head through a thick pane of frosted glass that separated two booths. The Prowler tumbled onto the table—a table still covered with the half-eaten meals of patrons who had fled when chaos erupted.

He tried to turn, to rise, snapped his jaws at Bill, trying to tear at his opponent with a mouthful of razor teeth. He missed.

With one powerful swipe of an enormous clawed hand, Bill batted the other Prowler off the table and on to the floor. His claws had raked the celebrity's face, and blood was pouring from the wounds, matting the beast's fur. Cantwell followed the other down to the floor, a roar of fury rising up from his chest. Bill snapped at his broken enemy, then snarled, baring his fangs as slaver dripped from them.

Arching its back, the other Prowler tilted back its head and exposed its furry throat. Bill ducked down and snapped his jaws closed on the other's neck.

"Oh, Bill, no!" Courtney cried.

Leaning on her cane, she hobbled up beside Jack. Molly was right behind her. The three of them stared across the restaurant at the awful scene being played out on the floor.

Jack held the Beretta steady, but now that the celebrity no longer seemed a threat, it was aimed at Bill. The man who had been a friend to him lifted his head and glared with yellow, feral eyes across at Jack and the others—the people who had composed his little family. Jack was stunned to see that the celebrity still lived, that Bill had not torn his throat out, as Jack had expected.

"Bill?" Jack rasped, shaking his head, his aim faltering.

The Prowler spoke. "He's done. He's given up. Ask him whatever you want to know. He'll tell you."

Jack, Molly, and Courtney only stared, paralyzed by the sound of Bill's voice—ragged and deeper than usual—coming from the throat of a beast.

"Get back," Jack snapped. He motioned with the gun, but kept it leveled at Bill. His mind whirled, trying to make sense of the situation, trying to decide what to do.

Jack glanced around in hope that Artie or one of the other phantoms might appear and offer some sort of guidance. There was no advice to be had. No ghosts offered to mediate in the war that was currently raging between his head and his heart. For Jack's head was telling him to shoot, to kill both of the monsters. But his heart . . .

In the distance, sirens blared. Only minutes had passed since it all began. Now the police were on their way. Bill's huge, shaggy head was tipped up toward the windows, his pointed ears pricking as the sirens reached them. His gaze swept across all three of them, a deep sadness in his monstrous eyes. Then he stared right at Jack.

"Shoot me, if that's what you have to do," Bill said

suddenly. He stood up to his full height, gave Jack a clean target.

Jack nodded slowly, steadied his aim.

Courtney cursed under her breath and said Jack's name. Her tone was enough to reveal her feelings. She was afraid, but she did not want him to kill their friend. It was the worst decision he had ever had to make, but if he let Bill live, how could they ever trust him?

"He's a monster," Jack said, his voice breaking. "He's one of them. They killed Artie, and who knows how many others."

Bill bristled. "I'm a Prowler, yeah, but I'm not one of them. Do what you have to do, but I'm not one of *them*."

"You can't kill him, Jack."

Jack flinched. He cast Molly a quick sidelong glance.

"All this time Bill's been a part of your life and you never knew this. He never hurt you guys or anyone else, as far as you know," Molly said gently, casting a wary glance at Bill. "Maybe he is a monster, and maybe he'll kill us all. Maybe. Or maybe he's just Bill. We don't understand Prowlers, don't understand what they are or if all of them are like the ones we've seen. If you let him live, we could pay for it with our lives. But if you kill him, it will haunt you forever. You'll always wonder if you did the right thing."

Jack stared at her. His entire body seemed clenched tight like a fist and he shook his head, completely at a loss as his mind and heart continued to war within him.

The sirens were louder.

"They're getting closer, Jack," Bill growled. He sniffed at the air with his long snout, ears twitching. His huge claws hung down at his sides. On the floor in front of him, the defeated Prowler had not moved, but his feral yellow eyes watched with great interest and cunning as the scene unfolded.

Closer. In his head he heard Artie's voice telling him that he had to take the Prowlers down, make them pay. But the monster on the floor, the one Bill had defeated, had information they needed.

The pistol wavered in Jack's hand. He stared at Bill. A dreadful certainty filled him. "You could take this gun away from me any time, couldn't you?"

"Jack—" Bill began.

"Couldn't you?" Jack demanded. "I've seen how fast you move. Even if you took a bullet, you could kill us all."

"What do you think?" Bill asked.

Still reeling, not at all content with his decision but feeling it was his only option, Jack nodded and turned the gun on the Prowler who lay on the floor at Bill's feet. The beast flinched.

"I can tell you where the lair is," it whined.

"I know where the lair is," Jack countered.

The celebrity's eyes widened.

"How long have you known?" Bill asked.

"Since this morning," Molly explained. "Jack's been keeping a lot of little secrets to himself."

Courtney took a step toward Bill, using her cane to

steady herself. She gazed at him with love and sadness, but without fear. "Jack's not the only one," she said.

Bill glanced away, unwilling to meet Courtney's gaze.

With that very human reaction, Jack truly saw for the first time the resemblance between this monster and the human facade he had always known. A sharp jolt went through him that was neither love nor anguish but perhaps a little of both.

After a moment's hesitation, Courtney moved closer to Bill. Close enough that had he been of a mind to kill her, he had only to strike out at her. A single blow would likely have done it.

"I . . . I don't know what it takes for you to change back," Courtney said softly. "But you'd better do it before the cops get here."

The gratitude in the beast's eyes was endless. With a sound like the crinkling of cellophane, Bill changed. The beast seemed to pull in on itself; bones popped, the jaw receded, and fur withdrew beneath a new sheath of human skin.

Then he was just Bill again. At least on the surface. In all of their minds, he would never again be *just* Bill.

Courtney went to him and Bill held her in a tight embrace. Jack wanted to shout to her to get away from him, his fear for his sister deeply embedded in him. But whatever Bill was, whatever monster hid behind his face, he loved Courtney. Jack understood that Bill would never harm her. Or any of them.

He had to trust in that. Bill was family. Jack wasn't going to let his family be shattered again.

"Jack, the cops," Molly prompted him.

With a nod, he stepped closer to the Prowler on the floor, Beretta steady in his grip, aimed at the beast's face.

"Your name?"

"Eric Carver."

Carver. So it had a name.

Molly stepped in front of Jack, gave him a hard look. "We don't have time for this. We have seconds, Jack."

She turned to Bill. "What do we need to know from him that you can't tell us?"

Bill glared at Carver. "How many are there? Who's the leader?"

"Fifty. Maybe slightly fewer now," Carver said quickly, as cooperatively as possible. "The Alpha's Owen Tanzer."

"Tanzer," Bill muttered. "Damn."

Tires squealed out on the street. Police cars pulled in, blue and red lights flashing through the windows of the pub. The shadows of patrons who had fled but stayed out on the street to see what unfolded played against the glass like ghosts.

Molly swore. "What will they do with this Carver creature?" she asked, studying Jack closely.

"I don't know," he admitted. "Probably they'll kill him. They're trying to cover this up."

"*Probably* isn't good enough," Molly said bitterly.

With one fluid motion, she tore the Beretta from

Jack's grasp, steadied it with both hands, and shot the Prowler twice in the chest.

The monster bled out on the floor as the police kicked through the front door, their own weapons drawn.

While the police cordoned off the area, the crime scene team descended on the pub. They took photographs, collected evidence, and dumped corpses in body bags. EMTs treated Courtney's wounds, which weren't as bad as they looked. Bill's wounds, too, had seemed far more significant when they were first inflicted.

Throughout the process, the police never said a word to them beyond the most bland comments. They were instructed to sit together at a table in the far corner of the restaurant, and they remained there in silence as the investigation commenced—if one could call it an investigation. Jack thought of it more as a continuation of the cover-up. The body bags were zipped up and the corpses of the dead Prowlers were carted off without even an odd look. The cops didn't wait for the medical examiner, and they sure as hell didn't call the animal control unit.

Twenty minutes after the police had descended upon Bridget's—during which police officers had taken statements from most of the patrons outside and then ushered them away—Jason Castillo walked in the front door. The detective glanced once around the pub, spotted Jack and the others in the back, and strode carefully through the restaurant toward them.

"This should be interesting," Bill mumbled.

His voice gave Jack a bit of a shudder. It was a reminder of the truth they had just learned about Bill, which was going to take a long time to get used to. But Jack supposed that visits from his best friend's ghost and the sight of Prowlers tearing apart security guards in Fenway Park had prepared him for it—if anything could.

"Mr. Dwyer. Looks like you've had quite a night," the homicide detective said casually. He pulled out a chair, turned it around, and straddled it, regarding the four of them.

"You think there's something funny about this?" Molly demanded.

Jack heard the bite in her voice, each word clipped off with a clack of teeth. In the back of his head he could still hear the echo of the Beretta firing, still see Molly draw down on Carver and pump two rounds into his chest. *Molly Hatcher. Molly did that.* He kept telling himself that but it was hard to accept. Not that he blamed her. After what they'd done to Artie and what they'd tried to do to her and Jack, he understood completely why she wouldn't take a chance that the cops would keep him alive, try to talk to him, give him a chance to escape without paying for all he'd done.

It was just that the suddenness and brutality of the act had stunned him. Molly had always been capable of handling herself. She was smart and quick and strong, and he would have chosen her to watch his back over any guy he knew. But she had also always been sweet and kind and good, and it had pained him to see the hatred and rage that drove her to fire those rounds.

Yet on some level it had thrilled him as well. Molly was not going to let things scare her. Not anymore. All his life Jack had felt that he was at the center of the world. He figured most people thought that way. And when he and his friends got together, he had seen himself as the leader, the one they counted on for answers and to figure out what to do next.

When Molly fired those rounds, however, he had to wonder if maybe if she hadn't been the decision-maker, the leader, all along. Either way, he would never underestimate her again. She was in this one hundred percent. Whatever he decided to do now, he knew Molly would back him up.

"Miss Hatcher," Castillo said. He scratched at the George Clooney stubble on his chin and offered an uncertain smile. "Seems to me that there actually is something funny about all this, but I couldn't put it into words. Maybe you understand what I mean."

"Maybe we don't," Courtney interjected.

Castillo frowned and regarded her carefully.

Courtney brushed a strand of her sandy blond hair away from her eyes and returned his hard gaze.

"You're Courtney Dwyer?" the detective asked.

"That's me. This is my place," she said. Then she looked at Jack. "Our place. If you have questions, get on with them. I want to be able to open for lunch tomorrow, if possible."

With a nod, Castillo turned to Bill. He narrowed his eyes as he studied the big man. "And you?"

"Bill Cantwell. I tend bar here."

Something about the way Castillo eyed Bill made Jack wonder if the cop knew more about the bartender than he let on. Then Castillo's eyes lit up.

"Yeah. Cantwell. You used to play for the Patriots, right?" Castillo said.

"That's me," Bill admitted.

"You were impossible to take down back then."

Bill grinned. "Still am."

Castillo nodded again.

The nodding was starting to get on Jack's nerves. The cop was eating up time they did not have if they wanted to stop Tanzer before he left town.

"Want to get to the questions, detective?" Jack asked.

The cop raised an eyebrow. "You in a hurry, Jack?"

"Like my sister said, we want to open tomorrow."

Castillo chuckled. "You guys are pretty cool, aren't you? Stone cold. After what went down here, you just sit there and tell me you're worried about lunch tomorrow."

"Maybe we are," Courtney snapped.

"Maybe," Castillo agreed. Then he focused on Jack. "But, see, a little more than a week ago two of your friends were murdered by a vicious killer. Or killers." He offered a tiny ironic smile. "Then yesterday some nasty folks tried to kill you two on the T. That *was* you two, wasn't it? You and Molly?"

Molly laughed. "If the police had treated it like a

crime and actually taken statements, you'd know, wouldn't you?"

"You killed two of these monsters."

"Monsters?" Jack asked, feigning surprise. "But I thought you guys said they were wolves."

Bill and Courtney laughed at that one. Molly only stared at Castillo.

For his part, the cop was not pleased. "Don't get coy with me now, Jack. All this stuff keeps coming back to you and your friends here, and that tells me you know more than you've let on. I want it. And then I want you to forget it."

Castillo's expression was grim.

Jack leaned back in his chair and shook his head. "You're something, you know that? You expect us to pretend we didn't see what we saw here tonight?"

The cop shrugged and glanced around the restaurant. "Who'd believe you? You have no proof, Jack, unless you've got a security camera you didn't tell me about. You can play ball with me, or I can arrest you for obstructing justice and maybe a few other things. Nothing will stick, but I can make things difficult for you and your sister and your little place here."

With a tiny growl—as if now that the animal in him had been loosened it could not be completely hidden again—Bill rose from his chair, about to reach for the detective.

"Bill, no," Jack said.

The big man stopped, but he glared at the detective.

In that same moment Jack saw movement out of the

corner of his eye. When he glanced up he saw Artie standing off to his right. Through his transparent form, Jack could see the crime scene team as they continued to gather evidence.

In the blink of an eye it all changed again. The world turned inside out and Artie had flesh. Jack was back in the Ghostlands, where the living seemed to be intangible phantoms and only the dead had substance. The cops and forensic techs were just specters now, as were Bill and Molly, Courtney, and Detective Castillo.

But the Ghostlands version of Bridget's was full. Several dozen people wandered through the pub and restaurant, some of them moving slowly, as if tired or anguished. Others, like Artie and Corinne Berdinka and Father Pinsky, stood and watched.

"Jack? You okay?"

He turned to look into his sister's eyes and was unnerved to see her this way, as nothing but a gossamer shade of herself. "I'm fine," he said.

"You can't believe the cops will handle this," Artie told him. His best friend's ectoplasmic form drifted over to him. "They just want to make this case go away. They don't care if the Prowlers move to another city, as long as Boston doesn't have to deal with them anymore."

Jack nodded.

"Well?" Detective Castillo demanded. He saw that Jack was staring off at nothing and tried to figure out what had caught his attention. "Hello? Jack?"

Jack focused on the detective again, and suddenly he

realized that the few figures that lingered around Castillo were somehow linked to the homicide detective. They were phantoms from Jason Castillo's own life. One of them was a girl no more than sixteen. When Jack locked eyes with her, the girl began to speak.

And Jack repeated every word.

As the others all stared at him, and Castillo's eyes widened with ever-growing horror, Jack spoke in a high, female voice, one filled with sorrow.

"In 1987. You were a rookie. My name was Annette Ramos and I screamed for help. You could have saved me, but you were afraid to go in without backup. They cut me up, mutilated me in the minutes you hesitated. When you finally went in, I wasn't quite dead yet. I looked up and saw the fear in your eyes, and then I died. You never told anyone I was still alive when you went in. You didn't want anyone to know you could have saved me."

Castillo recoiled, jumped up out of the chair, and glanced around as if the voice had come from elsewhere. Then he rounded on Jack, eyes wide and teeth bared in fury. "How the hell did you do that?"

Jack smiled at the insubstantial police officer, comfortable now with the vision of the Ghostlands that surrounded him.

"We all have our secrets," Jack said. Then he glanced at Bill and Molly and Courtney and winked.

"You son of a—" Castillo snapped and started toward Jack.

"They're in an old church tower converted to an

apartment in Copley Square," Jack said. "If I've got this right it used to belong to Eric Carver, who's one of the Prowlers your guys just hauled out of here. There are about fifty of them, give or take, and their leader's name is Owen Tanzer. If you kill Tanzer, you might be able to take the others, but with Tanzer alive, they're more dangerous."

Castillo stood staring at him. Then he shook his head. "Why?"

"Why?" Jack asked. "Isn't it obvious? Tanzer's the leader of the pack."

While the detective thought that over, Jack gazed around at the ghosts. He stared for a long moment at the specter of Annette Ramos. The girl was furious at Castillo and that anger had kept her here, in the Ghostlands.

"He's a good man," Jack whispered suddenly. "Even after you're gone, you'll still haunt him. You can go on now, if you want to."

Annette's spirit smiled gently, and a tear slipped down her cheek. She was solid, only a few feet from him, and he thought that if he reached out then he might be able to touch her, to lay hands upon the Ghostlands. But for some reason, though he had been touched by Artie once before, he thought that might be dangerous.

"Thank you," Annette whispered.

Then Jack blinked and the Ghostlands were gone. Only Artie's ghost remained, lingering in the background, barely visible now. Artie gave Jack a thumbs up. "Way to go, bro," he said.

Molly twitched and acted as if she had heard something. She shot Jack an inquisitive look, but he pretended not to understand.

"All right," Castillo said, "let's say I believe you."

"You do believe me. Don't screw around, now, Jace. We don't have the time for it. Here's what we're going to do. We'll give you brief statements, saying whatever the hell you want us to say. But we won't come down to the station. Leave us out of it as much as you can. The less often our names appear in your report the better. In return, none of us will say a word about anything. Just wrap this up as quickly as you can. Get over to the lair, slaughter the bastards, and be done with it."

The detective pursed his lips, which formed a tight white line. He didn't like being told how things were going to be; that much was obvious. But there was little in what Jack had said that he could argue with.

Castillo glanced at the other three. "Jack speaks for all of you?"

They all nodded, but both Bill and Courtney were staring at Jack with great curiosity. He had an idea their surprise had less to do with the hard tack he'd taken with the cop than with his channeling the voice of a dead woman. Jack felt bad for not having told his sister what he was going through, but Bill was another story.

He shot the bartender a hard look. Bill was the last person who should have been taken aback by discovering that Jack was hiding something.

"We all have secrets," he said again.

Castillo seemed to notice the tension among them. The cop frowned, then shook his head and waved a hand. "All right. We'll do it your way. But once you've given your statements, you all stay clear. Just keep your heads down until I say different, all right?"

Jack smiled. "We can do that."

CHAPTER 14

A little over an hour after their conversation with Castillo, Bridget's was empty again. The crime scene team had done a half-assed job at best, but everyone pretended not to notice. After all, they were trying very hard *not* to find evidence of the Prowlers, whose bodies would likely be cremated before dawn. Jack had no idea how the police were going to handle the eyewitnesses, but he figured it wasn't his business. And, after all, who would believe them? Particularly if the people who ran Bridget's Irish Rose didn't confirm their story.

While the cops were still around, Jack and Molly and Bill and Courtney circled one another warily. Revelations about Bill and Jack hung in the air the way secrets tend to do.

Now, though, Courtney locked the door behind the last of the cops and turned to face the other three, who had begun cleaning up.

"They're gone," she said.

The words echoed in the stillness of the pub. Jack was collecting the wreckage of a shattered table while Molly swept broken glass off the floor. Over at the bar, Bill was setting things right. They all looked up at Courtney.

"Funny how they didn't even bother with that yellow crime scene tape, huh?" Jack scowled and added a broken chair leg to the mess of the splintered table. Then he turned toward Bill, all his anger beginning to boil up in him.

Bill beat him to it. "You see the Ghostlands," the bartender said, his voice tinged with wonder.

Jack blinked. Then he frowned. "What do you know about it? They told me your kind couldn't see them."

"We can't, normally," Bill admitted as he stepped down from the bar area and the four of them converged again in the middle of the restaurant. "But then, neither can humans. I saw it once, though. Someone I . . ." He faltered, eyes downcast.

"Someone you what?" Jack demanded.

Molly stepped in toward Bill, and the big man, the Prowler, flinched. Then he saw the tenderness on her face, and he relaxed a bit as she lay a hand on his arm. "Someone you killed, right?" she said. "The person touched you somehow and you saw what Jack sees?"

Bill nodded. "Many of my race are no longer predators, but I doubt any of us come by the decision quite the same way. For me, it was that moment. I saw the anguish in the souls of humans I'd killed, and I found beauty there."

His eyes locked on Jack's. "We don't have souls. There's no Ghostlands for us."

"Good," Molly said simply.

Bill stared at the bitter expression on her face. Then he shook his head sadly. "You killed that Prowler, Carver, without a second thought. He deserved it, sure. But would it make a difference if he'd been a different sort? The cops don't care how many of my kind you kill, whatever their motivation. They can't even charge you with murder. Why is that?"

"Because you're animals," Molly said.

There was a sadness, a weariness in her voice. Despite her pain and anger, it seemed to Jack that she was not taking it out on Bill, just trying to work things out in her own heart.

Bill nodded. "True. But so are you. The truth is, we're a different sort of animal. I had the same disdain for human lives that you have for Prowlers. Our kind are almost extinct, mainly because of humanity. But then I saw the one thing that most separates us—that there is virtue in humanity that can't be found in other races of animals, including my own—and I knew I couldn't do it anymore."

Silence filled the pub. Rolled across it like swift thunderclouds across a darkening sky and equally ominous. Jack struggled with the emotions that roiled within him. His love for Bill warred with his anger. He glanced at Molly and saw in her eyes that she, too, did not know how to proceed.

Then he looked at his sister. Courtney was staring at Bill, her eyes filled with tears. It was the first time Jack had seen her cry in years.

"Court?" he whispered.

She ignored him. Instead, she went to Bill. When he met her tearful gaze, his own eyes began to fill and he reached out for her. She did not flinch or turn away. Rather, she dropped her cane and stumbled into his embrace, her shoulders shaking with her sobs.

For a long moment, the silence remained unbroken save for the small sounds that escaped her lips.

Then Courtney pulled away from Bill and reached up to stroke the contours of his face. "You're wrong," she said.

"I don't—" Bill began.

"You're wrong," she said again, more fervently, cutting him off. "You said the virtue of humanity couldn't be found among your kind and you are wrong, Bill Cantwell. In my head I know that this isn't your face, but your eyes don't change. And in my heart I know that means something. Everything I love about you I see in your eyes. Maybe your kind have no souls, I wouldn't know about that. But I bet you're wrong about that, too."

Bill held her close, breathing in the scent of her hair with a tiny smile on the facade he called a face. And yet Jack could not accept that it was just a facade.

"Thank you," Bill whispered to her.

"You saved our lives. Thank *you*."

Molly moved to Jack's side and their eyes met. He

slipped an arm around her, and she laid her head on his shoulder, her forlorn gaze matching the bittersweet ache in his heart.

Then Courtney turned to her little brother. "Jack," she said. "Can you really do this? Can you talk to the dead?"

He wanted to turn away but she held his gaze. "Not all of them. Only the ones who are still around, who haven't moved on."

"You never said a word."

"I didn't think you'd believe me."

"Fair enough," Courtney told him, a frown deepening the thin lines on her forehead. "But just so we're clear, I hope you never keep something like that from me again. Have a little faith in your sister, all right?"

Without much more discussion, the tension in the room dissipated and the four of them sat down together.

"We need to know what we're dealing with," Jack said, eyes on Bill. "What are we fighting, exactly?"

"We?" Courtney asked. "You just sent the cops off with their marching orders, Jack. The job is done."

He shook his head angrily. "Bullshit. Oh, they'll make a mess of the place, kill a bunch of them, but this Tanzer was already planning his getaway. If he's the pack leader, I doubt they'll catch him."

Molly sat up a bit straighter. "That can't happen. He can't get away."

"He won't," Bill growled. "We'll make sure of it."

Courtney reached across the table to take his hand. "Tell us about them," she said.

"I wish there was more to tell," Bill said. "But unlike humans, we have no recorded history. No universities. No professors. Only oral tradition. Tales told to young ones.

"Prowlers have been around even longer than mankind. At first we had only one form, but as humans began to spread across the planet, we had to evolve to survive. We are not truly shapeshifters; we're just physical mimics of humanity. As you've already realized, we aren't any more difficult to kill than, say, a grizzly bear. The difference is that we can think. That's a devastating variable. How much more difficult would it be for hunters to kill a grizzly if he were clever?

"I suppose my kind are the source of the myths about werewolves, though of course we are not wolves at all. In the distant past our packs were enormous, but as the human population grew, they were decimated. They lacked a strong leader, one who could unite them. Scattered far and wide, they hunted as best they could in the hard lands and the mountains, in places where their savagery could be passed off as the work of true wolves, or in the cities, killing homeless people and runaways, the ones no one would miss.

"One of the most brutal of my kind was Wade Tanzer. Europe became difficult for his pack, and so he brought them to America when its natives still roamed the mountains and the plains. Before white men ever set foot on American shores, Wade Tanzer led the largest pack then remaining. He was eventually killed, by a Sioux hunter, or so the legend goes.

"Tanzer had a son, Owen. He was not much to speak of, once upon a time—"

"Wait a second," Jack interrupted. "I'm missing something. You knew this guy?"

"Once," Bill replied. "But if it is indeed the same beast, he has evolved. What I have heard frightens me. Owen Tanzer wants to become greater than Wade was. He wants to unite the entire race, and to breed, and after that, who knows? I hesitate to guess."

Molly leaned toward Bill, arms on the table, staring at him as though her vision were out of focus. "But that was hundreds of years ago," she said. "If this Owen is the son of the original Tanzer, he'd have to be four hundred years old, at least."

Bill nodded calmly. He raked his fingers through his scraggly, graying hair. "That's not uncommon for my race. I knew Owen during the Civil War, and he was nothing more than a vulture then, preying on the battlefield dead."

Jack stared. "Jesus, Bill."

"How . . . how old are you?" Courtney asked.

The man—the beast they knew as Bill Cantwell—smiled. "Do you really want to know?"

"I do," Molly said quickly.

Bill had asked Courtney, and he waited for her answer. At length, she shook her head, eyes still wide with amazement.

"If you really want to know, ask me again and I'll tell you," Bill promised.

Then he returned his attention to Jack and Molly. "If this is really Owen Tanzer, and if he's evolved into a leader like his father, he can't be allowed to live."

"Agreed," Jack said. He stood up from the table. "That's why Molly and I are going to keep an eye on the lair. If the cops miss Tanzer, we'll make sure he doesn't get away."

Courtney leaned back in her chair and gave her brother an angry glare. "Just the two of you? I don't think so, Jack. Leave it to Castillo and his guys. They know what they're up against."

"Or they think they do."

Bill laid a comforting hand over Courtney's. "I'll keep them out of trouble. If it gets nasty, I'll—"

"Be here," Jack cut him off.

"Jack," Bill cautioned, "you don't know this beast. Guns, Tasers, whatever you want to bring, fine. Anything can kill him. But you have to surprise him or best him to do that, and, no offense, but I don't think you can do that. I'm coming."

"You're not," Molly replied firmly.

They all looked at her.

"Jack and Courtney love you, Bill. I've always liked you, but they're more inclined to trust you than I am. Not that I think you'd betray us, but . . . I don't know if I can bet my life on that."

"You'll be in more danger if I stay behind," he told her.

"Maybe," Jack put in. "I'd be willing to trust you, Bill. But there's something more important I want to trust you with."

They all looked at him curiously.

Jack looked at his sister. "They've come after Molly and me twice now. They know where to find us, and there's a good chance they'll come back. They may even be out there right now, watching us." He turned to Bill. "I don't think I could survive if I lost her."

There was so much weight to his words, so much more he could have said. But he didn't have to. Bill understood immediately. Protecting Courtney was as important to Jack as destroying Tanzer, maybe more so. And it was obvious that Bill cared for her deeply as well.

"We'll all go," Courtney said quickly, as if she had seen where the conversation was going and wanted to stop it.

But even as she said it, her gaze dropped. None of them had to tell her that she could not go along, that she would be a liability to them.

"I'll stay," Bill said grimly.

Jack let out a long breath. "Good. Then we'd better get moving. We don't want Castillo to beat us there."

They all began to rise. Jack started to turn away when Molly spoke up. "I just have one more question," she said, a quaver in her voice.

Jack raised his eyebrows as he regarded her.

"Bill saw the Ghostlands when a soul came back to haunt him," Molly began. She chewed her lip for a moment before continuing. "I just . . . Who did you see, Jack?"

He could not think of a response to that. He didn't want to lie to her after all they'd been through. But he had promised Artie he would not tell her the truth, and he understood why his friend's ghost had made such a request.

Jack swallowed hard. Molly's pain-filled eyes were locked on his. He reached out and took her hands and held on tight.

"If you really want to know, ask me again and I'll tell you."

CHAPTER 15

A light rain had begun to fall, a cold spatter across the city of Boston. Tanzer felt the drizzle begin to mat his hair but the feeling barely registered. Beneath the facade of flesh he wore, his muscles were taut. His chest rose and fell in deep, meditative breaths. He felt seared from within, as if his bones were ablaze with the rage that burned in him.

Below, tourists and suits opened their umbrellas. That felt like an insult to Tanzer, as if they thought they could keep him at bay with only a waterproof shield. Carefree, they moved on to their destinations this night, returning from dates and restaurants and late shopping.

Boston had been wounded by Tanzer's pack, but it was still alive. It had shaken the Prowlers off with the bored annoyance a dog might reserve for the least offensive of fleas.

"Damn you all," Tanzer growled, his voice carried away by the breeze, his masquerade of a face sprinkled with rain.

Jasmine had returned from her assignment to report the impossible. If she had been any other member of the pack, Tanzer would have slain her on the spot. But she was not, and he could not blame her for following his instructions. She and Carver and the others had set out to slay the humans who had killed Dori and the others. A simple enough task, he had thought.

How had it all gone so completely wrong? Tanzer doubted he would ever know. But Carver was dead. All of them had been killed save for Jasmine, who had been instructed to observe. The humans in the pub, whose names he still did not know, had killed them all. And Carver, Jasmine was convinced, had talked before they killed him. They had to assume he had compromised the security of the lair, that he had revealed the location of the pack.

There had been witnesses.

There had been police.

A growl of anger and remorse built in Tanzer's throat. A vision had come to him, a dream of the future, and he meant to fulfill it: to create a pack even greater than the one his father had led.

The vision seemed dim now, and all because of a few humans who'd proved hardier than most. Prey who had turned out to be hard to kill.

"They'll die," he snarled.

Then he sighed. They would die, but not soon

enough. For the moment there was only exodus. He sat atop the roof of the bell tower with the rain falling more heavily now, fat drops blowing into his face, and he knew that his first duty was to preserve the pack. He might put himself at risk, but he would never endanger the pack.

Below him, in the belfry, Jasmine appeared. She sat in a tall, arched window, then leaned out and pulled herself up onto the roof. It was an acrobatic feat few humans could have accomplished, but Jasmine performed it in one swift and beautiful motion. She slipped up beside him and folded her slender legs beneath her. Her skin was like milk chocolate and her eyes, which usually blazed a simmering orange, seemed duller suddenly, obscured by sadness, perhaps.

Or maybe it's just the rain, Tanzer thought.

"It's done," she said. "I've told the others. They're preparing now. In twenty minutes we'll be ready to leave. Where to next?"

Tanzer shrugged. "I don't know, Jazz. Carver had ideas, but suddenly I'm not inclined to take any of his suggestions. If he weren't dead—"

"You'd kill him," she finished for him. "I would kill him for you. I only wish I could be certain what he told the humans. We cannot take any chances."

"Doesn't matter," Tanzer said. "We're discovered. Immediate withdrawal is our only course."

Jasmine sighed. "I never thought it would come to this."

"After what Dori did at the baseball park, and my

killing the gangster, I knew we'd have to go soon, but not like this. We've got seven dead already, counting Ghirardi."

Jasmine stiffened. Tanzer frowned and studied her. She would not hold his gaze, and he snarled under his breath, for he knew what that meant.

"Others have left, haven't they?"

"Seven or eight," Jasmine confessed. "Cowards."

"They don't trust me as their leader anymore," Tanzer said bitterly. "Damn these humans! And Carver as well. It's all falling apart."

"Only for now." Jasmine touched his hand gently, a purring sound escaping her lips.

Tanzer nodded slowly, but it was hard to accept her comfort. All his grand dreams of unifying the Prowlers were crashing down because of the actions of a handful of filthy humans.

"I should have killed them myself, torn them to shreds and painted the walls with their viscera, brought their organs back as treats for the loyal pups . . . but I never thought them a threat," Tanzer confessed. He shook his head. "I will not make that mistake again. And I will rectify it. I'll destroy them."

"But not now," Jasmine said firmly. "I have their scent. We know where they live. You can get to them at any time. Revenge can wait until we have found a new lair and begun to strengthen the pack again."

As Tanzer gazed down upon Copley Square, he shuddered with anger and savagery. Then, slowly, he began to grin. Boston would think itself spared, think the nightmare was over. Far from it. Tanzer would return. It would take time to rebuild the pack. He had already begun to weave a new myth among his race, to draw forth those who wanted to emerge from the periphery of the world, to come out of the shadows.

"It's not over," he said aloud, though whether he spoke to the city or to Jasmine he was uncertain.

The city was silent, but Jasmine replied. "Not over. Only postponed."

When he had built the pack anew, gathered a vicious tribe around him, Tanzer would return to Boston and find a new lair. Then he and he alone would hunt the humans who had struck such a devastating blow against his dreams and his leadership.

As if she had read his mind, Jasmine whispered softly to him. "It will come. Your shadow will reach long across the land."

Tanzer turned to stare into her orange eyes and then dipped his face to nuzzle against her throat. She leaned her head back, offering to him the soft flesh there, and then they both began to change. The skin split and bristly fur tore through from beneath. Tanzer felt his fangs lengthening, jutting from his jaw even as the bones in his mouth stretched and popped.

Desire for his mate burned within him and he nipped at the furry skin at her neck. Her claws raked his back through the shirt he still wore.

Raindrops dappled their monstrous forms as the change swept over them.

Below, tires screeched, drawing their attention.

Breathless, Tanzer and Jasmine broke away from each other. He stared out over the edge of the bell tower. Below, on the pavement, police cars filled Copley Square, and the street in front of the church. No sirens. No flashing lights.

The police were not there on police business, not there to make an arrest. They were there to kill. The men in blue were no different from villagers with torches in the eastern European countryside or Sioux warriors on horseback on a campaign to reclaim their lands.

The roar came from deep within Tanzer's chest, and he bellowed his fury as he stood precariously atop the bell tower. So loud was his thunderous howl that the huge bell below them rang lightly with the sound. The change came upon him fully then, and his shirt tore as his muscles and bones stretched and popped, his arms lengthened and his talons extended into razor-sharp tips.

"It's to be war, then," he growled.

Jasmine's hand on his shoulder stopped him.

"No," she said.

She had changed as well, and his true body, his feral nature, responded to her lithe beauty. Though she still wore human clothing, the beast had been set free. This was his mate, a powerful warrior and hunter in her own right.

"I lead the pack," he told her. "I must defend them."

"The pack shatters beneath you. Some have already abandoned you," she said, her voice a rasp of anger and passion. "Your duty is to the dream, not to them. For the dream, you must live. One day humanity will scurry like rabbits from our predations across this earth, and it will be thanks to your strength, your will as Alpha. The flesh of the bravest among them will be your nightly feast.

"But for that day, you must live."

Tanzer's chest heaved with his anger, but her words struck deep. "We must live," he agreed. Then he took her long talons in his own. "Our pups will be born into a new world. I swear it."

"Then we must go."

With one last glance down at the police massing in the street, cowering behind their vehicles with their weapons at the ready, aimed at the door to the bell tower, Tanzer nodded.

"We go. For now."

Jasmine followed as he turned and clambered up to the peak of the roof, then over to the other side. They moved down the slanted surface, hung for a moment on the edge and dropped to the belfy window below. Far beneath them they could see the roof of the church attached to the tower. Beyond that, brownstones stretched out deep into the heart of Boston.

From window to window, belfry to seventh story and then sixth, they carefully climbed down the outside of the stone structure, even as chaos erupted within.

Through the binoculars he'd brought, Jack stared in horror. "You've got to be kidding me."

"What?" Molly asked.

He couldn't answer at first. He simply kept gazing

through the binoculars as if what he was seeing was somehow going to change. In the shadows of the enormous doorway of the Boston Public Library, which had closed hours ago, they had hidden themselves away from sight and from the rain and kept watch on the church tower the ghosts had led him to earlier.

The lair of the beasts.

From their vantage point on the concrete slab steps of the library, Jack had seen the figure on the bell tower roof. At first they thought the creature must be a lookout, but then he got a good look through the binoculars and even with the rain he saw the scars on the Prowler's face and knew it had to be Tanzer. Bill had told Jack about those scars.

Then the female had come up to the roof, and the two had been all over each other. And then the police arrived.

Castillo had the bullhorn out. He shouted something, but it echoed off the buildings around Copley Square so much that the words were garbled. Jack was sure it was some approximation of "Come out with your hands up." But of course, Castillo didn't want them to come out.

The police waited only seconds. Then four of them rushed up the steps dressed in riot gear and carrying a metal ram. The door shattered instantly, and the others swarmed around the front of the bell tower, armed to the teeth with shotguns and service weapons.

Jack swept the binoculars up and watched the windows. Watched the belfry.

Tanzer should have appeared in the belfry and then begun working his way down. But he hadn't.

"Damn!" Jack snapped.

He cursed again under his breath.

"What?" Molly demanded.

"They're bolting. Tanzer and his mate. They went over the roof and disappeared, didn't come back into the belfry, and I see no sign of them at the windows."

Molly shook her head. "That's impossible. How the hell did they get down from up there?"

"I don't know. But I know I'm not going to let them get away." Jack took her hand, studied her eyes again. He was reluctant to have her with him, but he knew there was only one way to do this, and that was together.

"Let's go," he said.

Side by side they ran down the rain-slicked library steps and dodged traffic as they darted into Copley Square. Jack felt the weight of the fully loaded Beretta against the small of his back and the extra clips in his jacket pocket. In a duffel bag he carried in his right hand was a shotgun Bill had dug up for him. Molly had another pistol and her stun gun.

Jack knew he should have been filled with terror.

And yet somehow all he could think about was Artie.

Now it ends, he thought.

On the street in front of the tower, Jason Castillo took cover behind a patrol car, his service weapon in his hand. He stood beside a Boston PD sharpshooter who kept his eye on the windows, just in case. Inside the building, shots were being fired. Things shattered, and there were human shouts and decidedly inhuman roars and howls of pain.

A third-story window exploded in a shower of glass, and a ravening beast plummeted through the air in a controlled fall. It landed hard, rolled with the momentum, and came back up again a dozen feet from where the tangle of police cars had lined up to block off the area.

The monster crouched amid the shattered glass, its blue jeans and black boots giving it an almost comically surreal appearance. But its eyes blazed and it snarled at them, and there was nothing comical about its razor-sharp teeth.

Then it bolted.

Castillo shouted for his men to fire, and the thirty-seven police officers lined up behind the cars did just that. The Prowler jittered, dancing like a flag buffeted by strong wind, as bullets tore through its flesh. The sharpshooter beside Castillo fired, and a high-caliber bullet punched through the Prowler's skull, shattering it like an overripe melon. The beast went down hard on the pavement, twitched once, and was still.

More of them crashed out windows, trying to flee. Then a couple made it out the front door. Which meant the cops he'd sent inside were likely dead already.

Castillo ground his teeth, revulsion and bitter anger

rising like bile in his throat. He set his feet apart, leveled his gun, and began firing.

"Kill the monsters!" someone shouted. "Kill them all."

He thought it might have been his own voice.

From a window ledge on the fourth floor, Jasmine leaped to the roof of the church below. Her animal reflexes allowed her to alight upon the building almost silently. She spun, sniffed the air with alarm, and then uttered a tiny bark to alert Tanzer.

More police were coming. They were moving around the building to watch for just this kind of escape.

With the rain dappling her fur and her ears pinned back, listening intently for humans coming closer, she looked up at the side of the tower and saw Tanzer there, ready to spring. His enormous form rippled with muscles and grandeur, and she knew she could not afford to lose him. His was the vision and his was the ability to inspire the most lowly cur among them. Jasmine had a mind of her own, and dreams of her own, but Tanzer was her mate, and she loved him.

Tanzer easily dropped down onto the roof of the church and landed in a crouch on the rain-slicked surface. Both of them wore boots, human constructions not made for this sort of thing. But Jasmine knew they could not simply throw off their clothes and shoes. They would need them to merge back into the flow of humanity, to get out of the city unseen. Tanzer's shirt was torn, but he wore a leather coat that hung nearly to his knees, and that would have to be buttoned closed over his shirt until Jasmine could get him another.

For the moment, the coat flapped around him, leather stretched over the bestial musculature beneath.

Jasmine caught his gaze, tilted her head, and growled low, an expression of her love and fealty. Tanzer nodded grimly, snout lifted to sniff at the sky. His ears were pricked up, listening to the din of chaos and death they were leaving behind, alert to any sign that their escape had been noticed.

"Come," Tanzer growled.

He loped carefully across the slanted roof of the church, and Jasmine followed. Her own steps were as silent as caresses on the slate roof, but she knew that Tanzer's passing would not go unremarked by those inside the church. She could only hope that the building was vacant, or that the reaction of the police would be slow enough to allow her and her mate to pass.

On the other side of the church the gap between buildings was too great for them to leap. Jasmine glanced around nervously, orienting herself. The church fronted on the street where the police cars were spread out. More gunfire tore through the night, telling her there was no escape for them in that direction. They could not go back the way they had come. They had two choices: climb down the side wall of the church and hope no one noticed—which was possible but not the most appealing of alternatives—or leap from the rear of the church to the building directly behind it, a structure she had paid little attention to.

The LaFayette Hotel had been a swanky place to stay in the 1930s. Its reputation lingered now like a faded Hollywood starlet; it was still a gem and could still draw a crowd, but all the real money went to the younger, more glamorous hotels. Jasmine remembered the place in its heyday. She had sung in the lounge when she was still traveling with Duke Ellington and his orchestra.

Another time. Another world. Another life.

That was the past. Tanzer was the future.

"This way," she said, pointing to the rear of the hotel.

Tanzer drew up beside her, crouched like a gargoyle on the edge of the church roof. "It's too high," he told her.

"The fire escape."

Jasmine pointed. The LaFayette was only five stories high, but they could not leap up to its roof. Even from where they stood, they would not be able to make it to the fourth-story fire escape.

"We can try for the third-story landing," she explained.

With a grunt, Tanzer studied the leap. It was at least twenty feet, probably more. Simple for a Prowler on the ground. But here they would have no running start and no margin for error. On the other hand, if they gauged it right and took gravity into consideration, they should be able to make the jump and grab hold of the third-story landing of the fire escape.

"You stay." Tanzer stroked the fur on her snout with his claws. "If I make it, follow. If I don't, stay here until it's all over. Stay until tomorrow night. Then climb down."

Jasmine nodded.

Tanzer crouched, stretched his legs and shoulders and arms. Then he sprang out across the gulf that separated the church from the grand old hotel. His talons lashed out, and with a clang he caught hold of the iron railing on the fire escape's third-story landing.

Someone shouted from below. They'd seen him, up there in the dark.

Police? Jasmine wondered. There was more shouting and she knew the answer was no. No police. But they would come soon enough.

Tanzer barely had time to move out of the way when she leaped across to the fire escape, hauled herself up, and snarled to urge him on. They could not go down the fire escape. Jasmine smiled to herself. It was simple now. Tanzer growled and turned to go down. He was tired of running, she knew. His nature was to stand and fight. But they had come this far.

"We have to go up," she said. "Or you'll never have the chance to pay them back for this."

Tanzer hesitated only a moment, then nodded. Jasmine led the way and the two of them hurried up the fire escape. It reached the fifth floor, but did not go all the way to the roof. Still it was a simple matter for the Prowlers to stand on the railing and leap the last few feet.

On the roof was a door into the hotel. It was locked but its frame shattered easily and with less noise than Jasmine had imagined. By the time the elevator doors slid open to admit them on the fifth floor, both Jasmine and Tanzer had once again retreated within their human facades and Tanzer had buttoned his jacket over the torn shirt he wore beneath.

When they stepped out into the lobby, Jasmine was amazed at how calm it seemed. The wall to her right was all frosted glass. Once upon a time an enormous lounge had been beyond it, but now there was only a small restaurant and bar. Only a handful of people were in there this late. On the far side of the lobby, a short white-haired man dressed in the faux-military uniform of the hotel staff sat behind a long counter looking bored. An exotic-looking woman with olive skin and braids stood at the concierge's desk. Otherwise the place was empty.

"We could just check in," she whispered to Tanzer.

He shook his head. "We'd draw too much attention, arriving this late. Without luggage and with the timing of what's happening."

Even as he whispered to her, Jasmine noticed the woman at the desk stare at them curiously. Tanzer was right. They had no time to waste. The sooner they left the city of Boston behind, the better off they would be.

Together they walked across the beautiful marble floor of the lobby. The front doors sensed their approach and slid open to allow them to exit. Jasmine reached out and twined her fingers with Tanzer's as they stood in the light patter of rain. She stuck her tongue out and tasted it.

Not far off, a couple of loud pops split the night. More gunshots. But they were slowing now. Whatever was happening back at the lair was almost over.

"Let's go," she said, and squeezed his fingers.

They turned away from the front of the hotel.

The wind shifted.

Jasmine caught a familiar scent.

With his heart pounding, adrenaline surging through his body, Jack wiped rain from his face and hurried around the corner. Molly followed hard on his heels in total silence. He wished he knew what was running through her head—thoughts of Artie, he guessed, and what these monsters had done to her boyfriend. What the Prowlers had tried to do to them, more than once. Jack knew he was a target. Molly too and probably Bill and Courtney as well. What they were doing now was not a choice, not some act of bravery. It was life insurance.

The cops had moved in. Attacked. Shot the hell out of the church tower and the Prowlers inside. But nobody had seen Tanzer and the woman, on the roof above the belfry. Nobody had seen them take off across the roof except Jack and Molly. They had sprinted across Copley Square, giving a wide berth to the police, and come up to the side of the church just in time to see the two monsters leap from the church to the hotel fire escape.

"It's time," Molly had muttered, her voice cold.

But she had been wrong. The Prowlers had gone up instead of coming down. The only escape route from the roof was through the LaFayette.

Now they stood, Jack on one side of the hotel's front door and Molly on the other. He had taken the shotgun from his duffel bag and stashed the bag behind a large planter next to the doors. He leaned against the wall with the gun behind his back. The Beretta packed a kick, but nothing like a shotgun.

His heart thudded in his chest as though his body were hollow except for that one frightened, fluttering, bloody muscle. That and a stomach knotted into a tight fist around a swirl of angry hornets.

Jack glanced around the tree that stuck up from the planter beside him and caught Molly's gaze. Her eyes were dark and cold, lips pressed together in a grim line. Despite all she'd been through, all they'd seen together, she stood there fearlessly awaiting the monsters. Rain spattered her face but she ignored it. Her wild red hair blew across her eyes and she shook it away. She nodded at him.

I'm all right, she seemed to say.

He fell in love with her, just a little, right then. In that very moment.

Which was when Artie appeared in front of him, a few feet away from the front door of the hotel. He was transparent, as always, the few cars on the street visible through him. The rain did not touch him, pattering the sidewalk beneath the phantom's feet without the slightest deviation.

"She's something, isn't she?" Artie asked.

Jack's mouth opened. Nothing came out.

Artie smiled. "It's all right, Jack. Just keep her alive. I want her over here with me, of course. But that would not be fair. It's cold here, and when people touch me, I can't feel them."

"I'm sorry, Artie," Jack whispered.

"Bro," Artie said. He shook his head, a small smile on his face, as if that one word was all that needed to pass between them.

Jack was surprised to realize that it was.

He glanced across the street and saw Father Pinsky standing on the other side, the ghostly priest gazing at him gravely. There were others. Too many others. Jack flinched, blinked, and the world inverted again, the ghosts taking on flesh.

"Jack?" Molly whispered across to him. "Are you all right?"

"Not now," Jack snarled. He blinked, hard, and shook his head. When he opened his eyes the world was back to normal and all the ghosts were gone except Artie.

"What?" Molly rasped.

Before Jack could respond, Artie snapped his name. Jack looked at him and saw that the ghost was staring through the doors of the hotel.

"They're coming," Artie said.

Then he was gone.

"They're coming," Jack muttered.

Molly's eyes went wide. So many questions. He knew she had so many. But now was not the time.

The automatic doors opened. Jack pinned himself back against the hotel, shotgun now held loosely in his right hand. He couldn't see them at first. Then they stepped farther out onto the sidewalk in front of the hotel, and the woman, looking human now, stared up at the sky, letting the rain fall on her face.

If Artie hadn't told him, Jack would not have been certain it was them. They looked so . . . normal. Until the man turned ever so slightly and he saw the three scars running down his cheek. Jack stopped breathing. Tanzer. This was the creature who led all the Prowlers, who set the monsters after him, who terrorized his city and many others. He was centuries old.

How the hell did I think we could go up against him? Jack wondered, terror seeping into his mind and heart. But then he remembered a horrible truth. They had no choice.

Molly, be careful! Jack thought.

Tanzer and the female turned away from him. They were about to pass right by Molly. Jack stepped out from the shadows and raised the shotgun. The female sniffed the air and hesitated.

"Jasmine?" Tanzer asked.

So that's her name, Jack thought.

Jack had his finger on the trigger when they spotted Molly. Tanzer stiffened and started to change. The transformation came so swiftly that Jack had yet to take another breath. Jasmine was changing as well, the beast erupting from within. Monsters tearing off their masks.

Molly shot Tanzer in the chest.

The Prowler stumbled back several steps just as Jack fired the twelve-gauge shotgun. Jasmine moved too fast for him. In the eyeblink it took him to fire she lunged for Molly and pinned her against the wall.

"Molly, no!" Jack screamed.

The monster with the pretty name slashed at Molly's chest with her talons, drawing blood and a scream. But Molly never lost her grip on the gun Bill had given her. Jack swung the shotgun over to blow Jasmine's head off, but the Prowler was too close to Molly and he hesitated.

Molly didn't hesitate. She fired three times at Jasmine's chest and torso. At least one bullet went wild, shattering the windshield of a BMW across the street. The other two shots were solid hits, one in the shoulder and one in the chest.

Blood spattered Molly's face as Jasmine went down hard on the sidewalk.

But it was far from over.

Tanzer roared in a voice that sounded almost like a human scream when he saw Jasmine shot. With a fury unlike anything Jack had ever seen, slavering jaws snapping, he went for Molly with talons flashing.

Jack pumped another round into the twelve-gauge and blew a chunk out of Tanzer's shoulder, splintering bone and sending the beast into a spin that drove him stumbling to the ground. Yellow-green eyes blazed with hatred. The monster, this ancient creature who had preyed on thousands of men, women, and children, gazed at Jack with pure hatred. "You'll die now," the beast growled.

"One of us will," Molly snapped.

She stepped in close to Tanzer, gun pointed at his head, just as Jack was about to fire. The twelve-gauge held five rounds. He had three left. More than enough to turn the monster into roadkill.

"Molly, get back!" he snapped.

Too late.

Despite the beast's wounds, Tanzer lunged behind Molly, slapped the gun out of her hand with a blow that snapped bone and tore skin, and then Jack was face to face with the monster, and Tanzer was holding Molly between them. With his damaged arm, the beast held her against his chest. Its snout jutted over the top of her head and bloody saliva slipped out into her hair from his jaws. Molly winced.

Tanzer growled low and deep, like a coming storm. But the storm was already here.

Yellow-green eyes blazing with fierce intelligence, the three scars torn across his face, Tanzer gazed at Jack. "Drop the shotgun, boy. Give me your throat and I'll let the girl live. You've cost me too much already. It's time for me to go, but I won't go without your blood."

Jack was frozen. He couldn't feel his pulse racing in his veins anymore. Couldn't feel the rain on his skin. Couldn't hear the sirens or the shouts. At any moment the police would be there. They must have heard the shots and they were just around the block. But seconds were an eternity.

Molly stared at Jack. Her eyes were filled with terror.

He was not sure if the droplets of moisture on her cheeks were rain or tears, and he did not want to know.

"Kill him, Jack," she said weakly. "It's the only way."

Tanzer laughed at that, deep and throaty, mouthful of razor fangs showing with the rhythm of his amusement. "Humans," he said, with a snorting chuckle. "Do you think she meant that? Didn't you hear the quaver in her voice?"

Jack wasn't listening to either of them. All he could hear in the surreal landscape where his mind and body now existed, a world where only Molly's eyes seemed to matter, was Artie's voice.

The voice of a ghost.

The voice of the dead.

It's cold here, and when people touch me, I can't feel them. Just keep her alive, Jack.

Jack held the shotgun out in front of him with both hands and let it drop to the sidewalk. The monster grinned. Sirens wailed. Tires screeched. The cops were coming.

The weight of the Beretta was cold and heavy at the small of his back.

"Go on and kill me then," Jack said staring at the beast in human clothes, its leather coat torn to reveal the fur beneath. Rain dampened the fur on its head, and its ears twitched with each new sound. A thick black tongue slid out of its mouth and over its lips.

Its grip on Molly tightened.

Its tongue snaked out again and tasted the flesh of her throat.

"Salty," the beast growled. "Sorry, boy, but I may not be able to control myself. I may have to eat her first."

Molly's hands had been moving all along. Jack had seen them, but the beast had not. With a grunt she thrust the Taser up into the monster's face and shocked it with thousands of volts of electricity.

"Eat this!" she screamed.

Tanzer roared, dropped Molly, and stumbled backward. Jack could see now how much damage he had done with his shotgun blast. One of Tanzer's arms was barely functioning and blood soaked down the denims it wore, dripping off its boots.

It recovered quickly, but not quickly enough.

Jack whipped the Beretta out from under his jacket. Without bothering to aim, he slapped both hands on the nine-millimeter and fired. The Prowler grunted as blood sprayed from its wounds. Jack fired again and again until he found himself standing over the beast in the rain with an empty gun.

Its blood eddied away in a little rivulet of rainwater and slipped down a sewer grating.

Molly snatched up the shotgun and looked around desperately. Prowler blood ran with the rain on her face like deep red mascara.

"Where's the other one? Where'd she go?" Molly demanded.

Jack looked around quickly, empty gun held useless in both hands. But despite the two bullets she had taken, Jasmine was gone.

"Damn!" Jack snapped.

Police cars, lights flashing, screamed around the corner. Jack tossed the Beretta into the sewer where it skittered and fell down into the dark. Molly dropped the shotgun and the two of them sat down on the sidewalk in the rain next to the corpse of a monster.

"Like to see them try to arrest us," Molly said, her voice pitched somewhere between hysteria and glee.

Jack slipped an arm around her and held her close.

EPILOGUE

Molly was taken to the hospital. There, with an officer keeping an eye on her, a doctor put stitches in her chest where Tanzer had clawed her. Jack spent only a single night in jail as a guest of the Boston Police Department. Both of them had been arrested on a variety of charges including unlawful possession of firearms, unlawful discharge of firearms, and hunting without a license.

"Hunting?" Jack had asked Jace Castillo, when the detective came in to question him.

Castillo had smiled. "Wolves."

There were countless holes in the cover story. Jack and Molly had been at the other recent shooting involving wild "wolves" wandering south into the city. Scavengers, the press was told. Their own hunting grounds offered only meager pickings this year, and at least five had been sighted in Boston in recent weeks. Four had been killed.

But there was no police report placing Jack and Molly at the previous wolf shooting, in City Hall Plaza.

Likewise, no connection was made between the gun battle with gang members in front of St. Luke's Church and the shooting of the wolf in front of the LaFayette Hotel. A block apart, the events had taken place almost simultaneously. No one seemed to notice. Or, perhaps they were asked not to notice, and complied.

Jack was certain that at least some members of the Boston media had to have been in on the cover-up for it to work. But work it did. Though it rankled him not to have the truth come out, he understood that as long as the threat was over, it would not serve the people to know there were monsters in their midst.

Panic would ensue.

Part of him believed that perhaps panic would be appropriate. Then people all over the country and around the world—could be on guard. That guy next to you on the subway with the hungry eyes? Maybe he really *was* an animal. In the end, though, Jack had to make a deal with Castillo. They all kept their mouths shut, and the gun charges went away. Jack assured the cop that none of them would say a word. At the hospital, Molly apparently agreed to the same thing.

What else would she have said?

Besides, no one would have believed them. Jack knew that much . They'd be laughed at, and that would bring Bridget's Irish Rose Pub the wrong kinds of attention.

Of course, at Bridget's they had proof right behind

the bar, but Jack wasn't exactly going to point that out. If people did start to believe there were monsters among them, they weren't likely to differentiate between the predators and the pacifists. The last thing he wanted was to endanger Bill.

All of these things went through Jack's mind while the long hours ticked by in the city lockup.

They let him out at just after eight in the morning. Molly met him at the front desk. Apparently they'd cut her loose from the hospital a lot sooner than they let him go, because she wore fresh clothes and had obviously taken a shower.

"You all right?" he asked.

At first she didn't respond. Would not even raise her beautiful sparkling green eyes to meet his. Then she pushed her hair away from her face and regarded him carefully.

"Do you think she's gone?" Molly asked.

Jack didn't have to ask who she was talking about. *Jasmine*.

"She's gone," he told her firmly. "She's alone now. And wounded. If it was Tanzer I'd say no. But he was the Alpha. Without him she's just another animal. She's on the run, most likely."

He only wished he felt as confident as he sounded.

But Molly was barely listening. She took his hand, twined her fingers in his, and together they walked toward the doors, moving around uniformed officers who all seemed in a hurry to be somewhere else.

"I'm not sure we should let her go," Molly said.

His hand on the door, Jack paused and stared at her. "What do you mean?"

"She's going to keep killing, isn't she? It's what they do. We should stop her."

The words echoed some of Jack's own thoughts from his long, sleepless night. They haunted him. But he shrugged. "There's nothing we can do. How could we track her even if we wanted to?"

"We could at least keep our eyes open," she countered.

He'd nearly forgotten that she was still holding his hand, and when she squeezed his fingers now he became self-conscious and pulled his hand away.

"We could do that," he agreed, staring at the floor. At anything except Molly's eyes. Jack knew he felt something for her. He knew he'd be constantly in her company from now on, that she'd be living and working at Bridget's with him and Courtney.

Artie had practically given his blessing to the idea of something developing between them. But Jack couldn't do that. It didn't feel right. At least not now. Artie's death had been a horrible trauma for both of them.

They needed time.

"We'll just watch the papers and the Net to see if anything turns up," Molly said. "Castillo and everyone else may be able to pretend it's over just because they killed a few monsters in this city. But I can't. We can't, Jack."

Jack looked up, gazed into her eyes. He smiled. "Absolutely."

On the concrete steps in front of the police station, Courtney sat waiting for them with her cane across her knees. The rain of the previous night had passed and the day was warm, with just a hint of the summer that was not far off now. The sky was beautiful and clear, and the sun glinted off the brass lion's head that tipped Courtney's cane.

Jack shuddered when he saw it.

Then Courtney was up and hobbling toward them, using her cane to help her manuever the stairs. Her eyes were wide and impossibly blue, as though they reflected the sky itself.

Without a word she threw her arms around him. He felt her cane thump against the backs of his legs. Courtney leaned on him a little to keep her balance and hugged him so tight that he could not breathe.

"You're killin' me, Court," he managed to choke out, along with a terse laugh.

Her grip relaxed, but she still held on. He could feel her warm breath on his neck, her chest hitching with emotion. But Courtney Dwyer did not cry.

"Nothing's funny here, Jack," she whispered to him, her voice shaky. "I was so scared for you last night. And scared for me. I've got nothing without you, little brother."

"Hey," he said softly. "I'm right here."

Courtney met his eyes, and brother and sister smiled knowingly at each other.

A car horn blew down on the street. Bill Cantwell's Delta 88 pulled up to the curb and he beeped again.

* * *

"God." Jack sighed. "A guy lives as long as he has, you'd think he'd learn a little patience."

Bill stepped out of the car and stood just inside his open door, watching them over the roof of the Oldsmobile. He raised a hand to Jack, almost a salute, and smiled. Jack grinned back.

It was the first time since discovering Bill's secret that he had been able to look at the bartender and just see Bill Cantwell, and not the other face he kept hidden deep inside. That was Bill, he realized. Beneath his skin, he might be something other than human, but Jack was somehow certain that when he closed his eyes at night and dreamed, Bill Cantwell was a man, a creature with a human heart and all that it implied.

They were all quieter than usual on the ride back to Bridget's. After the previous night, there would be a lot of work to be done, a lot of lies to be told, a lot of spin control to do. It was going to be a long day.

As they cruised through Boston, Jack gazed out his window at the sidewalks and storefronts, at the couples arm in arm, the suits swinging briefcases, the old matrons walking their dogs. All of them real and tangible, flesh and blood.

No phantoms.

He kept expecting to see Artie, hoping to see Artie. Nothing.

"What are you looking for out there?" Molly asked as Bill turned a corner near Quincy Market.

Jack looked at her quizzically, then glanced at

Courtney and Bill in the front seat. He shook his head and smiled. "Nothing. Nothing at all."

Damsel in distress.

Those were the words that went through Don Kramer's eyes when he saw the woman standing on the northbound side of Interstate 95 with her thumb cocked at an angle only slightly less severe than the angle of her outthrust hip. She was all legs and breasts, clad almost entirely in leather, and looked more like she ought to be strutting along a posh Manhattan street or stepping off a movie set than hitching a ride in southern Maine.

But she had no bags, not even a pocketbook. Nothing on her at all except the clothes she wore. Even for a knockout like this one, Don figured that meant one thing: she was on the run. Some guy had probably knocked her around and she was on the her way home to Mom.

Damsel in distress.

"Damn fool woman," Don muttered to himself as he downshifted his rig, braking as quickly as he dared.

The semi came to a stop fifty yards past where the woman had stood. In his rearview mirror he watched her jog up the breakdown lane and marveled again at her beauty. What the hell she was doing hitching along the highway was a mystery to him, but one he'd be happy to explore. Right after he gave her a little lecture about the perils of hitchhiking, particularly for a woman alone. If someone else had picked her up, he'd tell her, she might have ended up in a ditch somewhere.

Don rolled his eyes.

The young ones figured they were bulletproof. Untouchable. He had heard his share of horror stories in seventeen years on the road. He would share a few with this girl, maybe make her think twice about sticking her thumb out next time.

Without a word she hauled open the passenger door and hefted herself effortlessly up into the cab of the truck. Her skin was brown and silky, the color of milk chocolate. When she looked at him and thanked him for stopping, her smile dazzled him.

"Where you headed?" he asked.

"As far north as you go," she told him. "Don't worry, I'm good company."

Don chuckled. Her telling him not to worry, that was a laugh. "I have no doubt, darlin'. None at all."

The girl smiled again and Don was almost mesmerized by her eyes. They were the most incredible shade of orange he had ever seen, but he didn't think they were contact lenses. They were almost hypnotic, those orange eyes. And there was something else about them that struck him, sent a cold thrill running through him. They were playful, those orange eyes. Mischievous.

Wild.

ABOUT THE AUTHOR

CHRISTOPHER GOLDEN is the award-winning *L.A. Times* bestselling author of such novels as *Strangewood*, *Straight on 'til Morning*, and the three-volume *Shadow Saga*. His other works include *Hellboy: The Lost Army* and the *Body of Evidence* series of teen thrillers (including *Meets the Eye* and *Skin Deep*) which is currently being developed for television by Viacom. He has also written or co-written a great many books, both novels and non-fiction, based on the popular television series, *Buffy the Vampire Slayer* and the world's #1 comic book, *X-Men*.

Golden's comic-book work includes *Batman: Realworlds*, stints on *The Crow*, *Spider-Man Unlimited*, *Buffy the Vampire Slayer*, and *Batman Chronicles;* and the ongoing monthly *Angel* series, tying into the Buffy television spinoff. As a pop culture journalist, he was the editor of the Bram Stoker Award-winning book of criticism, *CUT!: Horror Writers on Horror Film*, and co-author of both *Buffy the Vampire Slayer: The Monster Book* and *The Stephen King Universe*.

Golden was born and raised in Massachusetts, where he still lives with his family. He graduated from Tufts University. He is currently at work on a new novel for Signet called *The Ferryman*. There are more than three million copies of his books in print. Please visit him at www.christophergolden.com.

Turn the page for
a preview of the next
Body of Evidence thriller
starring Jenna Blake

BRAIN TRUST

Available July 2001

"**H**ey Jude" was the last song Amalia Cheney ever heard. Had she known that at the time she likely would have appreciated the fact. Though she had already been in her thirties when they first appeared on American television on *The Ed Sullivan Show*, she had always loved the Beatles. It was that passion for their music that had led Amalia to name her place The Ob-La-Di Bookshop & Café.

"Ob-La-Di, Ob-La-Da, life goes on," was how the song went.

At the time, it had been her reflection upon her own life. Thirty-five years in science research and upon her retirement she had ditched it all, moved to eccentric but lovely Sedona, Arizona, and opened up the little store she had always wanted. Used and new books, fresh baked goods, and knockout coffee.

Ob-La-Di, Ob-La-Da. Sort of ironic, actually.

Even more so, if that had been the Beatles song on the CD player when Amalia's after hours customers came in. But it wasn't. It was "Hey Jude."

The seventy-two-year-old woman had long since flipped the Closed sign on the front door and shut off all the café equipment. Eight in the morning 'til eight at night, five days a week. They were long hours for a woman of her age, but Amalia enjoyed it. She was closed on Sundays and Tuesdays to allow herself time to rest, but the rest of the week she and the four employees who rotated through the schedule manned the counter and the bookshelves. Amalia loved Sedona. It had taken her a few years, but she had become a sort of fixture in the community, just as she had always wanted.

Amalia Cheney had never belonged anywhere in her life before she came to this town and opened The Ob-La-Di.

It was perhaps a quarter to nine. Amalia was back among the three aisles of books shelving the two boxes of used science-fiction and fantasy novels she had bought from Cal Vargas earlier in the week. Someone rapped hard on the glass door at the front of the shop.

With a frown, Amalia glanced toward the front but could not see around the end of the aisle.

"Tourists," she muttered, and rose to her feet with a bit of an ache in her knees.

Amalia knew that she owed at least half of her business to tourists, though she brought in a steady stream of locals as well. But the locals were considerate enough not to pester her long after closing time. She had even shut out the lights in the café area at the front of the shop and pulled the blinds that covered the broad windows and the door.

How much more closed could the place look? she wondered.

After she brushed off the front of her gray, cotton pants and made sure she had not left any books lying in the middle of the aisle, she walked out to the front. Even as she emerged among the half dozen round tables and their attendant chairs in the café area, the rapping on the glass started up again.

She walked past the glass counter upon which sat the cash register, coffee machines, and displays that held a few muffins that had not sold that day, and went to the door. With a steady hand she pulled the cord that opened the blinds that lay over the glass.

It was dark outside, and she narrowed her eyes as she studied the figures who stood just beyond her door. Two men in almost identical clothing, crisp dark blue jeans with black boots and navy blue cotton jackets. The older one had a doughy face and thinning hair and made her think of an actor; *the crazy one from Ghostbusters*, she thought. The younger had exotic, almost girlish features, olive skin and piercing eyes. Very handsome, if forty years too young for her.

"Sorry, gentlemen. Long since closed for the day," Amalia told them.

The older man smiled, increasing his resemblance to the actor whose name she could not remember. He pulled a wallet out of his jacket pocket and flipped it open, pressed it against the glass.

Federal Bureau of Investigation.

"I'm Special Agent Duncan, Professor Cheney. This is Agent Wilcox. We just need to ask you a few questions."

Amalia stiffened. Nobody had called her "professor" in a very long time. And she had not had a visit from government men in even longer.

With a sigh, she reached up and turned back the deadbolt on the door, then opened the lower lock as well.

"What's this all about?" she demanded as the two men thanked her and moved into the darkened interior of the café.

The exotic one flashed a bright, comforting smile. "Just doing a background check on an old colleague of yours. Nothing to concern you, but we need to do the job and thought we wouldn't bother you during business hours."

Amalia frowned, then shrugged a bit. "Thoughtful of you, I suppose. Been a while since my government days, but my memory's still pretty good. Shoot."

On the speakers piping music through the shop, "Hey Jude" had reached the na-na-na-nah part near the end.

"Can't shoot," said the sweet young man, Agent Wilcox.

"I'm sorry?" Amalia said, wondering if she had heard him right.

"Too messy," Wilcox informed her.

Even as Duncan slipped up behind her and placed a hand across her mouth. He punched the point of a needle into the flesh of her neck, and depressed the plunger.

Fighting against the powerful man who held her, Amalia screamed into the hand that was clamped over her lips. She stared, terrified, into the smiling, darkly handsome face of Agent Wilcox, and did not understand the tenderness she thought she saw there. The last strains of "Hey Jude" filled the shop and then the CD moved into that hissing, empty space between songs.

"Revolution" came on next.

Amalia did not get to hear even the first note.

The first thing Duncan did was lock up again and close the blinds over the front door. No one could see them from the street.

While Wilcox carried the old lady upstairs to her apartment above the shop, Duncan pulled on a pair of crime scene gloves and went behind the counter. There he put a small stack of napkins beside one of the big coffee makers. An inch or so of stale coffee remained in the bottom of the carafe which he dumped it in the sink, but he didn't rinse out the glass pot. Instead, he placed the carafe back where it had come from and punched the button that turned on the coffee maker.

The black ring beneath the carafe began to heat up.

A short while later, Wilcox came back downstairs. Duncan glanced at him, then looked back at the coffee maker. The two men stood there in silence as the empty glass carafe continued to heat up. After a number of minutes had ticked by, the glass shattered.

The plastic pouring ring around the top of the carafe slipped off to one side.

"Damn," Duncan muttered.

He walked over and picked up the plastic, which was hot beneath his latex gloves. Then he placed it back amongst the shattered bits of the coffee pot on the burning hot base plate of the machine. Within minutes, the plastic began to melt.

Then it lit on fire.

The fire touched the napkins.

And began to spread.

Duncan nodded contentedly, then glanced at Wilcox. "You ready?"

Wilcox sighed. "She seemed like such a nice lady."

"Yep." Duncan nodded. "Sure did."

Together they moved into the back of The Ob-La-Di, then into the store room. They exited through a back window, leaving no trace that they had ever been there at all.

The secret.

A week didn't go by that someone didn't ask Whitney Bannister what his secret was. At sixty-nine years of age he looked at least ten years younger and had continued on staff at Haviland College in Vermont long after he should have retired. He had voluntarily given up the top spot in the college's physical sciences department seven years before and since then had satisfied himself with teaching complex biology courses. Though the trustees at Haviland were vigilant about tenured professors staying on staff too long, no one had ever so much as whispered a suggestion that Professor Bannister give up the podium.

So what was the secret?

Whit smiled to himself every time the question came up. The answer was simple, really.

Action was his secret.

He kept his mind working, kept his body moving, and it kept him young. He worked hard to keep up with the latest developments in his field and challenged himself to remember all of the students in his rather large classes. He had Teaching Assistants, of course, or T.A.s as they called them. But while most professors would have let the T.A.s correct essay tests in classes as large as his, Whit Bannister read and graded all of those essays himself. He enjoyed seeing the way his students' minds worked.

It had become his habit to stay late at the physical sciences department's office in Benoit Hall rather than taking the tests home for grading. Not all of his work could be kept on campus, but he did his best to separate his life as a teacher from his life at home, where his garden and the piano were his great loves and boon companions.

Anyone who knew Whit Bannister had administered a test in his marine biology class that morning would have known to find him in his office that night. So when he heard a rap on the frosted glass door of the department's office, Whit thought little of it. He took a long pull off his Meerschaum pipe, put down the pen he had been correcting with and flexed his right hand, then proceeded out into the main office.

Only a pair of desk lamps burned in the office, but the hallway was still well lit. He would turn all of those lights out on his way home. But the lights in the hall silhouetted a figure beyond that frosted glass, and Whit frowned when he saw the diminutive figure, with its full, long hair.

Curious, he opened the door to find Bekah Savage fidgeting in the hall, arms crossed. Bekah was in his marine bio course—a brilliant girl with a future in the field if she chose to go that way. Brilliant, yes, and beautiful as well. Whit was an old man, but the fact that it made him feel like an old pervert did not stop him from noticing his more attractive female students. Bekah had pale skin and cupid's bow lips and the blackest hair he had ever seen that didn't look like it came from a bottle. He had taken her under his wing during her sophomore year and acted almost as her mentor ever since.

Now she would not meet his gaze.

"Bekah? What is it? Is something wrong?"

She winced, almost as though he had cursed at her, or even struck her. Her eyes were downcast and her lips were pressed together as though she fought with the words that might escape should she open them.

"Don't talk to me like that," she said after a moment, her voice tight.

"Like what?" Whit asked.

"Nice. Don't talk to me like that."

Whit lifted his hands in surrender. "Look, why don't you come in and we can talk about whatever's on your mind. I can make some tea if you like."

Finally, Bekah raised her eyes, and Whit flinched as he saw the fury in them, felt the rage and pain radiating from her gaze.

"I came, Professor Bannister. Like you asked. But I'm only here to . . ." her words trailed off, and Bekah bit her lower lip and wiped at her eyes. Fighting tears. "I only came to tell you I got your note. I'll be showing it to Dean Fassbender tomorrow morning. I thought you should know."

She turned to go.

Whit was rigid with shock and bafflement. After a moment, he shook his head and went out into the hall after her.

"Bekah, wait!" he called. "What is it? What note are you talking about?"

When she stopped and turned to regard him again, it was with an expression not of sadness or anger or even hatred, but merely disgust.

"Don't," she warned him. "Don't try that now. I worked so hard for so long, I knew what I wanted to do with my life. I wanted to be like you. You've taken all of that away from me now. So please, just let me go."

"But I don't—"

The slamming of the front door of the physical sciences building cut off his protest. With his mouth hanging open, Whit stood in the harsh light of the hallway and stared at the door Bekah had just gone exited.

"What in God's name?" he muttered to himself.

Whit reached up to scratch at the back of his head, his mind racing as he tried to decipher the incredibly bizarre scene that had just unfolded.

What was that business about the dean? he wondered to himself.

"Pretty girl."

Whit started at the words, at the introduction of another human voice into the vacant silence of the building. He heard his ankles crack and his knees pop as he turned too fast to face the pair of men who stood in the corridor behind him.

Old bones, he thought as he stared at the men.

"Can I help you gentlemen?" he asked, putting just enough pique into his voice to let them know that they were intruding. "The office closed two hours ago. You really aren't supposed to be here."

The man on the left had chubby cheeks and thinning hair and appeared to be in his mid forties. The other was ten years younger, thin and dark, possibly Greek or Turkish, Whit thought.

They behaved as if he hadn't spoken at all.

"Don't you think, Professor Bannister?" the older man asked. "Bekah, I mean. Pretty thing, isn't she?"

Whit froze. His eyes ticked back and forth, studying the two men. The way they carried themselves. The dark clothes they wore. The insinuating, almost amused tone of voice.

His chest began to ache, and nausea roiled in his stomach.

"You're from the government," Whit said.

Both men smiled.

Pretty girl, the man had said. *And he knew Bekah's name.*

"What've you done?" Whit demanded. His right hand curled into a fist at his side; the left gripped his pipe as though it were a lifeline.

They glanced at one another innocently. Then they turned back to him.

"Us, Whit? Why, we didn't do a damn thing," said the younger of the two. A Greek, he decided. "It's what *you* did."

"You sent Bekah a note today, after the exam," the other went on. "Told her about all the things you've wanted to do to her ever since you first laid eyes upon her, confessed your love and lust, promised to do all sorts of things to advance her career if she'd come and meet you here. Tonight. Right about now."

Whit Bannister felt like crying. He knew he should have been afraid, but he didn't have the energy for that. For once, he felt old and tired. Used up. And more than anything, he just felt sad.

"Why?" he asked, shaking his head. "Why did you have to do that? Hurt Bekah like that? Whatever you're supposed to do to me, you've hurt that girl, probably irrevocably. No matter what I say to her now, she has no reason to believe me."

The one with thinning hair reached into his jacket and withdrew an ugly blue steel pistol.

"You can't figure it out?" he asked. "I mean, you're obviously pretty quick on the uptake here, professor. I'm sort of disappointed in you."

Further confused, and anxious about the sudden presence of the gun, Whit shook his head again. "I don't . . . I don't understand."

"You needed a reason," the dark-skinned one explained.

The other nodded. "See, after you had finally professed your longing for Bekah, and she had not only rejected you but threatened to inform the dean, thus ruining your career and reputation . . . Well, you'd really have no choice but to kill yourself."

Whit closed his eyes and sighed. There was nothing he could do for himself now, but his sadness for Bekah was profound.

"So now what?" he asked. He opened his eyes and found that they both had guns trained on him now.

The older man smiled amiably. "Now? Now we go up to the roof."

Look for the next
Body of Evidence thriller starring Jenna Blake
by Christopher Golden and Rick Hautala
Available from Pocket Pulse
July 2001

BODY OF EVIDENCE
Thrillers starring Jenna Blake

"The first day at college, my professor dropped dead. The second day, I assisted at his autopsy. Let's hope I don't have to go through four years of this...."

When Jenna Blake starts her freshman year at Somerset University, it's an exciting time, filled with new faces and new challenges, not to mention parties and guys and...a job interview with the medical examiner that takes place in the middle of an autopsy! As Jenna starts her new job, she is drawn into a web of dangerous politics and deadly disease...a web that will bring her face-to-face with a pair of killers: one medical, and one all too human.

Body Bags
Thief of Hearts
Soul Survivor
Meets the Eye
Head Games
Skin Deep
Burning Bones
(Christopher Golden and Rick Hautala)

THREE NEW TITLES A YEAR

BY CHRISTOPHER GOLDEN

Bestselling coauthor of
Buffy the Vampire Slayer™: The Watcher's Guide

Available from Pocket Pulse
Published by Pocket Books

2071-07

"YOU'RE DEAD. YOU DON'T BELONG HERE."

Susannah just traveled a gazillion miles from New York to California in order to live with a bunch of stupid boys (her new stepbrothers).

Life hasn't been easy these past sixteen years. That's because Susannah's a mediator—a contact person for just about anybody who croaks, leaving things...well, untidy.

READ
THE MEDIATOR

BOOK #1: SHADOWLAND
BOOK #2: NINTH KEY

BY JENNY CARROLL

AVAILABLE FROM POCKET PULSE.
PUBLISHED BY POCKET BOOKS

3043-02

> *"I'm the Idea Girl, the one who can always think of something to do."*

VIOLET EYES

A spellbinding new novel of the future

by Nicole Luiken

Angel Eastland knows she's different. It's not just her violet eyes that set her apart. She's smarter than her classmates and more athletically gifted. Her only real competition is Michael Vallant, who also has violet eyes—eyes that tell her they're connected, in a way she can't figure out.

Michael understands Angel. He knows her dreams, her nightmares, and her most secret fears. Together they begin to realize that nothing around them is what it seems. Someone is watching them, night and day. They have just one desperate chance to escape, one chance to find their true destiny, but their enemies are powerful—and will do anything to stop them.

Available from

POCKET PULSE

Published by Pocket Books

Everyone's got his demons....

ANGEL™

If it takes an eternity, he will make amends.

❖

Original stories based on the TV show Created by Joss Whedon & David Greenwalt

Available from Pocket Pulse Published by Pocket Books

™ and © 2000 Twentieth Century Fox Film Corporation. All Rights Reserved.

2311-01